A DESCRIPTION OF THE BLAZING WORLD

A
DESCRIPTION
of the
BLAZING
WORLD

a novel by

MICHAEL
MURPHY

Freehand Books gratefully acknowledges the support of the Canada Council for the Arts for its publishing program. ¶ Freehand Books, an imprint of Broadview Press Inc., gratefully acknowledges the financial support for its publishing program provided by the Government of Canada through the Canada Book Fund.

 Canada Council   Conseil des Arts
for the Arts   du Canada

Freehand Books
412 – 815 1st Street sw Calgary, Alberta T2P 1N3
www.freehand-books.com

Book orders: Broadview Press Inc.
280 Perry Street, Unit 5 Peterborough, Ontario K9J 2J4
Telephone: 705-743-8990 Fax: 705-743-8353
customerservice@broadviewpress.com
www.broadviewpress.com

Library and Archives Canada Cataloguing in Publication

Murphy, Michael, 1982-
          A description of the blazing world / Michael Murphy.

ISBN 978-1-55111-730-0

          I. Title.

PS8626.U758D48 2011   C813'.6   C2011-900546-8

Edited by Robyn Read
Book design by Grace Cheong
Author photo by Joanna Thurlow

Printed on FSC recycled paper and bound in Canada

Table of Contents

For Joanna.

Nature's Works are so various and wonderful, that no particular Creature is able to trace her ways.

—Margaret Cavendish,
The Description of a New World, Called the Blazing World

I am dead. I am a dead man. A fraction of a second. Life comes and comes and goes. Then goes.

Hey-Zeus. What am I thinking?

I've been shot ninety times. The man holds the gun. Then puts a bullet in my gut. My temple. My solar plexus. Right between the eyes. It's happened eight times on the sidewalk, thirteen times at school, twenty-two times in a convenience store, a place with scummy tile floors and flickering fluorescents. There's a black glass camera bowl on the ceiling. The gunman pulls the trigger. I hear a popping sound. I watch myself receive the bullet on the store security monitors behind the cash, in grainy security greens. White light goes through me. That's the shot. My breath catches against my teeth. My dead body collapses onto the ATM machine, casing the screen in a thin sheen of blood. Bits of brain stick between the buttons.

I've had this death so many times. A death of light and blood and triggers. I prefer it above my other deaths. I also like knife death, cancer death, and car accident death. Those are the big three, after gun death. Less preferred are poison death, shark attack death, asphyxiation death, serial killer death, and any form of self-mutilation or suicide death. Even less preferred are being-buried-alive death, bleeding to death, starving to death, burning to death, and drowning to death. There are so many different deaths. I suppose they all work.

The first and only time I drowned I was seven, on the Scotia Prince with my family, going to the States. We were going to spend another family vacation on some cold New England beach. Dad took me on deck to watch for dolphins. He left me by the rail to go have a cigarette with my shirtless 'Uncle,' Ross, who drove a bright red Nissan that he had named Honda. I climbed onto the bars to see farther. The dolphins weren't swimming beside the boat like they do in the movies. Maybe they were a few miles off. I leaned out to get a better view, and my foot slipped against the sea-greased metal. I toppled headfirst into the waves and blacked out as soon as I hit the surface. I didn't even make a sound. I just hit the water and sank, upside down, air pressed out of my lungs. What little air remained escaped in tiny bubbles. Breathless and sleeping, I drifted down into the frozen, black belly of the ocean, where the whales sleep through winter.

My mom blamed my dad. Dad blamed me. My older brother watched TV and used my room as a storage space for his comic books and G.I. Joes. Five days they searched for my body. Some said the boat was in a warm gulf stream when I went over. I might've survived the temperature, as long as I had survived the fall. Of course, the authorities knew I was dead. The Coast Guard knew I was dead. My parents knew I was dead. The media knew I was dead. The entire country knew I was dead. Still they searched for my bloated corpse, hoping to find some material leftover, a piece of my shirt, my left shoe, something they could put in the solid ground, or burn to ashes. I don't know why they held out so long. My body was deep in the Atlantic and I wasn't thinking of them at all. I was under one thousand tonnes of water. I was dead.

If only I could've stayed that way, waterlogged on the ocean floor. But death never holds. I open my eyes and I'm fourteen, and I'm in my room, lying on top of the covers of my bed. I'm on the bus going to school. I'm eating dinner with Mom and Ross. I always come back up for air.

I do not need a name to tell my story. But if my story needs a name, I want it to be called *The Blackout Interviews*, or maybe *Apocalypse Never*. *The Letter Thief* or *The Stolen Letters*. Definitely not *Post: A Character Study*, which is about the dumbest name ever given to a story.

Morgan Wells saw his wife sitting up in bed, flipping through a magazine, her bedside table cluttered with unfilled subscription cards, three empty water glasses, her cell phone.

He saw her leaning against a telephone pole, unwrapping her scarf.

He saw her at the aquarium standing in front of the killer whale tank.

He saw her removing the lid to a pot of boiling water, the steam rising toward her face.

He saw her on the day she bought her first digital camera, taking pictures of the Toronto skyline, his reflection in the train window. Trees blurring past, leafless. Showing him the images after each was taken.

He saw her opening the refrigerator door, the light spilling into the dark kitchen. Inside, the shelves were full of things he would never buy on his own. Asparagus. Coriander. Chutney. Probiotic yogurts. He saw her reaching for the tomatoes.

In the bathroom: her bottles of contact solution, her moisturizers, anti-frizz hair oils, vitamin E creams, and lip balms cluttered around the sink, on the top of the toilet, rolling around on the floor. Her cotton balls, her brushes, her eyeliners, her mascara, her pink plastic razors, her body wash, her pumice stones, her water-resistant radio hanging from the shower rack, her shampoo, her conditioner, her nail polish remover.

He saw the dresses and sweaters and skirts that piled up on her side of the bed.

He saw the two of them at the beach, her hand on his forearm, on the day she decided to go. She had asked him to go for a walk. They made their way to the water, taking the usual route down Woodbine. At the Queen Street intersection she walked almost five feet in front of him, not waiting for the light to change, but he was the one who almost got hit. They walked beneath tangled stretches of telephone wires and streetcar lines, across a field of frozen brown grass. They sat on a bench dedicated to the memory of Lorne M.G. Laws, 1967-1999. A pair of gulls wrestled over a piece of plastic at their feet. The winter sun sat low and distant behind a matching set of condos.

She put her hand on his arm, then took it away. Said she blamed no one, but she was leaving. She had left. She was gone.

Well, thought Morgan, that explains all those U-Haul boxes.

He stayed on the bench for some time after she'd left, staring at the water, the cold, wet sand, trying to remember what she'd just said, exactly how she'd said it.

Once home, Morgan stood in the front hall for a moment—the vestibule, his wife called it—keys still in hand, unsure of his next move. Their downstairs flat smelled stale, unaired, like a dusty church basement. Standing in the vestibule, Morgan could see straight down the hallway, through to the kitchen and the sliding glass door that led into the empty backyard. The living room to his left, furnished with nothing but a couch and a small end table, bay window looking out onto the dark street. The master bedroom to his right, door slightly ajar, a lamp on a box beside the bed, clothes scattered across the floor. The two smaller bedrooms down the hall on opposing sides, doors closed. The cramped bathroom with its pedestal sink and weak water pressure just off the kitchen at the back of the apartment. Too many rooms for one person.

Her departure had been so sudden.

There she was: sitting at the kitchen table, flipping casually through the paper, chewing on dry unsalted crackers smeared lightly with peanut butter, her housecoat open ever so slightly at the collar, revealing the smallest triangle of pale pink skin. She looked out the window and wondered out loud, "What should we do about that broken blind?" Before Morgan could answer, there she wasn't: her seat empty, her cup untouched, not even a crumb to account for her sudden departure.

Most of the furniture was missing. She'd left the couch, but had taken all the chairs. The bookcases were gone; piles of books marked where they once stood. She'd taken the mirror in the hallway, the one they'd found in Leslieville. The woman who owned the shop claimed the mirror had been salvaged from a nineteenth-century shipwreck, and had given them 15% off because she liked Morgan's wife's handbag. They'd carried it back to the apartment together, Morgan in front, both of them wary of bad luck.

Newspapers crowded the vestibule table—the key table, she called it. The newspapers were still folded, bagged in plastic, cryptoquotes still encrypted.

PSPJACLP EBL FJPBT, BLF TIKQ OBSP FJPBTPF
OMK GOCHP HMUP, CU B DPJUPEQ
FIDHMEBQMCL CJ TIHQMDHMEBQMCL CU OMK
YPMLW, YIQ KIEO ECDMPK CLHA OBSP QOP
DCZPJ CU FJPBTK, BLF BJP FPKQJCAPF GOPL
CLP BQQPTDQK QC UCJEP QOP FJPBT MLQC
QOP JPBH.

RPBL YBIFJMHHBJF

Morgan decided that he would cancel his subscription. He no longer needed to know about bombs in Israeli cafés, or child labour practices in China. There were other more pressing issues at hand. He still didn't know what to do about the carpet indents from her chair.

Should he paint the walls? Would that make a difference?

That night, Morgan lay awake in his wifeless bed, a broken feeling in his chest, compiling a mental list of his wife's shortcomings. The Disasterologies.

1. Widens her eyes to emphasize a point.
2. Refuses to buy non-organic produce.
3. Verbalizes everything she thinks.
4. Takes the seat with the best view every time.
5. Thinks soy cheese is as good as real cheese.
6. Rates everything on a scale of one to three (one meaning Very Bad, three meaning Very Good).
7. Leaves lights on in the hallway when she sleeps.
8. Uses words like "detrimental" and "hegemony" on a regular basis.

9. Turns the volume down on the radio without asking first.
10. Hates raspberries.

The first few evenings, Morgan found himself wandering up and down the hallway of his apartment. The throat. The esophagus of his living arrangement. Sometimes he'd sit on the couch in the living room, counting the bricks the landlady had used to fill their fireplace. A fire *place* that was also, apparently, a fire *hazard*. He would sit there and listen to the sounds his neighbours made in the flat above him, wondering if their apartment had the same layout as his own. The vacuum running over the floor above his living room. The sound of something dropping and breaking in the room above his kitchen. A raised voice. It's not that he wanted to listen. His wife had taken the television. He tried the radio, but he couldn't listen for more than ten minutes. He couldn't put himself in a foreign country, couldn't stay focused long enough to know the conflict, the outcome, the purpose of it in the first place.

Books were worse. Even his favourites lost their shine. He attempted several times to reread his English translation of Hoffmann's *Nachtstücke*, but it was almost like reading the untranslated version. He would flip through the pages, read a paragraph or two, then set it down.

Had she taken his *Caleb Williams*?

For weeks, Morgan came home to his quiet apartment, only to stare at the empty walls. Silence was more bearable, he realized, when at least there was the possibility of eventual conversation. The occasional quiet cough. He longed to hear his wife talking on the phone in their bedroom, her small voice muted behind the closed door.

When they'd first moved in, his wife had scrubbed the place raw while Morgan carried the boxes in and lined them up in the vestibule. She came up to him at least three times holding a grimy black rag in her hand, smiling and giddy. "This was white when I started—white!" She was just as giddy when she came home one day with a painting that she'd found in a friend's basement. An oil painting of a pig jumping into a lake. Her friend had owned the painting for years, but had grown tired of it, or had run out of space, Morgan couldn't remember which. His wife had held the painting in front of him, asked him if he saw it. She made a noise like a pig. He said he could see it, but he was lying just to please her. The painting was abstract, just green and brown blotches of paint with a bright pink smear in the centre. Some blue along the top. Could've been anything. Morgan found it to be a bit ugly. But his wife held the painting against her chest when she showed it to him, her chin on the frame, proud of her find. She said she already knew where she wanted to hang it.

My mom and Ross are the two corniest people in the known universe. Like most people in Nowhereville, NS, they have orange faces and orange arms because they lie for many minutes a week inside body-shaped capsules that artificially burn their skins. If they dyed their hair green and their eyebrows white, they'd look like a couple of Oompa-Loompas. This town is full of Oompa-Loompas who possess a mentality in complete opposition to me. To mine? Ross and my mom happen to fit right in. They both laugh to kill themselves at the stupidest things, like dogs chasing their own tails on TV, and commercials where babies dance and talk.

I often wonder if it's possible for a person to laugh until his Oompa-Loompa head falls right off. Like when Ross does his moronic Super Mario impersonation whenever we order pizza—worst impersonation ever.

November 12 (Evening):

"Scusi mi, did-a somebody order a pizza pie?"
[Mom laughs.]
"Sí? Non?"
[Mom laughs more.]
"We have-a zee pepperoni, zee mushrooms, zee green peppers, and zee mozzarelli. Do you like-a zee mozzarelli?"
"Can I just have a slice please?"
"Ah, sí sí. But where I come from, it is zee custom to say 'grazie.'"
[6.3 second pause.]
"I won't say that word."
[8.2 second pause.]
"Grazie."
[Mom laughs so hard she almost chokes.]

This is something I should mention before I get ahead of myself: I own and carry with me at all times a Sony BM-610 Minicassette Dictator. I use it to maintain a record of all the absurd people I have to deal with in my life, so that when the judge asks me why I had to slaughter ten thousand innocent people, I can just press Play and he can figure it out from there.

The tape recorder once belonged to my dad. He probably owned about a hundred and one tape recorders in his life, and at least ten thousand minicassettes. I remember him sitting at the kitchen table, folders and documents spread out all around him, mumbling into his fist. Always working. He used to write for the *National Post* as a foreign correspondent, an embedded reporter. This basically means that he was sent on assignments around the world, to war-torn places, countries where they stone journalists just for doing their jobs, like Russia, Iran, and Fiji. Crazy places. Before that, he was a publicist for Michelin, and before that he worked in advertising. But that was before I was even born. He said he didn't like wasting his talents, and that's why he started writing articles. At first, he freelanced for the *Chronicle Herald*. Later he worked for the *Toronto Star*, and eventually the *Post*. The last job was the one that really kept him busy. He used to joke that maybe one day he would work for the CBC, so that even if he couldn't see his family, at least they'd be able to see him. Real funny guy.

My dad was gone so often that he lived in Toronto for almost a year before I realized Mom had asked him not to come home. Then he went to the other side of the world on assignment. Went missing after just three weeks. No one really knows what happened to him. He could be in Saudi Arabia, Pakistan. Bangladesh? No one knows. Now the Dictator belongs to me. I use it, as I said, to help explain my eventual insanity, but also because my memory is full of holes, and without the recorder I'd forget half of what I hear, which would be terrible, because soon I'm going to take all the things I have recorded and turn them into a bestselling novel, one that will eventually be adapted into a blockbuster movie that will break all the records and win all the awards. I already know what I am going to call it: *People Are Mangy*. That, or, *Not Guilty: Life Sentences*.

I am too young to have Alzheimer's, which is what my grandfather had. But I do not have a good memory.

I know it's only been a couple of years, but sometimes I have to fight really hard to remember my dad. I can only see him in bits and pieces, like he's a photo that's been cut up and spread across the floor, but some of the pieces have gone missing. I couldn't describe, for example, his teeth, or what his nose looked like when he was mad, and it seems to me that a person should be able to describe his father's teeth and nose, right? This is something I know for sure about my dad. He had the hairiest arms I've ever seen. Wiry black hairs, and he always wore a watch on his left wrist, a heavy silver watch. I remember driving to the beach, and Dad rolling his window down, and I was in the backseat, and I leaned against the door and watched the hairs on his arm dance around. He had one tape in his car, a George Harrison tape, and that's all he listened to that summer. He played "My Sweet Lord" and I watched the hairs on his arm dance around. That's something I know for sure about him. I can't remember if he had long ears or short ears, but he definitely had hairy arms.

The only downside about recording my days is that most conversations simply aren't worth taping. Some are just stupid, like my mom asking Ross, "Where did you put the remote?" Then there are the repeat conversations, words that are said again and again. The date and place might change, but the conversation is identical. On our way to school in the mornings, and church on Sunday, my mom and I are constantly repeating the same talk.

February 11 (Morning):

"Did you shower this morning?"
"Yes."
"Why isn't your hair wet?"
"Mom."
"I'm just asking."
"No, you're insinuating."
"You mean I'm implying."

"I mean what I mean."

"Don't bark at me."

"I'm not barking."

"It's just that something smells. Like seaweed."

"Maybe it's you."

"Maybe it's you."

"I showered, okay?"

March 18 (Morning):

"Sweetheart, didn't you wear that yesterday?"

"What? My jacket?"

"That shirt."

"I have lots of black shirts, Mom."

"But isn't that the same one?"

"No."

"There's a stain."

[2.7 second pause.]

"Hmm."

[5.8 second pause.]

"Did you shower today?"

"Yes."

"Use shampoo?"

"Mom!"

"It's just that it smells like scalp in here."

"Scalp?"

"Dead skin."

"I used shampoo."

"You need to rub it into your scalp. Really rub it in."

"I know that. You think I don't know that?"

To her credit, I may not be the cleanliest person. My doctor, this beluga whale of a man named Dr. Green, informed me that I have seasonal affective disorder, which Dave claims is a fake disease. He says that any disease with an acronymic name like SAD can't be real. For making fun of my weakness, I sent Dave a virus-encrypted email.

He did not open the attachment. Not because he's smart enough to know better, but because, in actual fact, I did not really send him a virused email. Surely he deserves it, but I refuse to be a stooper.

For lack of a better term, Dave is my brother. He's also my mortal enemy, my arch-nemesis, the Borg to my Picard. Everything about him is the opposite of me. He does not listen to music. He hates movies, especially movies that are based on books. He always compares them to the books they were based on, and will talk over the movie whenever something happens that didn't happen in the book. He says he hates TV too, though he watches more TV than anyone I know. Another thing he said, though I don't have a record of it, is that reality programs are products of lazy writing. I told him that didn't make any sense, and he said that's because I'm an idiot, which doesn't seem like a very good argument, especially coming from someone who dropped out of university after six years of wasted effort. He thinks that constantly reading detective stories and comic books, which he calls graphic novels, makes him an authority on everything. He has a whole bookcase in his office full of comics and he would definitely murder me in my sleep if he knew that I touched them. He sometimes falls asleep on the couch watching CNN, wearing idiotic tear-aways, or worn out jogging pants, his hand tucked under the elastic. It's not uncommon to find his marbled tighty-whities on the bathroom floor, and only mildly shocking to see them elsewhere in the apartment.

Dave works for this weird research firm most mornings and afternoons of the week. His job is to search for websites and companies that infringe the trademarks of other businesses. He says he must've inherited "journalistic genes," because his research skills are "off the charts." His words. He carries a green spiral notebook with him at all times, his proud account of his findings. It seems like such a ridiculous and pointless job for someone who went to school for as long as Dave went to school. But apparently there are thousands of thankless imitators out there floating around in cyberspace. He finds them, reports them to his boss, who then sells the information to the companies who own the original trademark. Dave acts like he's some kind of new millennium private detective; I think he's more like a glorified secret shopper. Does it really take a half-finished journalism degree to type key words into a search engine?

Meanwhile, Dave claims he invented the term "splash guard." That is (and only is) when you push the lip of your coffee cup lid into the cup, so when you're driving the coffee doesn't splash around and spill outside of the cup. I say this now only because it strengthens the argument that Dave is a ramrodded fuckerhead, and not my enemy simply for being my lookalike by a fifty-percent margin of error.

When he's not watching TV, Dave's usually in his home office, door locked, probably looking up pictures of sheep. I don't know anything else about what he does. He's gone most of the time, and when I see him he's virtually unpleasant. He smells like Tex-Mex. The odour has nothing to do with Val's cooking. There's not much else to say about this unwholesome man. He might weigh five hundred pounds. He probably only weighs about two hundred pounds, but when he sits on me, I certainly feel five hundred pounds. He will sit on a person just to prove his point. He sometimes takes my hands and slaps them against my face, then he says, "Stop hitting yourself," over and over in the most annoying voice known to earthlings. He will also sometimes pin me to the ground and breathe in my nostrils, and ask me if his breath stinks. If I say yes, he will burp in my face as punishment. If I say no, he will say, "Well then, I guess you won't mind if I do this," after which he will proceed to burp in my face.

Dave is probably the worst person I've ever met. Not only do I hate his guts, I hate his face, arms, legs, skin, his curly blonde hair, his disgusting half-beard, his stupid glasses, and the fact that he lives and has guts to begin with.

If I could have plastic surgery on any part of my body, I think I'd give myself a new face, because my current face looks far too much like Dave's. I don't care if the doctors made me into a movie star or a Ferengi, just as long as they took Dave's features out of mine. His hawkish nose. His miniscule eyes. Our similar faces might be why we hate each other so much. In my experience, physical similarities are enough of a reason to hate someone.

If I'd had a choice, I wouldn't have gone to stay with Dave in Toronto, that stifling pigeon-shit city. Near the beginning of August,

I heard my mom and Ross speaking in the kitchen. They were talking for a very long time and I know they were talking about me. I don't know what they said. I could hear Mom's voice. She never changes her tone. Ross is a nervous talker. His voice goes up and down and I'm never sure when it's going to erupt. When it does, it goes higher, into frequencies that even dogs would strain to hear. I kept hearing my name between small pauses. Then I puked all over the table and fell asleep.

The main reason that Mom wanted to break me in half was because I went for a walk in the woods. There's this old, abandoned farm about ten kilometres from our house, pretty much surrounded by forest. My dad took me there once when I was like nine or ten. One of the buildings is full of chicken coops and piles of rotted hay. The hay is practically black it's so decomposed. Another building is just one square room, and the last one looks almost like a prison. A long hallway with six rooms off of it, the floors all cracked and broken in. Seems like the type of place where people get tortured and no one hears them scream. Kind of creepy at night, but very cool in the day. My dad said it must've belonged to a farming family in the early 1900s. There were cattle skulls with moss growing on them wedged into the dirt, which clearly corroborates his theory.

We'd only gone to the farm once, but one day I started thinking about those rotting old buildings, and then I couldn't stop. I had to see them again. It's not like I had anything better to do. I made it there in about two hours walking, thinking the whole time that I would find something different when I arrived. Maybe see something my dad hadn't seen when he'd brought me there the first time. Pull up a loose floorboard to uncover a briefcase of money. A box of bones. A secret cache of weapons, a map, who knows what? But the only thing different was the spray paint on the walls, "Nick wuz here" written on the roof next to a skull and crossbones, and about a thousand smashed beer bottles everywhere. One of the buildings, the one with the chicken coops in it, had been burned down. A bunch of bastards must've been using the place for parties. The sight of it was so disappointing that I just sat right down and kept staring at it.

At around eight o'clock, just when it started to get dark, the group of partiers showed up. I heard them coming from a mile away, shouting and swearing. Howling like werewolves. I also saw them before they saw me. Three older high school kids, wearing black hoodies, faces impossible to make out. They were passing a bottle of something back and forth, pushing each other around. Completely wasted. I knew that was my cue to leave, but as soon as I moved, one of them saw me. This tall, lanky guy. Hair shaved close to his scalp. He alerted his two buddies, and the three of them went silent. The tall guy walked towards me, asking me what I was doing there as if he owned the place. He asked me if I was jerking off or something. His friends starting laughing, and called me a homo. I didn't respond. I tried to stand up. The tall guy pushed me onto the ground. I said I was just leaving, and tried standing again. He pushed me down again. I was about to tell him to eff off, was like a millisecond from saying it, when he spit into my face. The warm, thick wetness dripped down my cheek and into the corner of my mouth and I thought I was going to barf. The lanky one told me I was trespassing. I wiped the goober from my face with the back of my sleeve, and this time I told the guy to eff off, though he probably didn't hear me, because just before the words came out he kicked me hard in the ribs. Knocked the wind out of me. His friends passed the bottle back and forth. I tried to stand again, and this time the guy kicked me in the head. The arms. The stomach. All over. After a couple minutes, the other two guys came over, and started taking their shots too. Also, they had brought a Rottweiler with them. It started barking once the guy started kicking me, and that's when I knew I was finished. There were actually a few dogs, now that I think about it. At least three. It was dark, but there was definitely a Rottweiler, a Doberman, and a German Shepherd. They were barking and going crazy the whole time. Every few minutes the guys would stop kicking me, give me enough time to stand up. Laughing the whole time. Then they'd start hitting again, the dogs barking behind them, slobbering and howling, lunging forward now and then to take a piece of my face. Eventually they got tired of me.

That's when the fat one grabbed a rock. My brains looked like ground beef in the grass when he was finished. Hamburger Helper all over the place.

The dogs were hungry.

Somehow I lost track of time. Didn't get home until midnight. My mom came flying out of the living room when I came through the front door, and I thought she was going to push me down the stairs. Instead she gave me a hug that hurt, then yelled at me until my ears fell off. Her eyes were red and wet, and it was only then that I realized my stupidity. Caitlyn told me later I'd been a real jackass, that Mom had called her like a hundred times that night. But how could I explain why I needed to see those abandoned buildings?

The following morning, Ross decided to send me away for the rest of the summer until school started again. It wasn't just the disappearance. I also got suspended earlier that year for selling parsley to kids at school. It was just dried parsley, but because I was selling it as pot, the principal decided to pretend it was. He told my mom I was always starting trouble with other kids in my homeroom, but really it's the other way around. These two kids in particular, whom I will call Dick and Dickerson, are always on my case. Year after year, grade after grade, the same two morons making my life suck worse than it already does. Tripping me up when I walk to my desk, or throwing erasers at my head until I can't help it, I have to turn around and tell them to frig off. The teacher never takes my side, and never blames them, mainly because they play hockey, and comb their hair, and wear Tommy Hilfiger sweaters. The jackholes. With the suspension and the fighting, not to mention the fact that I also bombed all of my classes except English, I guess the disappearance was really the last straw. Mom called Dave, made the arrangements, paid for my ticket. Ross offered to drive me to the airport, but my mom intervened and said she would drive me. She bakes the best banana bread I've ever tasted, but I hate her choices.

August 6 (Morning):

"Do you have everything you need?"

"Yes."

"With only one bag? Do you have enough clothes?"

"I don't need a lot of things to keep me happy, Mom."

"That's good honey."

"Do you?"

"No."

"I'll bet."

[Window rolls down.]

"Are you looking forward to seeing your brother?"

"No. Are you looking forward to getting rid of me?"

"Sweetheart."

"What if I contract SARS?"

"You won't contract SARS."

"What if they put me in quarantine?"

"They won't."

"How do you know?"

[2.3 second pause.]

"Are you taping this?

[Silence. The radio comes on. Static.]

When we finally got to the airport, my mom parked the car to go inside with me. Not because she wanted to see me off, but because she didn't trust me. We spent ten minutes looking for a meter that already had time on it, and all we found was the worst location possible and five free minutes. It took five minutes just to walk from the car to the terminal. After checking me in, buying me a milkshake, and walking with me to the Departures area, my mom stopped me by taking a hold of my arm and said, "I'm not sending you away. I hope you don't think that." As a matter of fact, I was thinking that exact thought. "Look at me honey. This is just for a couple of weeks," she said. I said nothing. These were my mother's last words to me before my plane crashed into the Appalachians.

Approximately two and a half hours later—after the fuselage broke in half in a flurry of flames and human misery, after the media swarmed the scene with helicopters, ground crew, official Air Canada spokespeople, and experts in the field of aviation catastrophes, after the authorities finally reported there were no survivors, and a day of mourning for the victims was held in Ottawa and in select cities and towns across the country—my brother's wife met me at the airport in Toronto.

Val. That's her name. She was standing in front of this huge window when I came out, smiling and waving, a sea of concrete overpasses baking in the sun behind her. Dave was not there, because he had to work. Supposedly. I arrived on August 6, on what surely must've been the hottest, grotesquest day of the summer. Val might've been wearing a purple shirt with a neck like a V. About her attire on this day in particular I cannot be sure, but whenever I think of Val she's for some reason always wearing a purple shirt with a neck like a V. She was with Luís, who is her son, but not Dave's. His real father lives in Costa Rica. His name is Jesús, pronounced Hey-Zeus. It's Mexican for Jesus. That's all I really know about him.

I hadn't seen Luís since before he couldn't speak Spanish or English. About his attire I can be sure. He was dressed like Spiderman. A full bodysuit, feet included. He kept throwing his hands out in front of him, and singing made-up lyrics to the Spiderman theme song.

August 6 (Afternoon):

"*Spiderman, Spiderman, he can fly, he can land, he can jump, he's so fast, Spiderman, na na na, look out! Here comes the Spiderman!*"

Val gave me a hug when I came through the automatic doors. She came at me smiling, with her arms opened up, her Mexican piñatas swinging purple in the middle. I looked away but when I looked back they were still there. As she hugged me I could feel them push against me. This might be when I fell in love with her.

In many ways, Val is just like my friend Caitlyn. Completely and utterly a sexual goddess, but totally disgusting for wanting to do it with Dave.

It cuts me up, though it must be said that Val, Dave's wife, the person Dave left Caitlyn for, or for whom Dave left Caitlyn, is even more attractive than Caitlyn. She has the eyes of a rascal and sometimes I think of her without clothing, even though she is, by definition, my sister. Of course, in reality, she's no more my sister than Luís is Dave's son. I had to tell myself that like eight times on our way back from the airport, with Val in the front seat, her hair flying around in the wind, and my thoughts running in circles around her perfectly Mexican face.

Val is an elf. She speaks Spanish and is a fluent Mexican. Only she's not from Mexico, but Arizona. Everyone calls her Val. I think her legal name is Valeria, which I find a much more beautiful rendition, even though it rhymes with malaria. Malaria Valeria has deep-fried brown skin. She has a four-year-old named Luís. He speaks Spanish to Val, but Dave can't understand. Caitlyn says Dave has developed some kind of complex because of it, and that it serves him right. Whenever Val and Luís talk, always talking to each other so fast, at the table, in the car, my brother gets this look on his face like he's about to put someone in a headlock. He's always putting me in headlocks, so I know the look quite well.

Dave is twenty-eight, exactly twice my age, and Val is thirty, more than twice my age. I love her anyway. I've tried not to, but how can I not? Her voice, when she speaks, has no accent, even though she only makes spicy food. Only when she talks Spanish is she in her element.

Val does have a mole on her forehead, something I noticed as soon as we stopped hugging at Arrivals. I would never kiss it, but I love her still.

If he knew my feelings for Val, Dave would put me in a headlock and then twist. He would knock me on my ass and batter my lips and crush my facial structure with his enormous feet. I'm a dead man.

I didn't have any bags other than the one I brought on the plane, so we didn't waste any time getting from the airport to the parkade. Val opened the back of her hatchback for me, and while I was putting my bag inside, Luís shrieked "Shotgun!" in the most annoying voice I'd heard all morning. I half-expected it was a joke, but Val laughed and said, "He thinks because he's almost five he gets to ride in the front seat like a big boy." I watched Luís climb into the front seat and fasten his seatbelt. Then Val said, "I guess you'll be riding the hump," a phrase I was completely unfamiliar with, but I assumed was likely of Mexican origins.

On our way from the airport to their home, Val and Spiderman said things in Spanish to each other. Unlike Dave, I'm okay with that. Sometimes Val would translate, but I didn't find that necessary. I just pressed Record on my Dictator and closed my eyes, and pretended I was in a foreign country, on assignment, a carrier of confidential files, groundbreaking secrets, on my way to the Iranian embassy.

August 6 (Afternoon):

> *"Mamá, ¿podemos tomar pizza con aceitunas y champiñones esta noche?"*
> *"Cariño, eso lo tomamos anoche."*
> [Val says something fast and completely impossible to make out to someone who has just cut into her lane.]
> "Luís was just asking if we can have olive and mushroom pizza tonight."
> "Oh yeah?"
> "It's one of his favourites."
> "Sounds gross."
> *"Mamá, ¡quiero pizza con aceitunas y champiñones!"*
> "No, sweetheart, we had it last night. *De todos modos, viene un invitado esta noche. Voy a hacer algo especial para tu tío.*"
> [Val honks her horn at yet another person who has cut into her lane.]
> *"¡Díos mio!* I was just saying to Luís that … *¡Carajo! Pendejo, ¡escoge un carril!*"

Translation isn't one of Val's strong points. When she did speak English in the car ride, she went on and on about their apartment. How they lived on the bottom floor of an old three-storey house that was built in the 50s, but had been turned into a bunch of apartments in the 90s. "I can't wait for you to see it," she said, looking at me in the rear-view mirror, "I can't believe it's taken you two years to visit!" Val told me about the rustic hardwood floors, the baseboards, the claw foot tub, the built-in ironing board. "So much character," she kept saying. "The master bedroom looks right onto the street. It's so nice to wake up to the sun coming through the windows. And our kitchen leads right onto the backyard—we're the only ones with access to the backyard."

I was impressed a little until I saw the backyard. Not much bigger than a dinner tray.

Their apartment, on the other hand, is pretty big, though it's crowded with so much stuff that it feels small. It has two small bedrooms and one large bedroom. The room in which I stayed is really more like a glorified closet. Dark as a closet, that's for sure. Normally it's where Luís sleeps, but while I was there he stayed in Val and Dave's room. The other small bedroom is across the hall from Luís's room. Dave uses it as an office, though with the bookcases, Dave's desk, the washer, and dryer there's barely enough room for a person in there. Their bathroom's pretty big, but it's impossible to take a shower without rubbing against the sticky shower curtain on a regular basis. Plus, the door handle is a bit wonky, and sometimes the door just opens without the slightest touch. What's even worse is that the bathroom's basically inside the kitchen, which means zero privacy, especially when Dave is talking on the phone in the kitchen. It's like showering while he's in the same room. Impossible to feel clean when that happens.

After about thirty minutes of driving, we pulled up to the curb of their home in Pape Village, and I saw Dave looking at us through the living room window with this disappointed look on his face; turns out he was hoping Val had picked up some KFC, but knew it was a long shot. Luís jumped out of the car and started kicking the air. Val laughed and said something like, "Welcome to Camp David." I looked in the living room window and saw Dave glowering at me.

I knew in a flash that it was going to be a long two weeks.

Their apartment like a box. Their apartment like a mouldy, lidless box. The empty rooms. The quiet of the kitchen, only the refrigerator humming. The sound of the pipes yawning behind the walls. His upstairs neighbours watching television, listening to music, kitchen chairs scraping against the floor above when they have guests over for dinner. The clicking of the blinds against the windows when a breeze blows past.

Their apartment? His apartment.

Morgan went for a walk.

The cool air greeted him like an open palm. Snow falling around him like a million white lights. Drifting. He took a deep breath.

Morgan walked without direction. Most of the houses on Morgan's street had walkways that needed shovelling. Bicycles were chained to streetlamps, balconies, fences, covered in snow. At least half of the houses had long been converted into apartments. Flags from different countries, different provinces, different hockey teams were draped over the windows. Flags Morgan didn't recognize. Where was he?

As he walked, Morgan imagined dotted lines following him around the city, generating triangles and squares in his wake. Xs and Ts. Footprints in the slush.

St. Hubert intersects with Cosburn. Durant intersects with Sammon.

Trees heavy with snow, limbs crooked. A pink sky, the city almost quiet but never dark. Breathing. Everything wet.

Morgan crouched down and packed his hands with snow. Held them together until they hurt, then went numb. The cold turned hot. He wondered how long it would take before they became frostbitten. How long before they fell off?

He was somewhere between Pharmacy and Victoria Park when he saw a white light flash in the corner of his eye. He stopped walking.

The light flashed again.

Morgan stepped onto the grass and walked up to the window of the closest house. Through the sheer curtains, he saw a heavy-set man taking pictures of two girls, probably his daughters. One carried a lampshade on her head; the other had a green blanket tied around her shoulders. They looked familiar. Morgan wondered if he knew them, but that seemed unlikely. He didn't have many friends. His wife pretty much took the few ones he had, just as she'd taken the bookshelves, the chairs, the bath mat, and the curtains. During the first few weeks he'd had people around him who'd been supportive, as they'd been a year before, when his wife was in the hospital, feverish, losing blood, gaining infections. But after a while, one by one they stopped calling. And then his cordless phone went missing. He'd forgotten where he'd put it. He'd misplaced it. All that was left was the console.

The camera flashed and flashed. The girls walked back and forth, back and forth, like miniature runway models. Morgan watched them in the window for what seemed like a long time before one of them noticed. Before the girl with the blanket around her shoulders saw Morgan's face, a stranger's face, in the window. She stopped moving. Squinted her eyes. Smiled. Her father didn't notice. Not right away.

By the time she pointed, she was too late.

Morgan was already gone.

When he returned to his apartment, Morgan tried to remember the path he'd walked. He remembered turning onto Woodycrest Avenue, but had he gone left or right? He clearly remembered walking along a street called Wallington. Or was it Wellington?

The following night Morgan walked again. He passed by a gas station, brightly lit, full of trinkets and pins, ashtrays decorated with red maple leafs, stuffed beavers, bottles of gooey maple syrup, junk food, trashy magazines, batteries, stale bread, cigarettes. Morgan bought a map of Toronto there, which he later unfolded on his living room floor. He bent close to the map to inspect the streets. Line by line, name by number, he traced his paths with a blue felt-tipped marker. With each path imprinted he felt more connected, somehow, to the city. Rooted to the map, a part of the landscape now. Seeing his paths on paper. Mapping his movements.

Would this be enough? Was this enough?

He developed a system of rules for walking. He thought of them in no particular order:

Do not bring money.
Do not ask for directions.
Do not walk for less than an hour.
Do not stop moving.
Do not take the same route twice, not even in reverse.

Morgan focused on his map. He unfolded it and folded it back up again.

But when he pulled the covers back exposing the uninhabited tundra of his empty bed, he still felt it. He felt it when he moved the alarm clock from her side to his. He felt it when he forgot and cooked for two and, out of frustration and disgust, had to throw the remains in the trash. He felt it when he slept. That broken feeling in his guts.

There were things he couldn't forget.

1. On the day you first met. She said things to make you speak. To provoke a reaction, though not necessarily to upset you. At that Thai restaurant, when she told you she liked darker men. Men from Spain, Portugal, Italy. Men with sun in their blood. You said, "Wells is not a Spanish name." She laughed.
2. On the day you went to the ROM. How she insisted that you see the dinosaurs. "Which is your favourite?" she asked, "Which do you like best?" You said you liked the one you were looking at, whichever one it was, with the long neck, heavy body. A vegetarian. "Typical," she said. "I'm a T-rex. You wouldn't stand a chance."
3. On the day you first met her parents. She told them you were a paper pusher, because she thought it sounded better. Trying to be funny. She was an exceptional liar.

Morgan awoke dry-mouthed and damp with sweat. He sat up and drank the last drop of water from the mug on his bedside table, something his wife had bought at a yard sale for a nickel. It had a picture of two wolves howling on a snow-covered hill, a yellow moon rising above the trees.

Morgan's mornings progressed in five-minute intervals. Another one of his rules. Five minutes to get out of bed, five minutes to get cleaned up, five minutes to eat. He thought of them as "twitches." First lying in bed. Twitch. Next washing his face. Twitch. Now using the washroom.

Twitch.

Morgan stood in the centre of his living room, on a morning already three twitches old, and scribbled "potted zebra plant" onto a Post-it note. He stuck it on the wall beside the couch, just above where their old potted zebra plant once sat. Throughout his apartment, on the walls, the floor, the ceiling, the cupboards, the coffee table, the coffee maker, and the blinds, Post-its began to assemble a fragmented yellow brick road.

Bedside lamp: *light bulbs.*

Kitchen counter: *compost bin.*

Refrigerator: *eggs.*

Refrigerator: *cheese.*

Refrigerator: *mechanical pencils.*

Sink: *dish rack.*

Front door: *stereo.*

Occasionally, Morgan became conscious of the Post-its as a whole, the way they whispered when he moved. The way they folded out and away from the flat surfaces of his home, like wings.

The vestibule held the most Post-it notes in the apartment. From floor to ceiling, spreading even onto the inner surface of the front door, covering the eye in the centre. Covering each other, layer after layer. Breathing and growling, snarling.

Bristol board.

Shoe horn.

Black liquorice.

Morgan went into the kitchen and unplugged the boiling kettle. The phone trilled. In the apartment upstairs, someone turned on a vacuum cleaner. Morgan looked through his cupboards for coffee filters, but found only a pile of Post-its. He used paper towel instead, then he made his oatmeal in the same way he'd been making it for as long as he could remember.

Step one: Pour a drop of water into bowl and roll it around until the bottom of bowl is wet.

Step two: Pour one half-cup of oatmeal into bowl, beginning in the centre and moving out, clockwise, to the edges.

Step three: Pour hot water into bowl for two seconds. Stir until mixture thickens.

Step four: Pour rest of oatmeal into bowl, beginning along the edges and moving, counter-clockwise, toward the centre.

Step five: Pour hot water into bowl for three seconds, then stir eight times clockwise, eight times counter-clockwise, four times clockwise.

Step six: Add two tablespoons of brown sugar into the centre of bowl. Stir.

At the table, Morgan ate quickly, efficiently, eyes flashing from his oatmeal to the clock on the stove. He paused, took a sip of coffee. It tasted like boiled mud and vinegar. The phone started ringing again. Perhaps it hadn't stopped. Perhaps he'd tuned it out. Morgan took another soft and sticky bite of oatmeal.

Twitch.

In his bedroom, pulling his light blue company golf shirt over his head, Morgan struggled with the buttons on the front. They were hard to undo without seeing them, but he didn't want to take the shirt off and start all over again, so he fiddled with them blindly. A contortionist's pose, shoulders testing the boundaries of skin. Headless. Once he'd finally pushed his head through, he turned and saw himself in the bedroom mirror. "The Letter Shredders," the name of the document shredding company that he worked for, was written on the upper left pocket of his shirt, in either Times New Roman or Garamond. He couldn't tell which. His wife, a typographer, never missed a chance to criticize fonts. When she read books, or saw ads on the subway, she would comment briefly on whether she liked the typeface, tell Morgan what worked and what didn't. She had a longstanding thing against all the standard font choices, and would cringe when she saw Comic Sans used on a sign. Yet she'd never commented on the typeface his company used. He'd caught her staring at the letters on his chest, from time to time. "What?" he'd asked. "What's wrong?" She would just shake her head.

Morgan stared at his chest, in the mirror, trying to decide. Times New Roman or Garamond? He forgot which one she hated most.

Courier?

No.

Arial?

Twitch.

On the front step, locking the door, chewing down a grape-flavoured antacid, the rain falling lightly against the back of his neck, his key in the slot, his hand, that precise movement of pulling back, shaking, shaking. The sledge of the deadbolt sliding into place. The security of the locked door, keeping things in place. Keeping things contained.

Twitch.

Richard Cranley, Collections Supervisor, sat behind his steel-framed desk and rummaged around for something in his desk drawer for nearly a minute while Morgan sat quietly on the other side, watching him. Cranley was muttering something under his breath the whole time. Eventually he closed the drawer, and clasped his empty hands together on his chest. He wore the same company golf shirt as everyone else, but his was a darker blue. In the winter months, he sometimes wore a black turtleneck underneath. His office smelled like furniture polish and something else, something Morgan could never quite place, but something slightly reminiscent of his high school chemistry lab. Tiny brown bottles with corks in the necks. A sweetness.

Morgan worked for The Letter Shredders as a Collections Officer, which was the company's way of saying garbage man. He drove in a fifteen-foot cube van equipped with a black industrial paper shredder in the back. The shredder was screwed into the floor of the van, though half of the time it was out of order, so Morgan had to store the bags on top and beside the dormant machine. Wherever they could find room. The bags were full of bank statements, legal memos, customer lists, sales charts, business plans, unused blank envelopes with out-of-date return addresses; the occasional paper cup or brown lunch bag, or Kleenex, tucked into the mix. "If you don't want it read, give it a shred!" was stencilled in two-foot blue letters on the side of the van. The Letter Shredders had a jingle on the television; the radio too. Their clients included law firms, call centres, insurance companies, hospitals, schools, accountants, financial advisors, banks, mortgage brokers, securities firms. Some provided services Morgan didn't understand. Information management, corporate office solutions, risk calibration. He didn't know what they did, only that, like all the rest, they wanted the paper trail destroyed. Shredded and recycled. They were the people with the confidential information. The people with secrets worth keeping.

Normally, Morgan would've been climbing into a company van about now to do the morning pickups, but Richard Cranley had called Morgan into his office as soon as Morgan punched in. He'd made it seem urgent, but here he was, taking his time. He looked at Morgan for a good long moment before saying anything. His eyes, dull and glassy, gave nothing away. Cranley leaned back in his chair, hands still clasped on his chest. "How you holding up, Wells?"

Morgan had become used to questions like that since his wife had left. Even people he barely knew seemed to know about his wife's departure. His response had become more automatic, if briefer, with time. "Fine."

"I hear you've been slowing down some. Any truth in that?"

"I don't know what you mean."

"You used to come in fifteen minutes early, leave fifteen minutes late. But lately … not so much."

Morgan shifted in the hard plastic chair.

"It's not that I blame you for being slack now and then. I used to work for the city, so trust me, I know exactly what I'm talking about. It takes ten people to do a one-man job when you're dealing with government, because half the time nine of them are on paid leave for some bogus disability. Sore feet or restless legs syndrome, insomnia, you name it. Anyway, it's a problem but I get it. You think I spend every waking minute in here getting work done?" Cranley made a gun with his hand and put it to his head. He pulled the trigger, then held both hands up, defenceless. "Don't get me wrong, I work my share of overtime. But Scott says you don't listen. Says he catches you daydreaming. Says it takes you ten minutes to do what should be done in two. Not just on Mondays either."

Scott. Of course it was Scott. He was a fellow Collections Officer, a stick figure of a man who more often than not accompanied Morgan in the van. Morgan realized early on that he had about as much in common with Scott Parker as he had with the sacks of confidential papers, or "shreddies," they collected on their route.

"Okay."

"I've told you that my first wife wasn't much better than yours, eh?"

Cranley chuckled, leaned forward, and waited for Morgan to laugh. His smile pulled back over a set of straight, dentist-whitened teeth. He raised his eyebrows up until they practically merged with his curly blonde hair. When Morgan failed to take up the cue, Cranley settled back into his chair, a bit dejected.

"Point is I've been in your shoes. I know what you're going through. Not to mention that awful stuff with the baby …"

Awful stuff.

At the hospital with its squeaky white corridors standing above an isolette on no sleep while his wife made plans for her departure while tiny lungs collapsed on an unformed heart while bags of fluids and oxygen pumps worked uselessly to keep life inside that tiny see-through body.

Morgan nodded.

"Unfortunately, I can't give you time off. You're already over your limit, and understandably so, but still. You're over."

"I understand."

Cranley sat back in his chair. For a moment, Morgan felt sorry for him. Cranley was always like this, wanting to be everyone's friend. Most of the Collections Officers would've thanked Cranley for the friendly warning, promised to return with more energy. That, Morgan knew, was the normal reaction, the expected reaction. It wasn't his reaction though.

Cranley took a deep breath. "Good," he said, looking at the ceiling. "But I don't want to hear from Scott again. Don't make it any harder for yourself."

Morgan cleaned his apartment routinely, even scrubbed the rooms he never used. Every night, on his knees, lemon yellow gloves and special devices for cleaning the cracks, the grout between the kitchen tiles, removing the dead skin and the hairs. He spent hours in the bathroom, scrubbing the toilet, the rim of the tub, the faucets, the mirror, the walls. He invented rules for himself, things he could rely upon. Rules for washing dishes—with hot water only, right hand holds the sponge. He could not always rely upon his ability to follow the rules, but at least he knew they existed. Rules for entering a room. Rules for brushing teeth. Rules for ordering food at a restaurant. Rules for coming up with rules. He wondered how far he could go, if it was possible to map out an entire day before it even occurred.

The rules continued to multiply, rules sprouting from rules, an incredible system, a means of straightening things up, renewing, keeping order, understanding how one moment leads to another, rules to build a life by, until one day a new diversion came to Morgan. He no longer would need to search for a distraction. One day, one found him.

It arrived in the form of a postcard from France.

My first week in Toronto was completely happenless. Day after day of endless nothing. A whole seven days of sweating and stinking and not doing anything at all. A week of just waiting for time to pass so I could go back home. Indeed, my premonition about the visit being a long one had been true.

I barely saw Dave, because he spent all of his time in his home office, doing God knows what. Val and Luís were around most of the time, but they always wanted to do kid things. Play with Luís's toy cars and watch scatterbrained kid cartoons. Since no one really knew how to deal with me, I was pretty much on my own.

Right away, I started going for long walks in the middle of the day just to get the heck away from Camp David, my annoying fake nephew-in-law, and his so-called parents. One day I was so bored I actually went downtown and walked from one skyscraper to the next. I rode the elevators to the highest possible floor. When I got to the top floor of the TD Centre, I found the door to the roof and jumped. It felt longer going down than up.

I'd be lying if I didn't say that August 14 started off as just another hot, suffocating day of nothing. Val and Luís were at the beach. Dave was working in his office. I was on my own. So, not surprisingly, I found myself sitting in the food court at the Eaton Centre, as usual, a real pro by now at loitering. I went to the Eaton Centre often because it was air-conditioned. It's basically like any other mall in the world, times a thousand. Anyways, I was in the food court, I'd just picked up some batteries, a three-pack of minicassettes, and a giant pretzel dipped in animal fat. I was sitting there questioning my love for burgers, because Val had recently got me thinking of E. coli, and a death of tubes and plastic and rubber. She'd come into my room the day before, or the room I was staying in, the room in which I stayed, and talked to me about her plans for Luís's birthday party. His birthday was in a few days, and she was already making plans. She talked about food. I recommended burgers and she made a face. I don't know exactly what words she spoke because my recorder was turned off. She definitely wanted me to kiss her.

She might be older than most people I know. And she's married to my brother, which might be an indication that she's also in love with him. But I think if I kissed her, she might change her opinion on that matter. I'm guessing she smells like lavender, though I'm not sure how that smells. Purple, maybe.

Val thinks burgers are evil. Meanwhile, she eats veggie burgers like it's nobody's business but God's.

Val said she definitely wouldn't be serving hamburgers at Luís's birthday party, though soy burgers were a possibility. Now it was my turn to make a face. Val mentioned something about scientists creating scents artificially, which they inject into meat and vegetables and things. She said that burger meat has no nutritional content whatsoever, and is injected with pheromones and hormones, fake smells and flavours. She also pointed out that beef cows live really sad lives, and die by the horriblest conditions. Rifle to the head. Val's lecture made me wonder if anyone had patented rotten corpse smell. I'd like to market rotten-corpse-scented deodorant. That way if someone told me I smelled like a rotten corpse, I could say, "I am one," and they would leave me alone. I'd also like to patent the smell of Val's skin.

Even though Val pretty much convinced me that burgers are Satan's preference, I still wanted one. I was trying to decide between a regular burger and a cheeseburger in the Eaton Centre food court when the lights flickered, then went out. The whole place was suddenly dark, except near the dead escalators, where slices of light cut through from the glass ceiling four floors up. At first no one made a sound, but then a few people starting hooting a bit, laughing, and I didn't move at all, just stood there like an idiot, looking around in the bluish dark. Then the security guards with their flashlights and loud voices came around. They proceeded with the evacuation, but couldn't tell us anything. Everyone was in single file, walking up the escalators, but it might've been different had we known that the entire city—and not just this one building—had lost air conditioning.

Some people might've started pushing. Especially if they knew that New York had also lost power. Detroit, Chicago. The Pentagon too. We could've been trampling each other.

I was reminded of a bar fire that happened on Channel 5 News a few years ago. Apparently, a smoke machine exploded. People in the audience had their cameras and they caught it all on tape. I saw footage of a burning stage, people trapped in the doorway, stuck there, burning. Seventy-six casualties. Most died of asphyxiation. A fire marshal told reporters that if everyone in the bar had only remained calm and exited in an orderly manner, everyone would've lived. Except the band, who died instantly when the smoke machine exploded.

I am a huge fan of standing in single file. It's the most efficient social invention since the can opener.

Once outside the mall, we stood near the entrance, holding shopping bags close to our legs. Confused. Hot. In single file. We lined up right there on the sidewalk, waited for someone to give orders. When no one did, I imagined myself walking into the Centre, raising my voice, pushing my hands into the air. Smiling. Confident. Leaderish. My picture on a billboard. I was thinking this long after we dispersed.

I made my way to Union Station. The trains were melting, congregating with the tracks. I watched people melt into their luggage, their boxes, their laptops, their purses, their coffees. Arrivals and Departures. Literally thousands of people with these lost looks. The trains weren't coming or going. Everyone was stranded. I talked to a man who was on his way to Montréal. He told me his name but I forgot it instantly, a rookie mistake. I hadn't yet put new batteries into my recorder.

I left the bus station at around five and headed home. The sidewalks were choking. Rivers of people. The subway was shut down, there were stranded commuters everywhere, briefcases and bookbags floating along the surface of the city. I've never seen that many bodies all in one space. All drowning. The traffic lights were out. The bodies, the cars, the metalized air. No one knew what was happening. A bunch of idiots sat in a stopped streetcar, just looking out the window as though any minute the thing was going to start moving again. As though any minute the entire city was going to restart itself. Or spontaneously combust.

I walked the whole two hours to Pape Village thinking about weapons of mass destruction and the Middle East. Remembering the time I was captured by terrorists in Iraq. They grabbed me off the street, beat and starved me. They pissed on me and published pictures of me on the Internet and the Al-Jazeer network. Eventually, Abu helped me escape. But I got caught. Had my head beheaded. I recorded a video on the Internet to say goodbye to my mom before they killed me and slung my headless corpse over a bridge, the words "Get out US" carved into my chest.

By the time I reached Dave's place, I was still thinking about the desert. I went into the kitchen, poured myself a tall glass of water, and drank it in one gulp. If our bodies are 75% water, mine was hovering at around 20%. Out on the back deck, Val was sitting in one of their fake plastic Adirondacks that they had picked up at Canadian Tire. Each was a different colour. Blue, red, green, and orange. Val was in the green one. She was sitting so wonderfully in her chair, Buddha-like, the sun reflecting off her body as though it were wrapped in aluminum foil. Luís leaned against her bare legs. He was colouring. He can speak two languages, but has no idea what it means to colour inside the lines. Worst colourer ever. Through the screen door, I heard Val say something in Spanish, which made Luís giggle.

I was about to finish up my second glass of water when Dave came into the kitchen wearing his faded grey joggers and a black T-shirt. He had a plate full of crumbs in one hand, his green spiral notebook in the other. "Hey little brother," he said, hitting the back of my head with his notebook. "Where were you when the power went out?"

Dave never uses my name when he talks to me. Caitlyn thinks it's because me and my dad have the same name. What a genius. Either way, when either Val or Luís or my mom or Ross are within earshot, Dave calls me "little brother." When we're alone, he calls me "little fucker."

I told Dave I was downtown buying the special little tapes for my recorder, which is true. These specific tapes were brand new, though sometimes I buy them at garage sales and flea markets. Used tapes are great for two reasons: they are cheap, and they are interesting. I like to see what the previous owners recorded on them.

Undated (woman's voice):

> "This course is, uh, cross-listed with Engineering 2035, and so, um, and so if you are in that class, then you shouldn't be in this class. I am assuming of course, that, um, that you would have already looked into this, but, um, if not, then now is the time to do so. Question?"
> [Someone in the class asks a question, but it's indecipherable.]
> "You don't know what cross-listed means? You don't know that and you're taking Applied Differential Equations? Seriously?"

Sometimes I listen to my dad's old tapes too. He just talks about his stories, his reports, and most of the time I have no idea what he's saying. But I haven't taped over any of them, because they sometimes help me fall asleep when I'm being an insomniac.

Undated (Dad):

> "Need to work on the HaloCorp story. Get in touch with Mike Taylor before six tomorrow evening to set up a meeting."

I showed Dave the bag from Radio Shack to corroborate my story about buying minicassettes. He tried to grab it from me but I am poetry in motion.

August 14 (Evening):

> "I got batteries too."
> "Good for you. Was it crazy down there?"
> "Where?"
> [Sound of dirty plate being placed in the sink.]
> "Where do you think?"
> "Oh. Same as usual."

[Tap turning on.]

"Don't be a fucking smartass."

"Dave!"

"Val?"

"Watch your language."

"Would you prefer Spanish?"

"… Don't be a smartass."

"Val, I'm only having a conversation with him."

"You're calling him names."

"I'm not. Thanks for refereeing though."

"Just knock it off."

[Tap turns off. Fridge door opening. Closing. Opening again.]

"Val, we're out of milk."

"Bought some yesterday. Look harder."

"Oh."

[Fridge door closing. 5.2 second pause. Loud slurping.]

"Ah!"

"Disgusting."

"Delicious."

"Now you've polluted the whole carton."

"I paid for it."

"Val paid for it."

"I paid for it."

"Is it warm?"

"The power hasn't been out that long you idiot."

"David!"

"You're such a dick."

"That's enough! Come out here. Both of you."

[Dave laughs. 4.2 second pause as we walk outside. Distant traffic sounds. Grackles cawing and other bird noises.]

"Can I ask you for a favour?"

"Ask whom?"

"Can one of you please go find some candles before it gets too dark?"

[Grackles suddenly get a lot louder, start cawing repeatedly back and forth.]

"Those goddamn birds."

"The little tea lights, Dave."

"Why have a birdfeeder if this is all we see? Greg and Vanessa get cardinals. Hummingbirds."

"Dave, are you listening to me?"

"Yes. Why not a flashlight?"

"I'd prefer tea lights."

"Where are they?"

"Luís's room … the guest room. Should be in the top right corner of the desk. There's a whole pack of them in there."

"How many do you want?"

"Por lo menos tu padrasto es útil para algo."

[Val and Luís laugh.]

"What? *Padrasto* what?"

[More laughter.]

"Just bring them all out, Dave."

"Okay. Sure. You heard her, little brother."

"What? You said you'd do it."

"Apparently, Dave wants to be a big baby today. Maybe his little brother wouldn't mind filling in for him?"

"Hey-Zeus. Okay."

There is only one window in the room that was formerly Luís's but was temporarily mine. This window is rather high on the wall, and lets in insignificant light. I was so stupid as to try and turn the light on when I entered the room, even though all I'd been think-ing about for the past however many hours was the blackout. As it was already well past seven, I could barely see anything in the desk. I checked the drawer that Val mentioned but no candles. I looked quickly through the rest of the drawers. Zilch.

I did find a half-empty pack of AA batteries, one pearl-beaded rosary, a broken one made of wood, two decks of unopened play-ing cards, Old Spice, a tourist money belt, a pile of strange-looking change, and a flashlight with a cracked bulb. I found an old movie stub, faded and curling, three rolls of film, a felt box with a tube of Krazy glue in it, some of those little pins with the multi-coloured balls on the top and a pile of pens. A Mad Libs book. A box full of photos: my brother getting confirmed; my parents, sitting together on the front step of our old house, my mother's hand on my father's knee; a black and white one of my dad standing in front of a mountain, looking young, about Dave's age. No candles.

It was then that I decided that Val must've lied about the candles being there, just to make Dave go away. Or to make me go away. To separate us. Either way, there were no candles in that room. But I didn't want to go back empty-handed. It was frustrating, because all I wanted to do was tell both of them to die. But Val would've been disappointed, which would've made Dave happy on two levels: first that I had failed, and second that Val had been proven wrong. I could not let this happen.

Even though I'd been staying with Dave and Val for a week, I still didn't feel comfortable in their apartment. When I did the dishes, I kept forgetting where the glasses and cups were supposed to go, and which drawers held the cutlery. Obviously, I didn't have the first clue where to look for candles. If I'd been home, with Mom, I would've found candles right away, not because I know where she keeps them, but because I would know where she might keep them. But at Camp David I didn't have a clue where to start. I thought for a millisecond about calling my mom, because I hadn't talked to her for almost a week. Not that she would care. She probably hadn't noticed. Had been too busy doing her marital duty with idiot Ross. I almost picked up the phone to call, just out of spite, just to waste her time. But then I remembered that Val was waiting for me. If I took too long she'd probably send Dave in, and then he'd find the candles and would rub it in my face and say, "What did I tell ya?" Moving as quickly as I could, I checked the living room, and then the bathroom, and finally the kitchen. I looked through all the kitchen cupboards, and drawers, and was *this* close to giving up. I was so frustrated with not finding the candles that I pulled one of the drawers right out of the counter. It crashed to the floor, silverware spilling everywhere.

My terror alert went from yellow to orange. I waited for someone to yell at me, but the sliding door was now closed. Dave and Val were standing out there with Luís, facing the burial plot they call a backyard. Oblivious. So I picked up all the forks and spoons and knives and things and put them neatly into their plastic tray. I left that on the counter, while I tried to push the drawer back into its place. But it would only go about halfway. I pulled it out and tried again. Half of the drawer still stuck out. It was dark, so I couldn't see what was blocking the tracks. For a brief moment I imagined there was a severed hand or a dead rat in there, just waiting to give me rabies or the plague. I pictured myself foaming at the mouth, my pupils dilating, and then falling to the linoleum, shaking and writhing and dying under the table, my groin swelling with buboes. I reached into the hole and felt around. I moved my hand around rapidly at first, hoping to scare whatever animal was hiding in there, should it happen to be alive. Then I felt along the tracks until I came upon what I first thought was a small box. I grabbed the box and pulled it out, only to discover that I was holding a book.

It was slim, less than one hundred pages. I had to peek inside the cover to see the title, as the jacket was missing. *The Description of a New World, Called the Blazing World.* I could tell the book was written a long time ago by the way the words looked on the page; some of the 'S's looked like 'F's. Plus, underneath the title, it said the book was written by "the thrice noble, illustrious and excellent princesse, the Duchess of Newcastle." The author's name was Margaret Cavendish, and the book had originally been published in 1666.

Once, on a class trip to a museum in Nowhereville, we saw this ancient copy of the Bible. The Bible was from the olden days, and was in a glass case to keep assbrains like Dick and Dickerson from touching it. The pages looked brittle, slightly brown along the edges, ready to fall apart if anyone tried to turn them. *The Blazing World* might've been written in the same time period that that old version of the Bible was published in, but the copy in my hands couldn't have been more than a few decades old. Older than my mom, but not necessarily older than her mom. Still the cover felt kind of gritty and grainy in my hand, like it had been left outside for months before being hidden in the drawer. On the first page, someone had written an inscription, although the letters were faint and a bit hard to pick out.

This is totally weird, right up your alley. And incredible. Written by a woman (you'll thank me later). Don't you lose it! Love, Myrna.

Myrna? I'd been staying with Dave and Val for a week, and not once had I heard the name Myrna mentioned. She'd drawn a little bubbly heart next to her name. Was it even possible for another woman to be in love with Dave? Why was he hiding this book behind a drawer?

I put the book on the counter and gently replaced the drawer. It slid in easily. Then I carried the book to the other end of the apartment, into the living room. I did this for three reasons. Number one, to get a better look; number two, to get as far from Dave as possible, who was still standing out on the deck. The third reason came from one of my all-time favourite movies: *The Neverending Story*. This kid named Bastian finds this old book and basically gets sucked into a different dimension, into this place called Fantasia. The circumstances behind him finding the book at a used bookstore and me finding the book in my brother's apartment weren't completely unalike. It's not as though I thought I was about to enter another dimension. I'm fourteen, I know better. But I figured if there was even a slight possibility, I wanted to be comfortable when it happened. I stretched out on the couch and opened the book. The pages were stiff. I read the first page.

This present Description of a New World, *was made as an Appendix to my* Observations upon Experimental Philosophy; *and, having some Sympathy and Coherence with each other, were joyned together as Two several Worlds, at their Two Poles. But, by reason most Ladies take no delight in Philosophical Arguments, I separated some from the mentioned Observations, and caused them to go out by themselves, that I might express my Respects, in presenting to Them such Fancies as my Contemplations did afford. The First Part is Romancical; the Second, Philosophical; and the Third is meerly Fancy; or (as I may call it) Fantastical.*

It took me almost five minutes just to read those first few lines. I could tell by the way this person wrote that I wasn't going to like the story. I don't read a whole lot, but when I do, I read Choose Your Own Adventures. My dad used to buy them for me because he thought "active reading" was better for brain development. I couldn't agree more. They're pretty much the only books worth reading, because the main character is me, and I get to make the choices and decide what will happen. In most stories there are over twenty-two possible endings. I could end up rich, or dead, or locked in a golden box for all eternity. That's what happened in one of my top three favourite books, *The Underground Cavern*. I ended up getting locked in this golden box that doesn't allow you to age, but is also impossible to open. Worst possible thing that could happen to me, I think. But that's the beauty of choosing my own adventure. If my character has to make a choice between walking down a dark alley or not walking down a dark alley, I get to choose simply by turning to the appropriate page. I have the power to decide how it all goes down. Plus, if I don't like the ending, I can just read the story again. It's different every time. Talk about a neverending story.

What happens next in the story? It all depends on the choices you *make. How does the story end? Only* you *can find out! And the best part is that you can keep reading and rereading until you've had not* one *but* many *incredibly daring experiences!*

So I wouldn't say I liked Cavendish's writing. Hard to understand, with capital letters everywhere. It was like code. Mostly I was skipping words that were spelled funny, and even whole sentences, because not a lot of it made sense.

But I kept reading, and I'm glad I did. Admittedly, I didn't read the thing word for word, but I gathered within the first few pages that the story was about this woman, this super hot Lady with a capital L, who gets kidnapped by some foreigner for sex slave purposes. He and his men grab her while she's out walking along the seashore collecting shells, because that's apparently what beautiful young women like to do.

After the woman is captured and loaded onto the foreigner's boat, a terrible storm comes along and sets the boat off-course, straight north, towards the Arctic, where the captors all freeze to death. But somehow the Lady doesn't freeze, because when the captors kidnapped her they tied her body in a thick, wool blanket, so that, after they all died, she was still comfortably asleep, and completely unaware of the blizzard that had killed them. By the time she wakes up, the ropes the captors had used to tie her up have come undone. That's when she crawls out of the blanket and realizes she's hit land, and sees these strange creatures that look like bears and talk like human beings walking around. She calls them bear-men. Only then does the Lady realize the ship has passed into another dimension, because, according to the author, our world is connected to a second world, the blazing world, at the North Pole.

I dropped the book onto the coffee table. My first impression was that this was fate, that I was meant to find this book. True, it wasn't about to take me into another dimension. But I couldn't help but see the parallels between what was happening to me in my life, and what was happening to this woman. Like her, I'd also been taken prisoner. So to speak. And I was in a new world, a hostile environment, a humid garbage town full of strange creatures. The story reminded me of being downtown. Of seeing so many people from so many places looking so lost.

My second impression was that this book must belong to Dave. Who else would read science fiction from the 1600s? Was he hiding it behind the drawer on purpose? For what purpose?

I was asking myself such questions when I heard the deck door slide open, then close. I held my breath, worried Dave was about to come in and tell me off. If he found me on the couch, he would think I hadn't even looked for the candles. I instinctively slipped the book under my shirt. Luckily, it was just Luís who had come inside. I could tell it was him from the sound of his light footsteps padding down the hall.

"Mom and Dave are having a private discussion," he said as he walked into the living room. "You can't go out." He then dropped to the floor a foot or so from the coffee table and opened his colouring book.

I sat up on the couch.

August 14 (Evening):

"Private?"

"They told me to come inside."

[5.5 second pause.]

"Wanna colour?"

"No thanks."

"Can you time me?"

"What?"

"I can run from that wall to that wall in ten seconds. That's my
record. Wanna see?"

"What's that, like, a foot a second?"

"Huh?"

"Nothing."

"Do you know it's my birthday in five days?"

"You've only told me four thousand times."

"I'm turning five."

"Yeah. Hooray."

[11.4 second pause.]

"Wanna play with my cars?"

"Definitely not."

"Did you know I have about one hundred cars?"

"Hmm."

[4.2 second pause.]

"Did you find candles?"

"No. Still looking."

Luís nodded, looked at the ceiling for about half a minute, then
went back to colouring outside the lines. He made high-pitched
whispery sounds as he coloured, and sat with one leg bent at the
knee so he could rest his head against it.

I got up off the couch and went back into the kitchen. Val and
Dave both had their backs to the sliding door. A private discussion? I
walked right up to the sliding door, but I couldn't hear what they were

saying. So I put a brand new tape into my recorder. Then I strategically placed it next to an open window and pressed Record. A good idea but it didn't really work in the end. Just fuzz, and the occasional car honking. At one point, you can almost hear Val say my name. My name, and then, "Is it really so hard … a little bit … and it's not like he's …" The rest of the sentence is mutilated by fuzz, and you can't hear what Dave says in response. He can be a bit of a mumbler sometimes.

One day I would like to upgrade my tape recorder and get a digital voice recorder, probably a Sony, which is the best technology company in the world. The Japanese are a brilliant people. Dave says I'd need a computer to make my Sony digital voice recorder worthwhile, so I would probably get a Sony of that too. My plan falters, however, when I remember that I need money, which is always my problem. I don't have any money. The extreme poverty of youth is the second worst thing about my life.

After Dave and Val came inside, I collected my tape recorder from the windowsill and went to my room. Val asked me about the candles, but my headphones were on and I pretended not to hear her. Didn't work. She followed me right down the hallway, still in her bathing suit, yellow flowers on a green background, and tapped me on the shoulder just before I went into the guest room. Luís's room. My room. Whatever it is.

"Did you find them?"

I kept my eyes desperately pinned to her face, the ceiling above her head.

"No."

"Did you look in the bathroom closet?"

I shrugged.

"Thanks for trying."

Val started to walk away, then turned around. "Don't worry about Dave," she said, quietly. "He doesn't mean it. Not really. He's just feeling a little frustrated lately. He's been under a lot of pressure."

Then she turned around, and I watched her go into the bathroom. She came out ten seconds later with a big plastic Ziploc bag full of candles and a satisfied smile on her face. She winked at me.

Could've been a bomb exploding in my chest.

"What's the next address?"

"1200 Ossington. It's a school."

"High school?"

"I don't know. Grade school, I think."

"Catholic?"

Morgan checked the name on the sheet. St. Mary's Grammar School.

"Think so."

"Then I don't wanna go in. Can't stand the collars and the habits."

"Okay. Turn here."

"I can see, fuckhead."

Scott reached for a lighter and lit a cigarette without putting his window down. Morgan put his finger on the window button. He wanted to push it. But the rain was coming down. If he opened the window, the rain would come in. Why wouldn't Scott put his window down? Air circulation in the van was already limited. With the smoke, it became nearly impossible to breathe. The company had a no smoking policy. Morgan rubbed the window button, felt its ergonomic design receive his finger, a perfect fit. He wanted to push it. To let the smoke out. To let the rain in. But he didn't.

"Hey," said Scott. "You heard the one about the mule with Tourette's?"

Morgan said nothing. After a long pause, Scott tried again.

"Hey, Wells."

No response. Scott was about to tell the story anyway when a sudden coughing spasm overtook him. His cigarette danced within inches of Morgan's shoulder. Morgan watched the street, and made a game of counting the umbrellas. They looked like bouncing black beetle shells moving up the street. He'd counted up to fourteen before the coughing faded into a kind of heaving, breathless whimper. By the time Morgan had counted seventeen beetles, Scott's cigarette went back into his mouth, and he turned his attention back to the road.

"So there was this mule with Tourette's, walks himself into a gay bar. Don't ask me what the fuck a mule is doing in a gay bar, that's just how the story goes. He sits down and says to the bartender, 'Excuse me, motherfucker, may I please have a glass of your finest cocksucker?' Bartender looks at the mule for a blip, then says, 'Well, if you're gonna be an ass about it ...'"

Scott started coughing again. Morgan wasn't sure if that was the end of the joke, but Scott clearly had nothing more to add. He waved his hand at Morgan, dismissing him.

They knew they were close when they saw the first cluster of uniformed children walking down the sidewalk. A minute later they parked in front of a small elementary school, fenced in. Morgan opened his door.

Scott lit another cigarette. "Take the walkie," he said. "Lemme know if it's more than you can carry."

Morgan got out of the van and shut his door. "There are just a couple bags anyway," he said to the closed window.

Morgan stood there for a moment, watching Scott push the radio buttons, thumbing the dial. Repeatedly. The motion was vaguely neanderthalic, and Morgan began to wonder if his co-worker had ever had a thought that wasn't completely and utterly focused on the present. He sometimes imagined they'd been placed together as some kind of test, to see who would be the first to flinch. Morgan rarely complained; Scott had opinions on everything from the weather to the whereabouts of Elvis. His fits of aggression were bloated, noisy, and impossible to ignore. He seemed to have no social filters, and spoke at length on subjects that would have been deemed inappropriate by even the most liberal of listeners. To top it off, he smoked constantly. Morgan had a hard time determining which was worse for him to be exposed to, the vitriol or the carcinogens. Both constricted the airflow inside the van.

One thing about Scott Parker: he could only refer to things in synecdoche. Women were legs, asses. Men were heads. Houses were roofs. Cars were wheels.

The list goes on.

Scott was also equipped with a large arsenal of quotidian phrases, one for every occasion. If they were late for a pickup, Scott would mention something about cookies crumbling. If they were early, a quick bit about birds and worms.

Morgan wondered how Scott would describe his meeting with Cranley. Would he say the shit hit the fan?

Morgan: Was talking to Cranley the other day.

Scott: Yeah?

Morgan: Backstabber!

Scott: Excuse me?

Morgan: You told him I was slowing down. What does that even mean?

Scott: It means you're not pulling your own weight.

Morgan: I don't know what that means either.

Scott: It means you're not putting your nose to the grindstone.

Morgan: Can you be more specific?

Scott: It means you're not using enough elbow grease.

Morgan: I hate you.

Scott: Put the pedal to the metal, son.

Morgan: Stop talking like that.

Scott: Give it one hundred and ten percent.

Morgan: You're ridiculous.

Scott: When life gives you lemons ...

No. It would never happen. Morgan wasn't the confrontational type. Whenever he attempted to confront people, his throat would swell up, his voice would soften, become wispy. His heart would start to pound, and the corners of his vision would go white. Blank. It was a confusing and completely sickening experience. If a store clerk gave him not enough change, he'd put it in his pocket and keep walking.

After gathering up four large bags of shreddies from behind the secretary's desk, Morgan exited the school and returned to the van. There were no children walking along the sidewalks. Except for the odd parked car, the street was empty. Scott got out of the van to help Morgan toss the bags into the back. Transparent sacks full of old class lists, outdated, confidential student files. A few computer disks. Crumpled-up napkins. Unfilled report cards.

"Jesus H. These are heavy."

"What do you think all this stuff is?"

"Who gives a fuck, Wells?"

Scott heaved the last bag into the van and slammed the door. A resounding metal hum rang out in response all along the empty, wet street.

The postcard. When Morgan came home from work that day, he'd almost overlooked it in the mail, thinking it was just some gimmick, a "Wish You Were Here" from a local travel agent. But then he got stuck on a thought: what if it was from her? So he gave the postcard a closer look.

On the front: the Eiffel Tower in broad daylight, and a man wearing a beret, giving the camera the finger. Above him, "Vive la France!" in the ugliest typeface Morgan had ever seen.

Morgan smiled smugly. Copperplate Gothic, likely.

Morgan stopped smiling. Even though the handwriting was vaguely familiar, clearly the postcard wasn't from her.

Hey Morgan,

There's a million of them out here, they all look like you! Or a mix between you and Haley (remember her???) Haha! Was out on the Champs-Elysees the other night, passed by the Arc de Triomphe, saw this postcard, decided you were worthy. Bonjour, bonsoir, bonne nuit, etc. I have taken about two thousand photos. Tell Nat I said Hi, or bonjour, whichever.

K.

P.S. You better put this on your fridge ma merde! See you in Sept.

Who was K? Morgan walked into the kitchen and read the post-card again. And Nat—Nathaniel? Natalie? He knew a Nadia once. She smoked menthols. But she wouldn't remember him.

The only thing he could be somewhat certain of was K's sex. The cramped, heavy cursive.

And Haley? Ma merde?

Or was it someone who went by last name only? Krieger? King? He used to work with someone named Kasaday. Kelsey? Kevin? Keenan?

Morgan pinned the postcard to the fridge with a magnet shaped like a fish. The fish had a big smile on his lips, and was wearing a chef's hat. Morgan positioned the magnet so that only the edge of the postcard was concealed. The Eiffel Tower and the ugly bereted Frenchman looked back. A glitch. A gift. He didn't know which.

A Post-it under the coffee table: *coffee table.*

And one under the kitchen table: *kitchen table.*

And another under the garbage can: *garbage can.*

But something was still missing.

Once his wife had slammed the bathroom door against his chin. They'd just come home from a Northern Ontario vacation. A quiet, one-street town with a black lake, orange trees, green and red canoes. He couldn't recall the name of the town, but he remembered they'd stayed at a place called the Adirondack Inn, a large green and white building surrounded by forest. They'd bought some postcards with the inn on the front. She'd said she wanted to send them to her parents, her sisters.

Morgan didn't know if his wife sent the postcards or not, but he remembered the train ride home. A disaster. She didn't speak to him, and when they got home, she dropped her suitcase and went straight down the hall toward the bathroom. He followed her. He kept saying her name, grabbed her arm, squeezed it hard to make her stop moving, but she pulled away, and went into the bathroom. He tried to follow her in before she could close the door, but she slammed it, hard, and the door cracked against his chin, knocked him back into the hallway. She opened the door and they both stood there, frozen for a moment, her in the doorway staring, Morgan touching his fingers to his bloody chin. The blood on the front of his shirt. The blood on the floor. He couldn't believe how quickly it dropped, thick black gobs sticking to his fingers.

Morgan stared at the postcard. The postcard from K. The ugly Frenchman stared back. *There's a million of them out here, they all look like you!*

A million of them, thought Morgan. A million of them just like him.

Morgan removed the postcard from the fridge. Turned it around in his hands. For the first time, he noticed that the street name was smudged. It could've said Mortimer, which was where he lived, but it might've spelled something else. Wasn't there a Morton Road near Danforth Village?

He'd heard a story several years before about an ER doctor in Vancouver who'd performed a lifesaving operation on a woman with an aneurysm, only to find out afterwards that they both had the same name. Apparently, the doctor wasn't even on call that night. She just happened to be at the hospital, and was the only person on staff capable of conducting the procedure.

Morgan knew that things of that nature happened occasionally. In a city of five million, there had to be a few Morgan Wellses around. Two of them living on similarly-named streets wasn't any more coincidental than winning the lottery with the first six positive integers. Logically speaking, it could happen.

Couldn't it?

Morgan went to the computer, but he no longer owned the hard drive; the monitor remained, a closed lid. It took Morgan twenty-seven minutes before he found the phonebook. It was under the bed. He saw the cordless under there too, but when he pulled it out into the open it became a sock.

He turned the pages in chunks. Abdou. Campsail. Hernandez. Gallo. Kenchammana. Nguyen. Sissoko. Quincy. He found W, trailed his finger down the page. Walters. Walton. Weir. Wells. Morgan scanned through the Wellses until he found just one name identical to his own. The other Morgan Wells lived in the Annex, on a street with a name completely unlike the one he lived on. Even if part of the name on the postcard was smudged, the first four letters were not.

Morgan scanned the names once more. Was there really only one other Morgan Wells in the city? He found himself wondering how many there were in the world. And how many came before him. How uncommon was his name?

Morgan closed the phonebook on the table and glanced at the cover. "1998" was written in bright blue letters on the top right corner. Morgan was busy discerning the font—Verdana?—when he realized his error: the phonebook was out of date.

In the phone booth outside the Tonka Gas Bar down the street. The phone hung upside down, its jaw smashed out. Morgan chomped on a banana-flavoured antacid and watched the passersby. Stared at a bike pole covered in torn-off sticker residue. He then slid the phone-book out of its case. Though worn, the book was recent. Morgan flipped with calculated ease to the back, to Wells. He found himself and the other Morgan Wells, the one he was looking for. The one he knew he would find. A Morgan Wells that lived on Morton Road.

For how long had this other Morgan lived in the city? A year? Two years?

Morgan wondered if they'd ever spoken to one another, or at least passed each other on the street. Perhaps they'd ridden the same subway without knowing it. The addresses were nearly identical, and seemed to reflect each other, one right on top of the other, differing only by a few letters. For a moment, all of the people outside the phone booth became potential Morgans. That purple-skinned man in the gas station buying lottery tickets. That guy walking his dog. Potential selves. A dizzying effect. About as likely ... as likely as ...

Morgan tore the page out of the book.

By the time he got home, he decided to return the postcard to the correct Morgan Wells. The improbability of the postcard demanded this reaction. A chance to set things right. Although not many right things had happened to him lately, Morgan felt compelled to do good by his other. The other Morgan Wells would surely appreciate his effort. Perhaps they'd become friends, like that Vancouver doctor and her patient with the aneurysm.

To get to the address, Morgan would have to take a route he'd already taken.

Do not take the same route twice, not even in reverse (unless you already know exactly where you want to go ...)

He decided to make an exception.

Feeling, for the first time since his wife had left, a shift. A movement toward something new. A subtle relief, this predetermining.

Well, it was a start.

Nearly three weeks would pass before he went to the other Morgan's address. Before he committed his first federal offence.

August 15 (Morning):

"Someone has to take action. Whether in Ottawa, or here in the ..."

August 15 (Morning):

"Our office is twenty-two floors up. When the power went out, we filed down the stairs. We all thought it was just a usual power outage, nothing serious. It wasn't until we were at street level that we realized the extent of the blackout. I've never seen so many people walking. People directing traffic and—"

August 15 (Morning):

"Hi, I'm Asha. I just graduated grade seven. Last night, me and my sister, she's nine and a half, were both excited when we discovered the elevators didn't work, so we had to take the stairs, which we never did, so we did. Many people in our building placed candles along the stairway, so we could see, which was dangerous, so we blew each of them out as we went up. We stayed up until midnight, and from the balcony we could see lights, but from my window only darkness. It was a lifetime memory I will never forget."

BLACKOUT, DAY 2.

Incredibly dull. I cut my wrists twice just to sharpen things up, which isn't normal for me, since I'm really not a fan of suicide death. Once in the kitchen and another time in the bathtub. In the kitchen, there was so much blood. I couldn't believe how much there was. The blood spurted out with the force of a firehose. I painted the cabinets purple before falling to the floor. In the tub, I stuck my wrists underwater when I cut them open, and saw the blood move through the water, mixing with the suds, a current under the sea. My death sounded like a Jacuzzi, and then the water turned so red I could see my own reflection. I passed out thinking I was bathing in Kool-Aid, my mouth and nostrils filling with blood and warm water.

Boredom alert red.

Frigging Toronto.

At home, when my mind is working on too many thoughts at once, or when I wake up earlier than everyone else on a Saturday, I walk around our house examining everything that I see. I open my mom's cookbooks and skim through her recipes. I open Ross's laptop, and see what sorts of programs he's been using. I climb the steps into the attic, open old boxes, and see what I can see. I can be such a wanderer sometimes. My point is that when I'm home I can usually find something to occupy my time. But in shithole Toronto, lame-ass media capital of Canada, there is nothing to do but sit on the couch and watch TV. And then the blackout interrupted that. And then the media went on talking about that.

Other things that get old quick: playing Scrabble, Boggle, and Trivial Pursuit all in a row; throwing cards at the wall; looking at my face in the mirror; thinking of Val; thinking of Caitlyn; snooping through my brother's magazines; his hockey cards; looking out the window; talking on the phone to Caitlyn; timing how long I can hold my breath underwater in the tub (1.43 minutes); lying on my back on the kitchen floor; wandering around; and other things, things so dull I can't even remember doing them.

The day after I found Cavendish's book, Dave and I were supposed to go to this flea market in Scarborough, but Dave changed his mind. Of course. He said he had work to do, though without power I'm not sure how many trademark infringers he'd be able to find. The lazy brute. He would've been fired a long time ago if it weren't for the Internet. Dave walking around in the hot sun looking for trademark infringers? Never going to happen. I said something to this effect, but he just closed his office door in my face. This was especially annoying because he said he'd seen "lots of those mini tapes" the last time he was there, but we would definitely need to drive there since it was in Scarborough. I guess it didn't matter in the end anyway, because the power was out, and the market was probably closed. Still, I would be a liar to say I wasn't disappointed.

To be honest, I wasn't at all surprised when Dave broke his promise, and in fact saw myself choking him at that very moment. I saw myself choking him with my arm, and standing behind him like he does to me when he puts me in headlocks. And shaking him and saying right into his ear, "Does my breath stink?" Choking him until his face starts to bleed through the pores, until his eyes pop out of his skull, which is something I've taken from a movie. Personally, I've never died like that.

Val cooked Eggos on the barbeque, which she called our "blackout breakfast." I smothered mine in peanut butter. That's pretty much the only way I eat Eggos. Pancakes too. Peanut butter is also amazing on sandwiches, no need for jam. Jam is for sissies.

While we ate, Val said I could come with her and Luís on some errands if I wanted. But I politely declined her offer. I hate errands. Mom sometimes takes me on errands, and she spends an entire afternoon at the bank, and I sit in the car and listen to the radio and wonder why I said I would come along. Plus, Val's errand had something to do with Luís's birthday, which is about all either of them had talked about since I arrived in Toronto. I've never heard of a person putting that much effort into a birthday, let alone for such an insignificant birthday. Five? What's to celebrate about being five? We never really did birthdays growing up. My dad always said they were just an excuse to spend money on things no one needs, and I completely agree. I suppose cake is always welcome, but it's not like it makes birthdays more fun. Especially not vegan cake.

I ate my peanut butter Eggos, then called my mom just after Val and Luís left. But we didn't talk for long. And all she asked about was the blackout. She wanted to know if we could see the stars in Toronto, which seemed like a pretty dumb question, considering it was morning. I told her I was bored, that staying with Dave and Val was already a chore, a fact only made worse by the loss of power. No TV. No money. No friends. She sighed. Told me to go for a walk. That pretty much ended our conversation.

I spent the next thirty minutes listening to the radio. It got its energy from the sun, but only one station came in clearly, and all they talked about was the blackout. The blackout this and the blackout that. 50,000,000 people with food rotting in their fridges, a real tragedy. Buffalo, New Jersey, Mississauga, et cetera. Over and over, the same stupid conversations, different writers and analysts and critics and politicians and stupid jerks with a telephone and nothing better to do. Sit and complain. Complain and say, "The power is still out," and "They're working on a solution." Or talk about seeing the stars.

August 15 (Morning):

"I am not from this country, but from Hong Kong, and so have no friends, and when the blackout happened, I did not know what was going to happen, or if this was happening all over everywhere, and I needed to call my family in Hong Kong, but my cell phone did not work, and no cell phones did work. So I went around asking, but no one could help, until I went into a hotel, and asked to use their phone to make long distance call. They didn't want to let me, but then they did, and when I heard my wife's voice, I started to cry, to know that she was okay, that this was just the power out, and we would all be okay. This was my best terrible experience in Canada."

With the radio alternating between complaints and boring first-hand accounts, I decided to go into the room where I was staying and give Cavendish's book another chance. For me, reading is the only effective medicine for the real world. Cavendish's book wasn't my first choice, but the only books Dave and Val own are geeky computer manuals and books about women who love to shop. I took *The Blazing World* out of my bookbag, where I'd hidden it, sat down on the floor, and read for an hour.

I found out that after the Lady meets the friendly bear-men, she meets a bunch of other weird animal-human hybrids, like fox-men, and wild geese-men, and jackdaw-men, though I have no idea what a jackdaw is. She also meets humans with grass green faces, which made me think they'd get along great with my mom and Ross with their orange Oompa-Loompa skin. All these weirdoes eventually send the Lady down a river on a boat that is really just a giant bird's nest. At first she worries that this strange Adventure with a capital A will lead to her certain death and destruction, but then she starts to fall in love with the land and everyone in it, especially after she meets the Emperor of the Imperial City, whose face I think was also green. He thinks she's a Goddess and marries her on the spot. As far as I could tell, from this point on, the story is basically about the Lady, now Empress, interviewing different creatures in order to discover more about this new world.

I flipped ahead to a random page, hoping for some action. Like maybe the Emperor turns out to be a total psychotic mass murderer, or some of the hybrids start a war, or who knows. Something more interesting than a person asking other people questions.

The Sun, as much as they could observe, they related to be a firm or solid Stone, of a vast bigness; of colour yellowish, and of an extraordinary splender: But the Moon, they said, was of a whitish colour; and although she looked dim in the presence of the Sun, yet had she her own light, and was a shining body of her self, as might be perceived by her vigorous appearance in Moon-shiny-nights.

My English teacher from last year, Ms. Rossbach, says stories always have to be read in context, and in the context of the last few days I could see these lines were clearly related to the blackout, to the fact that the sun, by being so vastly hot, had caused everyone to jack up their air conditioners, which caused the blackout, and led to a moon-shiny-night in Toronto, the first in decades. Yes, I saw the connection. And it could've just been a convenient, coincidental cor-relation, like how horoscopes always seem to say something relevant and specific, but could be applied to just about anyone, regardless of whether they're Capricorn or Cancer. That is, after all, how sassy shamans like Miss Cleo, also known as Youree Harris in a crazy Jamaican headdress, make a living. But I couldn't shake the feeling that the book was trying to tell me something. In Choose Your Own Adventures, the clues are always there if you look for them. People don't just *happen* to look in a drawer hiding a secret book. I didn't just *happen* to pull the drawer out too far. I knew the story had to be important, that's why I'd found it, even if the paragraphs were way too long and there were too many commas and capital letters in the middle of sentences. There had to be some reason Dave was hiding the book in the back of the cutlery drawer. I wondered what Ms. Rossbach would think of all that context?

I flipped to the first page again, where Myrna had written her note. I then noticed, for the first time, an address written inside, on the top left corner of the cover of the book. 479 Palmerston Avenue. How had I missed this clue the first time I'd opened the book?

I closed the book. I sat on the floor with my back against the bed, staring at the wall, trying to sort through the thoughts in my brain. If Dave did not live at 479 Palmerston (he did not), then maybe Myrna lived at 479 Palmerston, owned the book before she gave it to Dave, and might know what the book was all about (*This is totally weird, right up your alley. And incredible*), and why Dave was hiding it in the back of a drawer. But what if she was (*Written by a woman*) Dave's mistress? Would she just deny any (*you'll thank me later*) knowledge of the book?

Of course, there was also the small possibility that there was no connection, or that Myrna had moved since giving Dave the book, or that Myrna had given Dave a used book, second-hand, bought at a garage sale or a flea market.

Then again.

I do not mind walking. Since the government deems me too young to drive, walking is my only option. I could take a bus, but who has the money? I used to own a bike, but someone stole it from me and Mom won't let me get another one because she suspects I sold it. Needless to say, I've resigned myself to being a full-time walker, at least until I'm old enough to drive. As a result, my calf muscles are about fifty percent stronger than most people in my age group. I can also run like the wind.

But even though I was really decently walking, as soon as I left Dave and Val's, and picked up some speed, I felt a great sense of disappointment threatening to slow me down. I'd expected people to be everywhere downtown, chaos in the streets. I'd kind of hoped to see broken-out windows, burning bodies everywhere, riots, that sort of thing. But everything had pretty much returned to normal. A few shops were even open. The blue and white flags on Danforth hung like they always had, not tattered or torn. Flower shops sold flowers, pizza places sold pizza. Utterly normal. The traffic lights were working again, even if they could only blink in red. The rows of identical brick duplexes hadn't changed at all. As per usual, the air was full of tar, hard to breathe, like someone had wrapped a plastic bag around my head. Within minutes, I was hot and dying, completely losing control over my body, lungs disappearing. I felt like I could die any minute, with too much heat in my chest, suffocating on summer. After just thirty minutes of walking, I stopped at a Dairy Mart on the corner of Pape and Gerrard to get some liquid caffeine to cool me down. The headlines on all the newspapers were pretty much identical.

Blackout 2003.

Heart of Darkness.

Lights Out.

They made me stand there forever, the guy behind the counter and this cab driver. I cleared my throat like three times, but neither of them noticed me.

August 15 (Afternoon):

"When did your power come back?"
"This morning. Six o'clock, maybe. Had to throw away all the ice cream bars in the freezer."

"That's nothing. I had this one woman in the cab, and it was a killer rush hour. Even before it happened. Just me and this woman, caught on Bathurst. Worst, the worst I've ever seen. And she wouldn't stop talking."

"Some people don't know when to shut up."

"Said she was having hot flashes, her car was stuck in a parking garage. Said I don't need this, I don't need this. Crazy, I said. She wouldn't stop about terrorists. They're going to kill us. I don't want to die, I don't want—, and she was like, The phones aren't working, I need to call my husband, it's so hot, oh God. And of course all the traffic lights were out, random people in the middle of the street telling us when to go when to stop. I'm just two seconds away from pushing her out. She was like, They've taken the power we're going to die."

"White people always think they're going to die."

"Of course! Sure, I felt nervous too. That's me being completely honest. But there's no need to take that out on me, a guy she's paying. For a service."

"You want to buy lotto with that too?"

"No thanks. Like it's my fault we're stuck as though I'm the fucking terrorist. I have the AC on but she's still on me. On second thought, I'll take one ticket. You never know."

"I just read about a Canadian girl, this girl from Calgary, who was in New York when it happened. She was on the subway, and said it was so dark down there, and not even the emergency lights worked. People were screaming, banging on the doors. Some were crying. They thought it was a terrorist attack too."

[The cashier laughs.]

"I don't know what's worse, a stopped train or a menopausal woman."

"*I* know."

Just because the power is out doesn't give people the right to spill their guts. To be honest, I was surprised that these two morons saw the blackout as nothing more than a monumental inconvenience. It was such a letdown. Didn't they realize what was going on? The blackout was clearly only the beginning. A test. They were talking in past tense, like there was nothing left to be afraid of. But any idiot would know better. First take the power out, see what happens. Wait a day or two. Then cut the power for good before sending in the nukes. It seemed so obvious. We'd be picking the flesh off our faces before the week was up. I knew it.

I began to wonder what other people were thinking. I wondered if I took a poll, how many people would say the blackout made them happy. How many would tell me to go eff myself?

Even after he paid for his stuff, the gabby cabbie and the storekeeper kept talking about the blackout, as if there was nothing else to say or do. I wondered why survival of the fittest hadn't yet eradicated boring storytellers from the human gene pool. I thought of how great it would be if human beings adapted an innate ability to stop talking once a boring story started coming out their mouths. Our voices would start to fade out, or would cut out completely, when people lost interest in what we were saying. So bad storytellers would know when to shut up, instead of rambling on and on and wasting everyone's time. They wouldn't even have a choice. Their throats would simply constrict, they'd run out of air, and the volume would get turned down. No more words. I waited for the cabbie's voice to fade, or at least for the man behind the counter to notice me. Three minutes later, I did the logical thing and left without paying.

Then, as I walked out of the place, a van that was driving 70 km/hr skidded out of control on the main road and I put my hands up and then that was it and the last thing I saw was the driver's face, stupid father type of guy, glasses and wide face and mouth smooth like an O. Like he was yawning. My face and hands were completely destroyed as soon as the minivan hit. My body was crushed, flung back against the store window, a lump on the pavement. Big shards of glass stuck in my back, my neck. I pictured Dave driving past in the hatchback, seeing my bloodstains on the ground, continuing to live, and driving around, maybe whistling to himself and scratching his crotch while the paramedics scraped my body off the sidewalk.

After putting some distance between myself and the store, I gave my legs a break at a park, which wasn't so much a park as it was the front lawn of a three-storey brick barracks, also called an apartment building, property of the Toronto Community Housing Corporation. I sat in the shade across from Lin's Burger and drank my cola in long, throat burning gulps. I sat there for a while, just watching people walk by. It sounds stupid, but sometimes when I'm in a crowd I find myself looking for my dad. Not really looking for him, but noticing people who sort of look like him. Who dress like him or maybe walk like him. It's a stupid game, but it helps to pass the time.

Before he disappeared, my dad sent me a postcard from the other side of the world. The picture was of an old bearded man wearing a turban and a pair of gas station sunglasses. He was almost smiling. On the back, my dad had written the following:

Hey buster,

It's all sun and dust and hot air out here—you'd hate it. When I get back to Canada, I hope you'll come visit me in Toronto. In the meantime, keep up with your homework, and try not to give your Mom too hard a time. Sound like a deal?

Miss ya, love ya, give my best to Davey.

I keep the postcard in my bookbag at all times.

I found my way to Palmerston—lots of old houses, big trees. A much nicer street than the one Dave and Val lived on. 479 Palmerston was also a heck of a lot bigger than any house I'd seen in Pape Village. It was white, and I estimated nearly two hundred years old, which was also the age of most of the people in it. Weirdly enough, the doors to the house were wide open, and there was jazz music coming from inside, like they were throwing some kind of party. The place was swarming with people, mostly old ladies wearing jogging pants and white running shoes. Track suits and fanny packs. But this one old bird really stood out from the flock. She was wearing her red carpet best, this maroon and grey number. Looked like an old Hollywood actress. I wanted to take her hand in mine, maybe kiss it. She seemed like royalty, just in the way she held her arms. Perpendicular to her body, wrists limp. I've never seen a woman of that particular vintage look so exquisite. Hair in a bun. She smelled like perfume and mouthwash. She was standing in the doorway, at the back of the line waiting to get in, and throughout our entire conversation she kept turning away from me after each thing she said. It was exhausting trying to keep her attention.

If I were forced to name this woman, I'd call her Sophia. Or Virginia.

August 15 (Afternoon):

"Excuse me, are you the owner of this house?"
"Pardon me?"
"Do you own this house?"
"This is an estate sale."
"So?"
"The owners are dead."
"Dead?"
"Yes."
"How can they own the house if they're dead?"
[5.3 second pause.]
"Well, *they* don't own it anymore, but their family does."
"Do you know who they are?"
"No. I live a few streets over. I probably saw them before, but wouldn't have known them from Adam."
[3.4 second pause]
"Have you heard the name Myrna before?"
"I have."
"Did you know her?"
"I said I've heard the name, not that I know anyone by it."
[6.9 second pause.]
"Why are all these people here?"

"It's an estate sale."

"I'm still not sure what that means."

"The family is selling the house and everything in it."

"Oh. Is that normal?"

"Sure, I guess, if you have a lot of stuff."

"Can anyone go in?"

[6.8 second pause.]

"Excuse me? Can anyone go in?"

"Yes, anyone who plans on *buying* something."

[3.2 second pause.]

"Uh ..."

"Yes?"

"Do you happen to know when the owners of the house died?"

"I told you already, I didn't know the owners."

"I know. But I thought you might know when they died."

"All I can tell you is that this house has been vacant for almost two years now, so I would guess they've been dead for two years."

"Two years? What took the family so long to have the estate sale?"

"Honestly, how would I know?"

"Well, you knew when they died."

[4.5 second pause.]

"Okay, young man. Are we done here?"

I nodded. Needless to say, I was disappointed to know I wouldn't be able to speak with Myrna. I considered turning back. If Myrna wasn't around, what use was there in going into the house? But then I had another thought: if Dave wouldn't take me to the flea market, maybe I'd find tapes here. I figured since I sometimes found used minicassettes at yard sales and garage sales, there was a good chance I might find a few at an estate sale too. It was definitely worth taking a look.

I stood there in the doorway behind Sophia for a while longer, before realizing that I wasn't waiting in the line to get in, but the line to buy. This guy with fingers thicker than rolls of loonies sat behind the cash table next to these two girls, not much older than

Luís. The kids were serving lemonade out of these plastic pitchers. The guy, I guess, was just the cashier. He looked as though he was hiding a garbage bag full of fast food under his Iron Maiden T-shirt. I looked at Sophia, and realized for the first time that the purse she was clutching so tightly to her hip did not yet belong to her. No wonder she held onto it so nervously. At any moment some other granny might see it and snatch it from her hands.

At the front of the line, this woman put a porcelain dish down in front of old loonie fingers and started haggling. Apparently, two dollars was too much for a dead person's thing.

I pushed past Sophia, out of the waiting-to-buy line, took a sharp right, and ended up in the dining room, where china dishes and crystals were laid out on a long table. Twelve to fifteen people were stuffed into that room, rooting through the display cabinet, opening drawers and lifting gravy boats up to get a better view. "This one's chipped," I heard one woman say, "no way I'm paying five dollars for it."

A rolling blackout had just shut the power down on this particular street, but the house had lots of tall windows, so the place was well lit. If only they'd open the windows. The whole place smelled like one hundred years of dampness. Dampness in the wooden picture frames, the brick fireplace, the paisley wallpaper. I walked through the dining room and into the living room. The green shag carpet and sleigh-shaped furniture made me think of Polident commercials and women with blue perms. A young couple, probably Dave and Val's age, were sitting on the sofa.

August 15 (Afternoon):

"Do you feel that?"

"Yeah. It's stiff."

"It's been sat on about three thousand times too many."

"I know, but it's so beautiful."

"Sure, it looks good, but it's so uncomfortable. I don't know how anybody could own a piece of furniture like this."

"What if we got it reupholstered?"

"Sweetie, it's as hard as slate, and definitely not worth two hundred and fifty dollars."

[5.7 second pause.]

"Do you see that stain?"

"Ugh. What is that?"

"How did they ever get comfortable on this thing?"

[The couple's conversation gets interrupted by the battery-operated, motion-sensitive Elvis fish hanging on the wall above them. It plays a recording of "Love Me Tender," but the batteries are dying, so the song is slurred and blurry, the voice all drawn out and slowed down. Totally demonic.]

"That fish—God."

"I know, right?"

In the family room, everything had a price tag, a piece of masking tape with a dollar amount written in marker. Lamps, end tables, toy keyboards. There were people everywhere. Scavengers. This old British guy with wiry hair and glasses and a younger man were crouched over a set of mildewed cardboard boxes full of old LPs, flipping through them.

My dad had listened to vinyl long after the invention (and intervention, if you asked him) of CDs. He told me once that it all came down to sound quality, "the texture of the sound" is the phrase he used, though I have no idea what that really means. He liked the objects themselves; liked to hold a record in his hand, place it onto the turntable, position the needle into the groove. He used to lie on the couch in the living room with his headphones on, eyes closed, hands clasped on his chest, listening. He sometimes bought two copies of a single album, one to play, the other to store, to keep in its finest form.

I looked at the two men sorting through the sad box. My dad would never have allowed his collection to grow mould. Not in a million years. The two assholes crouching over the soggy cardboard box.

August 15 (Afternoon):

> "I'm tempted to buy a couple of these just to hear what they
> sound like. But not really."
> [Laughter.]

I could not find mini tapes anywhere, only a shoebox of regular
cassettes.

I went upstairs. The staircase was old and winding. The steps
creaked as I ascended.

I kept hearing noises coming from the ceiling, thumps and thuds.
I figured people must've been in the attic, but I had no idea how
they got up there, I didn't see another staircase or even a ladder
anywhere. I went into one of the upstairs rooms, a former office or
study, hoping to find a hidden staircase, but instead I found a beat-
up old desk, a chair tipped upside down, and wall-to-wall shelves.
The plaster in the ceiling above the desk had broken off, revealing
a heavy black water pipe with rust along the exposed joint. At one
point the bookshelves were probably lined with books, but the room
had been pretty much raided.

What was left: some mysteries. True crime novels. Some sci-fi. You
could tell by the covers—like the romance novels, with pictures of
women being molested on the front. A set of old encyclopedias. A
travel guide to Europe. Someone had written, "You'll need this where
your going" on the front page, and I had to fight the urge to correct
the error. I might've failed grade eight Social Studies, and Math, but
I can spell and punctuate like a motherfucker. Seeing stupid mistakes
makes me twitch like a diabetic with low blood sugar.

I was staring at the inscription, thinking about how easy it would
be to slip an apostrophe between the u and r and add an e on the
end, when it hit me. The handwriting was familiar.

I took *The Blazing World* out of my bookbag (what if I forgot the
address on Palmerston at the last minute? What if I mixed up the
seven and the nine?) and compared the two samples. They were
identical. The travel guide inscription wasn't signed, so I started
looking through all the other books too. It took a few tries, but

eventually I found a copy of a book called *The Tiger in the Smoke* by Margery Allingham. It had a dagger on the cover. Cool. On the inside, Myrna had written the following:

> Okay, so I know you haven't read this one ... but someone put it in the throwaway bin as part of the annual purge, and it's in good shape, and I always think it's a shame for something that you can still read to end up in a dumpster. I know. Typical librarian. Love you. Myrna.

So *The Blazing World* had come from Palmerston. The second inscription proved that beyond a doubt. Did that mean Myrna was one of the house's owners, or was she merely the dead man's daughter? Or just a friend?

Was Myrna dead?

Of course, it was possible that Myrna the librarian didn't live on Palmerston at all. In any event, what was Dave's connection? How did a gift from Myrna to the owner of the Palmerston house end up at Dave's place, hidden in the back of his kitchen drawer?

This whole situation got me thinking. I wouldn't go so far as to say I thought I was receiving a message from beyond the grave or anything, but it seemed strange to me that on the day when the power went out, when everyone in the whole city thought the world was about to end, I'd found a book that seemed to be about the world coming to an end. The world burning up. I'm not a flaker, but things often happen for a reason. I thought finding the book, reading that title, might've meant something; knowing that the book had once belonged to a dead guy *must've* meant something. I was meant to find *The Blazing World*. Meant to use it somehow.

But how?

If you choose to purchase The Tiger in the Smoke, *turn to page 126.*
If you choose to set the house on fire, turn to page 25.

After a millisecond of hesitation, I decided not to buy *The Tiger in the Smoke*. One crazy old book was enough.

The chalky sky hung heavy like a headache. Half-lit and dripping.

Morgan ran up his front steps and let himself into his apartment, nearly leaving his key in the lock. He went directly into the office. He bent over the heavy legal desk with the wood chipping off the sides. The junk desk. At least fifty years old. It must have weighed six tonnes. Its drawers were full of things that should've been thrown out. Empty pill bottles, faded receipts, tapes without cases, two broken computer speakers, dead batteries. An unstoppable phalanx of junk. Each time Morgan tried to clean the drawers out, he would get no further than one or two items before he found something that distracted him, and kept him from completing the purge.

Today, however, Morgan had no intention of cleaning out the desk.

His actions at the other Morgan's house had been unplanned. Beyond his control. He didn't know what he was doing until he'd already done it. But now was not the time for gut reactions. He would need to be more careful.

He covered the scarred, inked surface of the desk with a fresh tablecloth. The tablecloth was brand new and had been purchased for this precise purpose: to conceal the desk, to cover its face and its drawers. He no longer wished to reclaim it. He would be satisfied with simply pretending it did not exist.

The tablecloth draped over the desk gave it the impression of an operating table. Morgan was pleased with this impression.

On the floor next to the desk, Morgan set up a two-drawer file cabinet he'd found at a discount store, the kind he often saw in the office buildings and hospitals he visited on his route with Scott. The cabinet had seen better days, but at least the drawers were empty. That's all Morgan could really ask for. On top of the cabinet Morgan arranged his tools, side by side: an ivory letter opener; three blue pens; one red pen; one black marker; one yellow, lined notepad; a pair of polyethylene gloves. Morgan pulled the gloves over his hands, snapped the band over each wrist like he'd seen on television. The element of opening, of prying, of tearing into and examining, of moving and replacing. And he, a mortician of sorts. An archaeologist.

Do not open the envelopes with your fingers.
Do not open the envelopes along the long edge.
Do not tear the letters.
Do not smudge the ink.
Do not open the desk drawers.

Morgan switched the desk lamp on. Not bright enough. He removed the shade and worked under the bare bulb. He took the pile of envelopes that he'd stolen from the other Morgan Wells's mailbox out of his pocket. He placed them in the centre of the desk, the unreturned postcard on top—later, he would have to put it back on the fridge, where it belonged.

The first envelope he opened came from Visa. As he slipped the letter opener beneath the fold, Morgan wondered what the other Morgan would think when he realized he hadn't received his monthly statement. Would he say something to Nat? Would he call Visa after a couple of weeks? Not likely. He probably wouldn't even notice it was missing. He would never suspect stolen.

VISA Classic

MORGAN WELLS 4520 xxxx xxxx xxxx
STATEMENT FROM FEB 02 TO FEB 27, 2000

NEW BALANCE: $4,104.23
MINIMUM PAYMENT: $93.00
PAYMENT DUE DATE: March 14, 2000
CREDIT LIMIT: $5000.00
AVAILABLE CREDIT: $895.77
ANNUAL INTEREST RATE: 18.50%
AMOUNT PAID:

FEB 04	RED DRAGON RESTAURANT TORONTO ON	$34.00
FEB 04	BELL MOBILITY INC MISSISSAUGA ON	$67.63

FEB 07	DUPONT SUPERMARKET TORONTO ON	$15.17
FEB 10	HOME DEPOT TORONTO ON	$134.11
FEB 14	GREYHOUND LINES TORONTO ON	$15.52
FEB 14	MCCORKS LONDON ON	$78.00
FEB 15	COLES #451# LONDON ON	$51.24
FEB 16	GREYHOUND LINES LONDON ON	$15.52
FEB 21	FOODSMART TORONTO ON	$32.12
FEB 25	LCBO TORONTO ON	$22.34
FEB 26	WOODGREEN DISCOUNT TORONTO ON	$62.50
FEB 27	MCCOY'S TOYS TORONTO ON	$15.32
FEB 27	PAYMENT – THANK YOU / PAIEMENT – MERCI	-$150.00

The first thing Morgan noticed was the Greyhound purchase, and the subsequent charges in London. What was in London? A job interview? A conference? Friends? Maybe that's where Morgan was from. Apparently, he liked Chinese food and Irish pubs. Seventy-eight dollars seemed like a lot to spend on one night at a pub. He must've gone with friends. His credit card was nearly maxed out. Was he the type of guy to buy the rounds? If so, thought Morgan, he couldn't be married. Then who was Nat?

Morgan opened the remaining three envelopes he'd slipped into his pocket. There was one from Blockbuster threatening legal action (the other Morgan had an outstanding balance of eleven dollars), and another announcing that Morgan Wells had just won a Carnival cruise. After scanning through these two letters, Morgan put them, along with the Visa statement, into a file folder, and put the folder into his cabinet.

He then scrutinized the last remaining envelope. A white one, the addresses written in pen. Sent by Heidi York, post-dated March 1. She lived in Markham.

Morgan carefully cut along the crease. When he opened the envelope, along the short edge, he wondered how the other Morgan Wells opened his mail. The long edge? Did he even think about it, or did he simply tear the envelope open? The folded paper inside the envelope was neat and crisp. Morgan expected the letter to have a sweet smell, like women's perfume, scented oils. The gloves made

slipping the letter out of the envelope difficult; with the Visa statement, he hadn't worried as much about folding or tearing the paper.
But this letter was different. Its reception deserved the same care
its sender had obviously put into sending it. Ultimately he decided
to remove the letter using a pair of tweezers. He then put his nose

deep into the envelope and breathed. It smelled like glue and fibres,
and made him feel chilly.

Morgan put the envelope down. He unfolded the letter, massaged
its creases between rubbery fingers. And he read.

Dear Morgan,

Hi! I've been trying to keep in touch with you, but I couldn't
find your phone number. I tried emailing, but no luck, so I'm
thinking it probably went into your junkbox. I hope you still
live at this address.

How're things? I'm back in Markham now. Obviously. Montréal
didn't exactly pan out. I can tell you about that some time?
I'm working for my father. Yes, what progress eh? I've been in
contact with OCAD and will probably go back to school, finish
up, maybe even as early as June.

What about you? Still studying economics? How's your collection of old textbooks? Last I remember it was massive. You
were such a dork!

Well, I wanted to say hello, because it's been a long time and
I'd love to see you again. My number's at the bottom here, if
you want to call, or you can just write. Personally, I like letters,
even though they're not eco-friendly, or all that efficient. At
least they give mail carriers something to do.

Don't feel pressured to respond.

Gerberas rule, Heidi.

Don't feel pressured to respond? Until he came across this line, Morgan assumed Heidi was just a friend. But wouldn't a friend say just the opposite? "You better respond," or "I can't wait to hear from you." Only an ex-girlfriend would provide a disclaimer.

Morgan read Heidi's note again.

Touch
Phone number
Address
Markham
Montréal
Maybe
Economics
Love
Respond
Gerberas

Morgan went into his kitchen and poured himself a glass of cold water. He took small sips on his way back to the guest room, letting the liquid warm in his mouth before swallowing. He wondered how long it had been since Heidi had last spoken with the other Morgan. Obviously, they were students when they met. Was Morgan still a student? If Heidi had taken some time off, apparently to become an artist in Montréal, would that have given Morgan enough time to graduate? Enough time to find a new woman and settle down?

She didn't lose his phone number. Of course she still had it. If she was an ex-girlfriend, then she was making excuses. There had probably been lots of times when she held the phone with his number already dialled, her thumb hovering above the call button. Squeamishly debating the pros and cons. His response, the tone of his voice, would tell her too much too fast. Morgan smiled to himself. We've all been there, he thought. It's completely understandable why she would prefer to send a letter.

If she was too afraid to call, Morgan could only assume that she was somehow in the wrong. Perhaps she'd broken up with him. Perhaps she'd cheated. Maybe she'd disappeared.

Morgan realized that when he tried to picture what Heidi York looked like, the first image that came to mind was that of a small animal, a hamster or a guinea pig, running in a lab maze.

Beyond the picture he gained of Heidi, a more nuanced image of the other Morgan also emerged. An Economics Major, but no longer a student, which made sense (if he was still a student, how could he own his place?) He was in his late thirties, but most likely carried himself like a man who worked, made money, believed in time management. He probably played squash, still owned his textbooks. He was the type who saved everything, from kindergarten up until now, any assignment, test, or scribbler he'd ever owned. The type of person who buried a time capsule when he was ten years old and still remembered where he buried it. Morgan could see the inside of this other Morgan's closet, boxes and boxes of old report cards, photographs, and textbooks, the man's entire history, two metres cubed. Nothing under the bed, not even a sock. His squash racquet leaning against the wall beside the front door. Pictures of his friends on his refrigerator, and postcards like the one from K. Old Christmas cards he didn't have the heart to throw away.

Morgan folded Heidi's letter back into its envelope. A few moments later, he started writing:

Dear Heidi

Hi! It's been so long. I didn't expect to hear from you at all. But I have to say, this is quite a nice surprise. I definitely remember you and

Morgan crumpled the page and started again.

Dear Heidi

Hi! Yes, the textbook collection is alive and well. As am I. I was happy to hear from you this morning. Are you happy to hear back from me? Are you happy?

Morgan stopped. Should he agree to meet with her?

Two hours later, Morgan finished the letter. In the end, it was only a few lines long.

Heidi—

It's good to hear from you. I'm glad to hear you're pursuing the artist thing. I'm working in the marketing department for Leeman and Welsh. I make pretty good money, and get to travel. I'm not sure which email address you have, so I'll have to give you my new one. It's morganwells2@gmail.com. Flip me an email. We should seriously get together.

Gerberas do rule,
Morgan

Morgan read through the letter. He thought he captured the essence of the other Morgan Wells. Leeman and Welsh was a firm Morgan collected shreddies from. He wasn't entirely sure what they did, but he assumed that Heidi York wasn't the type to over-investigate letters from lost loves. At first he was going to sign off with something casual, such as "later." But this Morgan Wells was certainly not the type of guy to finish his letters with "later." Especially those to an ex-girlfriend. Then he remembered that Heidi had signed her letter with "Gerberas rule." It must've been a thing they did, a reference about which Morgan could only speculate. Perhaps those were her favourite flowers? Or the type of flowers he used to buy for her? Morgan almost started laughing as he wrote "Gerberas do rule." He didn't understand the reference, but he appreciated, when he said the words out loud, the way they seemed to fill the room.

As for the email address, Morgan hadn't checked his inbox in months. He hoped the account was still active. His wife had set it up for him a year or so before, but he rarely used it, even when they'd had an Internet connection. He'd have to use the Internet at the public library to see if she responded.

Morgan realized the other Morgan didn't seem like the type to use conjunctions. He'd have to correct that. Also, if Heidi had dated him, she would likely remember his handwriting. Probably had a few old love letters stashed away and might even double-check if she became suspicious. He would have to type the letter before sending it.

Morgan packed up his kit and put the loose tools in a Tupperware container. He spent the rest of his evening outside, walking and thinking about Heidi. About the other Morgan Wells. Trying to figure out what would happen next.

Eventually, he passed a thrift shop and saw an old typewriter in the window. A Smith-Corona Coronet Super 12 with a half-full cartridge. He bought it for $19.99.

The following morning, Morgan typed his response to Heidi. He made sure to put his own address in the top left corner of the envelope before mailing the letter.

I don't believe in prophecies, but after I'd left the estate sale, before I'd passed Jarvis, I'd come up with a brilliant idea. I still had a week left in Toronto, a week before everyone would disappear, and it seemed pertinent that a record be made. Something to leave behind for future archaeologists, something they could find three hundred and thirty-seven years after civilization as we know it had disappeared off the face of the earth. I saw the men in hazmat suits combing through the smoking ruins of Toronto, a place still radioactive and crawling with subhuman winged creatures, airborne zombies, drooling, slobbering Torontonians desperate for a taste of human meat. I saw the hazmat men searching the grey, broken city for remnants of intelligent life, a city-wide estate sale where everything was free. They would find my recorder buried in the wreckage, somehow spared from damage. Miraculously. What insights would that tape reveal?

I decided to spend the rest of my time in Toronto interviewing people, recording their thoughts on the blackout. Like the Lady does in *The Blazing World* after she becomes an Empress and interviews all the different creatures. Also my investigation would be different; it would be an investigation of how the world was about to end. Not about a new world, but a world about to be no more. A dead world.

When the lights went out, bombs could've easily started dropping from the sky. Six hundred and sixty-six bombs, suddenly descending, totally flattening the skyscrapers, turning the entire city into molten flesh and rubble. The nuclear power plants all Chernobyling at once, sending clouds of Black Death from one city to the next. The Great Lakes turning toxic in a half-second, bubbling and seething with biochemical diseases. People with flesh hanging from their faces, eyes putrid and rotting in their skulls, teeth falling out, feeding on the gore of their family members. Mothers eating their babies and vice versa.

Okay, so the power was back in most parts of the city, but with so many people wanting to talk, with the entire city on the verge of a complete grand mal, the story would pretty much write itself.

Even if the world didn't end, at the very least I'd walk away with a *New York Times* bestseller. Or, better yet, an interview with Oprah. I'd play myself in the film, and would win all the awards.

I already had a title in mind: *From Their Eyes: Descent into Chaos.* All I would need to do is press Record.

August 15 (Afternoon):

"They say it happened in Ohio."

"I heard it was up North."

"No, Ohio. Some kind of explosion."

"Really?"

"Lightning. Natural disaster."

"No shit. That's all it takes to kill the power to most of North America's major cities?"

"Yep."

[2.3 second pause.]

"I mean, if it was an attack or something, something would've happened by now. You know the Pentagon was running on emergency generators?"

[1.6 second pause.]

"I heard someone saying it was some kind of plasma weapon."

"A what?"

"Some kind of weapon that delivers an electromagnetic pulse, kills the power. Completely dismantles the grid."

"Oh my God."

"But it was probably just a computer malfunctioning."

"Or lightning."

After hearing that conversation, I decided to alter the title slightly. It would now be called *From Their Eyes: Death by Lightning Bolts.*

Val was in the living room when I got back to Camp David. She was sitting on the paisley armchair, reading. Her legs curled up under her. Something I have noticed about Val: she reads all the time, and never the same book. The covers change from day to day, and, until I found out her secret, I used to think she was the fastest reader on the planet.

Val stopped me as I passed through the living room. "Hey," she said, without lowering her book. "I need to talk to you."

I tried not to look at her brown, brown legs and her bare sunburnt arms. "Yeah?"

"Come here." She closed the book on her thumb and used it to wave me over. I didn't want to go. I wanted to go to my room. But her chair was suddenly next to me.

Lavender.

August 15 (Early Evening):

"What do you think of pirates?"
"Pirates?"
"Yes."
"They're okay. Kind of dumb."
"No. I mean, for a theme. For Luís's birthday?"
"Ahoy!"
"He wants to be Johnny Depp."
"Then it's probably a good idea."
"I guess so. Can I ask you a favour?"
"What?"
"Can I trust you? Can you keep a secret?"
"Yes."
"It's Luís's birthday in a week. I want you to buy him something."
"I don't have a lot of money."
"Don't worry about that. I'll give you money."
"What should I get?"
"I'll give you twenty dollars. Get him something he'll like."
"How's this a favour to you?"
"It is. Believe me. Promise not to tell your brother I gave you money."

I had no problem lying to my brother. Especially when it involved getting money for nothing. So that was Val's plan. For confiding in me, I wanted to say something important. Something to make her laugh. Something to make her trust me. I wanted to tell her about the way people were acting downtown, about the weirdoes at the estate sale. About finding the rare book. About my plan to interview people about the blackout. I also thought about warning her of the impending doom. The end of time. I thought about recommending that she stock up on canned goods. But Val is not someone I even pretend to understand. She's a hot sex rocket, but that doesn't mean I trust her. Instead, I asked her about the book she was reading.

August 15 (Early Evening):

"Is that the same book as yesterday?"
"No."
"Really?"
"Yes."
"You finished it? Already?"
"Sort of."
"Sort of?"
"I didn't finish it. But I am finished with it."
"Oh. So it wasn't very good. It didn't look very good. I mean, the cover had a photograph of a man holding a baseball bat and giving the thumbs up. How good could it be?"
"I see your point."
"You should really try reading Choose Your Own Adventures."
"Do they still publish those?"
"You can find them at most used bookstores."
"That so?"
"For like a dollar. And they're all good."
"But aren't they for kids?"
"What? No. Ages ten and up."
"Hmm. Okay. You'll have to lend me one."
[7.8 second pause.]
"Why didn't you like the other book?"

"I liked it. It was funny."

"Then why'd you stop reading?"

"I don't like finishing books."

[4.5 second pause.]

"I know how it sounds. But I only like the first one hundred pages or so. They're the only pages worth reading."

"Really?"

"Yes."

"Why?"

"Just are."

"That's not a good reason."

"It's my reason."

"*Hey-Zeus.*"

[She laughs and I think she's never sounded younger.]

"I don't trust endings. I can always tell exactly what the author is doing. Even the good ones. I've never read a single book that has made me believe in the end. Endings are either bad, or they're just contrived. Even the ones that are, you know, 'surprising yet logical' or whatever. Really the writer was just planting hints all along. It's all been staged. Endings aren't honest."

"But beginnings are?"

"I couldn't have said it better."

"If you don't like endings, you'd probably hate Choose Your Own Adventures."

"Why?"

"That's all they are. There are probably about twenty different endings for each book."

"Yikes."

"But if you make the right choices, you can usually be finished in less than one hundred pages."

"I see."

"I think 'The End' is the most important part of a story."

"Middles are the worst."

That night, when I couldn't sleep, I lay on my bed, stared at the ceiling, and counted the little sticker stars someone had put up there.

Forty. I looked out the window and counted real stars. Supposedly, about six thousand of them are visible to the human eye. At sixty-three I gave up. I began to wonder what my mom was doing. NS is an hour ahead of ON, so I knew she was probably in bed. She and Ross tend to go to bed way before midnight. It's not that she would've minded being woken up. But the last voice I wanted to hear right then was Ross's, and since the phone is on his side of the bed, I knew he'd be the one to pick it up. Since Caitlyn keeps late hours, I decided to call her instead.

Caitlyn is Dave's ex-girlfriend, but she's still my friend. She is perhaps the exact opposite of Val. Her hair is not dark and Mexican, but light and completely Canadian. Her skin is light, but not pale like mine. The freckles on her shoulders are an unwanted feature I deliberately overlook.

Caitlyn. Yes, it's pretty nauseating to know that she once loved my brother, but if it weren't for Caitlyn I would've totally disappeared by now. Unlike everyone else in the Nova Scotian village of wolves, she does not have orange skin. Her skin is for the most part untanned because she works inside, and, like me, does not think much of the sun.

Caitlyn and Dave broke up not long before my dad went incognito. That was almost two years ago, when Mom got busy with Ross, and Dave got busy with Val, so I did the expected thing and got busy with Caitlyn. But only as friends. Caitlyn is a listener. I told her that when she applies for jobs, she should put that down as her special skill. She studied Psychology at university, which she thinks caused Dave to leave her, because when they broke up he accused her of overanalyzing him. She's a teacher now.

Even though we're not even close to being in the same age group, I have a serious suspicion that Caitlyn wishes she was ten years younger, boyfriend named Gary or no boyfriend named Gary.

An interesting factoid about Caitlyn: after my brother dumped her, Caitlyn became a bit born-again for a while, and decided to pursue her second virginity. According to her church, a church my mom calls "a weathervane faith," a person can become a new virgin after six months of abstinence. Presumably, Caitlyn didn't make it past month five, because she started dating Gary, high school softball coach extraordinaire, and then stopped going to church all at once. Probably just as well, because it's stupid to think that you can just wait for time to pass for things to go back to the way they were.

Although she doesn't call me that much any more, Caitlyn has never screened my calls, or stopped answering the phone when I call her, even though I know for certain that she has call display, because when I call her, the first thing she says is "Hello there, kiddo," which is what she always calls me. I think if I had to listen to one thing for the rest of my life, it would be that line, "Hello there, kiddo," in her voice, in just the way she says it. That would certainly suffice.

On this particular night, she and I talked for the first few minutes about the blackout. She told me she'd been watching TV, and that apparently lots of bars in Toronto were giving away warm beer on the first night of the blackout, and people were celebrating in the streets. Then she told me about a party she went to with Gary, which sounded boring. She asked when I was coming home and I told her maybe never.

I was in bed. Caitlyn was somewhere in her house in NS. I didn't know where, but I imagined she was in bed. I closed my eyes and pictured her lying next to me.

August 15 (Evening):

"So I heard you guys can see the stars now."
"What do you mean?"
"They're saying it's like camping in a city."
"Who's 'they' anyway?"
"Seems sort of spooky, really. All those tall buildings. Like a ghost town."
"I don't see what the big deal is. They're just stars."
"Can you see them from where you are?"
"This isn't a Volkswagen commercial, Caitlyn."
"But now is definitely the time for the murderers to come out, don't you think? Wielding axes and stuff."
"Yeah. There are probably two or three just outside my window."

"With the power out, having to go into the bathroom without a light. Who knows who is waiting for you in there."

"Some serial killer with a machete."

"Ha! Or maybe he just puts the machete in the toilet bowl, and then waits to hear you howl before jumping out from behind the shower curtain."

"Strangles me with the shower curtain or something."

[Caitlyn laughs.]

"Have there been a lot of crimes?"

"What do you mean?"

"Crimes. Criminal activity. Thefts, vandalism."

"No. Well, I don't know. Maybe. Haven't heard anything."

"Oh."

[7.7 second pause. Caitlyn yawns. Says something to her cat in a sleepy tone.]

"So … what about Dave and Ms. Mexico? Any news?"

"They're pretty lame, as expected."

"Is he still doing that web job?"

"Yeah. Though I have my doubts if he really has a job. He does all his work from home."

"Sounds like Dave. Lazy, sluggish cognitive tempo Dave."

"Yeah."

"No surprise to hear he hasn't changed. Good old never-wants-to-go-out Dave."

"Yeah. Anyway …"

[5.2 second pause.]

"Well, it's getting late so—"

"Caitlyn, I'm going to tell you about my four major scars. I have more than that, but I'm going to tell you the stories behind four of them and I want you to tell me which one is false."

[2.9 seconds of static.]

"Is this a test?"

"No. It won't take long."

"Are they all true?"

"No."

"Is there only one false story?"

"I have a scar on my knee. That's the first one. It's small but wide. It happened when Dave used me as a bike ramp."

"Used you as a bike?"

"A ramp. I was too young for a bike. He told me to lie on the driveway in front of our house. He walked his bike to the other side of the street and told me not to move. I shouted that I was ready and he came pedalling at me. The next thing I remember is my mom and dad taking him to the hospital in the station wagon with a broken arm, blood on his sleeve. They didn't notice the gash on my knee, which is why the scar is so wide. I sat in the backseat picking the rocks out of the blood."

"Hmm. True."

"Maybe."

"What's the next one?"

[2.5 second pause. The pause is a figurative pause, representing the years that passed between the scars.]

"Hello?"

"The next scar is a surgical scar. Happened when I was ten. I had appendicitis."

"My sister had that."

"Lots of people get it."

"What side is the scar on?"

"This kid in my grade got it the same year I did. Except his happened during the school year. Mine was in the summer. The day he came back, after being out for weeks, everyone congratulated him. They all wanted to see his scar."

"What side is the scar on?"

"Left."

"False."

"But I haven't even told you the story."

"I'm tired."

"Have you ever noticed the scar on my forehead?"

"Does Dave still wear that ugly blue bandana?"

"What? You mean the headband? I dunno."

[5.5 second pause.]

"He looks like such an idiot with that thing on. Do you think she knows I'm the one who bought it for him? As a joke, but still. Does she know that?"

"What does that have to do with the scar on my forehead?"

"Oh, false. All false."

"But you need to hear about this one. It happened one night when me and a friend from school broke into this old house to steal booze."

"Which friend?"

"A friend from school."

"False."

"So we just walked in and went straight for the liquor cabinet."

"False."

"We found a bottle of whiskey and were about to leave when there's this loud shout in the dark, asking us what we think we're doing. A man standing there in his underwear, and we're scared so shitless we actually run into each other as we head for the door."

"False, false, false."

"My forehead slams right into the door frame and I'm suddenly stumbling against the kitchen table, blood on my hands and face. Totally slapstick. I don't feel the cut, don't even notice it until we're in the clear. But first I have to fight with this old man who's grabbing onto me. I'm hitting him in the face, pushing him off me. He's strong. I can't shake the old fucker. He's telling me he's going to call the cops. He's got me pinned to the floor. Can't see anything, right?"

"Blinded by all the blood in your eyes?"

"Now I know I'm done for but I don't stop struggling. He's cursing at me, knees on my shoulders. Then he's quiet. I hear this smash and I'm free. The old man's on the floor beside me and I don't know how he got there but I don't really care. My friend pulls me up and then we're outside, laughing and running. When we're far enough away, I ask for a drink of whiskey. That's when I found out how he got the old man off me."

[Caitlyn laughs. For almost ten seconds.]

"Why do you do this? You're so full of shit."

"They're all true Caitlyn. Caitlyn? I still have another one."

"I have to go."

"Do you want to listen to my tapes?"

"Goodnight."

"Caitlyn?"

" … "

33. Double Foam Mocha Latte w/ cinnamon stick and chocolate shavings.
34. Pronounces espresso "expresso."
35. Avoids black cats.
36. Doesn't wear white after Labour Day.
37. Prefers spring over summer.
38. Slurps her tea in the morning.
39. Reads the same three books over and over.
40. Brushes her teeth with baking soda.
41. Opens envelopes from the short side, always.
42. Collection of identical black V-neck sweaters.

Morgan's stomach turned. He followed a woman wearing a headset down a long, brightly lit corridor. The floor had been recently polished. It was the colour of rust. He didn't know what it was made of. The ceiling was white, as were the walls, both made of gypsum board. Every now and then they passed a window that looked onto the city thirty-six storeys below.

The woman's heels slapped rhythmically against the floor. *Crack-ca-crack-ca-crack-ca-crack.* She kept looking at Morgan and Scott, to make sure they were keeping up. Looking at them, but not bothering to catch their eyes. Not seeing them, not really.

The bottom half of the white office walls were panelled in fake wood. The hall, as a result, reminded Morgan of an old station wagon his parents used to drive. He reached out as he walked and traced a line along a panel. Car door.

They were at an advertising firm, a place with a made-up name. Dynamix or Dynametre. Dyna-something. Scott had decided to come in. He was especially hard to work with when he had to deal with businesspeople. In their presence, he smiled and chatted amiably about the weather. When they weren't around, he'd talk in monosyllables. He'd act cagey and smoke twice as many cigarettes. Like most everything else, he referred to office workers in synecdoche. They were suits. Sometimes, suitcases.

"Assholes."

Scott stopped a few feet ahead of Morgan. He was looking through a glass partition, into a boardroom full of smiling men and women. All wore some article of blue clothing. Blue skirts, blue pants, blue ties, blue blazers. They were sitting around a large wooden table, facing a projection screen lit up with an image of a tornado tearing apart a farmhouse. A narrator's voice droned on, but was muffled and impossible to understand. From the back of the room, a blue pinpoint of light beamed into the darkness. Morgan moved closer to the partition, one hand playing with his collar, the other pressed up against the wall. By the time he got to Scott's elbow, the farmhouse had disappeared completely. Then a company logo popped up on the screen. Lighthouse Insurance Co., with the slogan "The stormy weather people" written below. The people at the table started clapping. Then the lights came on.

The woman leading them down the hall noticed the two of them standing there, but she kept walking and speaking into her shoulder. She adjusted her headset.

Scott turned away from the window. "Let's get this over with."

Morgan didn't move.

"Wells?"

"Is this real wood?"

"What?"

"It looks fake."

Scott put his face within inches of Morgan's. His breath smelled of cigarettes, and something else. Sandwich meat. He looked for a few seconds like he was about to say something, but changed his mind.

"What does it matter if the wood is real or fake?"

Morgan could barely concentrate. The mess in his guts. The texture of the wood under his thumb.

A few people in the boardroom had noticed him standing there. They were looking at him, looking at each other, then back at him again. Must've been wondering who he was, the same person they saw nearly every week unloading their printed emails, their price points, their detailed strategies. Must've been wondering why he was standing there, hand on the wall. Why he wasn't already gone.

When Morgan and Scott finally walked around the corner, they found the woman waiting there, next to an open closet. Her headset rested around the back of her neck. She turned the light on and gestured to the bags, six or seven in total, full of CDs, old newspapers, magazines, invoices, spreadsheets, forms. Bags and bags of information. Useless, supplementary data.

They spent ten minutes down in the van, trying to get the shredder to power up. Scott kept feeding the data into the machine. It would sputter and spin for a moment or two, then slowly die out. At first they just turned the machine on and off, hoping that would solve the problem. Eventually, Scott resorted to banging it with the flat of his hand. For a moment or two Morgan thought he was going to spit on it in frustration. But just as quickly as it tightened up, Scott's face relaxed.

"We'll have to bring it back to the warehouse," he said, climbing down to the street. "Fucking piece of shit."

Perfect. Everything according to the plan. Morgan wondered what the technician would think when he found the thumbtacks.

They delivered their cargo to the warehouse on Hendrick Street, a nondescript building near the lake. One section of it used to be an old textile mill. It looked like an oversized pink cardboard box.

After unloading the morning's pickups, Morgan went around to the front office. He needed to speak with Cranley. If he didn't speak to him soon, his whole plan would fall through. He could already feel the tempest stirring, and wondered if anyone could see signs of the coming storm in his face, the way he moved. The way he held his hands against his legs, fingers clutching intermittently at the collar of his golf shirt. Each time he opened his mouth he had to take deep breaths before speaking. Steady the winds.

"Hi Tabitha."

She was on the phone, doodling on the back of an envelope. When she wasn't on the phone, Cranley's assistant spent most of her time feeling sorry for herself. Morgan was sympathetic. He worked for The Letter Shredders too.

Morgan looked at Tabitha's postcards. Tabitha had at least sixty of them pinned to the inner wall of her cubicle and taped against the drawers of her desk. Cancun, Vienna, Jerusalem, Ibiza. Cathedrals, bikinis, busts, and skylines. The Statue of Liberty. Big Ben. An enormous effigy of Christ on the cross. Hanging. Morgan looked at the two Post-it notes stuck to Tabitha's calendar. *Cancel Friday Do Thurs?* and *Baby Brussel Sprouts*.

"Tabitha, can I—?"

"Just a minute."

"Exactly a minute?"

"What?"

"Exactly a minute? Or more?"

She shifted her weight in her chair. Changed ears. Clicked her pen.

"Tabitha?"

"Less."

Morgan walked to the front door and surveyed the parking lot. He kept his hand tight against his stomach. Two blue cars, one red, four silver, two white. The word miscellaneous came into his head. He remembered hearing the word for the first time in school, and knowing its meaning before it knew him. Miscellaneous cars.

Morgan moved from the door. The wall to his left boasted a Monet poster, a bright one. Lots of floating colours and indistinct forms. Hopeful. Morgan saw a company business card in the upper right corner of the company bulletin board. A thumbtack keeping it in place.

If you don't want it read, give it a shred!

To his right, three immobile fish named by Tabitha—Oscar, Wally, and Sam—floated inside their home. Morgan was drawn toward the fish, and though he knew not to he tapped his fingers against the glass, trying to draw their attention. None of them moved. He flipped the lid back and dipped his hand into the water, watched it grow as it sank, watched the warm ripples spread out in concentric circles. He stirred the water around. The fish were still. When he reached for one, it glided away unblinking.

Morgan's stomach moved against his ribs.

Wiping his hand on the back of his pants, Morgan closed the tank lid and wondered if he'd just contaminated the water. He was reassured by the hum of the aquarium's power unit. There was no need to worry. It wasn't really a self-contained environment, he thought, looking at the tank, no longer thinking of the fish. Thinking of the isolette, that medical aquarium, and the tiny purple-skinned fish it had housed. Not a fish, but equally incapable of breathing oxygen, of surviving on dry land. An artificial being, a form without content. He thought of the hair, dark patches, pressed against the skull. He thought of the fingers, pink and translucent. The necessary parts, made to function by green and blue buttons, white wires, brain monitors, environment modulators. An end without a beginning.

Lightheaded, Morgan rested his fingers against the lip of the tank. The aquarium's power unit cut out for a moment, then resumed humming. Like the isolette, the tank might've existed in itself, but it only existed because of what happened outside, the multiple tubes, timers, and lights. The fish existed because Tabitha fed them. If Tabitha did not exist, there would be no fish. Morgan scratched his chin. As he did so, he caught a whiff of his hand. It smelled like a moist dishtowel.

Outside, the rain broke against the windows—a thousand falling light bulbs, popping in sync.

His baby, needles and wires scaling its hand-sized body, modern medicine's attempt at gills. The purple splotches on the chest.

Tabitha was looking in his direction, phone tucked against her shoulder, asking "What's wrong? What's wrong?"

He opened his mouth to say, "I don't feel good." What came out was a pound or so of semi-processed waste.

"Oh Jesus, Morgan!"

The true violence of vomit isn't its smell, or its consistency as it passes over the teeth, or even the way it looks. The true violence of vomit, thought Morgan, is that it reveals what I pretend is not inside me. A mess of organs. A mess.

Included in the mess that now pooled around Morgan's shoes was a single breast of chewed-up raw chicken. He'd eaten it that morning along with his usual bowl of rolled oats. He needed the afternoon off. He had wanted to save the episode for Cranley's office, or even just when Cranley was around. Payback. The violence of the vomit in exchange for Cranley's insincere, safe attempt to empathize with Morgan's "situation." The boss no longer in control, but scrambling desperately to avoid the mess, the stench, screaming at Morgan to use the garbage can.

On his knees, coughing and spitting waste, pulling the phlegm from the back of his throat and drooling it out, making a show of it for the security cameras, practically choking on the bile, the burning battery acid on his tongue, Morgan only regretted the lost opportunity to see the mess spattering all over his boss's cluttered desk.

The gallery was in Oakville. It belonged to Heidi York's aunt, or second cousin, her email wasn't entirely clear.

Cranley had given Morgan the rest of the day off. When Morgan had asked for it earlier in the week, Cranley had refused. Barely even looked up from his desk to say no. Morgan wondered if Scott had been telling more lies. All Morgan had asked for was one afternoon. Heidi had invited him, or rather, the other Morgan, to an art gallery for what she'd called an "afternoon rendezvous." Just like old times. He couldn't let her down.

Heidi and the person she arrived with were both fashionably attired, carrying purses the size of their torsos. Morgan watched them from his position near the reception desk. He saw them walk in, saw Heidi looking around, looking for Morgan. The other Morgan. The two girls moved around as one, arms linked, from one exhibit to the other. Heidi looked and seemed so much like his ex-wife. Her dark curls, her Irish nose. Not a single piece of jewellery around her neck, wrists, or fingers.

Morgan chewed on a mint antacid tablet, leaned against the wall. The blonde girl behind the reception desk kept looking at him. He stared right back until she looked away. Morgan had been at the gallery for more than twenty minutes, standing in the same spot, waiting for Heidi to arrive. Now that she'd finally arrived, he didn't know what his next move should be.

He decided he needed something to drink. A glass of water. He went over the small café located off the main exhibit area. He asked the twenty-something behind the counter for a glass of water, to which the guy replied, "What? Not wet enough already?" The waiter laughed, but Morgan said nothing. He took the glass of water and drank it in one gulp, then put the glass back on the counter. Morgan then walked back into the main exhibit area, but not toward Heidi. She had to come to him.

Do not write letters by hand: type them with the Coronet Super 12.
Do not meet with subject.
Do not mention too much about yourself.
Do not respond to more than one letter at once.
Do not use email (unless required to do so).
Do not ask for photograph.

Morgan went to the nearest exhibit. The painting was ten feet high and five feet wide, and depicted a naked woman in a swimming pool, a swirl of blood willowing from her knee. Her mouth covered with cotton. Upon closer inspection, Morgan discovered that the entire work was painted over old newspapers.

In a side room, a handful of cubicles had been set up under a falsely lowered ceiling, buzzing with fluorescents. The desks were empty. Paintbrushes glued to the walls.

Morgan stared at a picture of a floor plan for three minutes, looking for the artist's signature, before he realized he was actually looking at the gallery's floor plan. Fire exits clearly marked.

A sculpture of an owl, made from recycled car parts.

A flock of paper geese flew out from under the hood of a rusty '56 Ford.

Morgan sat on a conveniently placed bench. Heidi, hair pulled back, smiling nervously, looked closely at a painting of a purple chainsaw. Relaxed her jaw. Tilted her head slightly to the left. She seemed distracted. Morgan counted the number of times she looked around, looked toward the door. Eleven. He noted the way her right hand clasped her purse strap, while her left hand hung loose at her side, moving when she spoke. She spoke infrequently. Her friend carried most of their conversation. Morgan wondered if Heidi was always this reserved. Had she told her friend her ex-boyfriend was coming? Who were they expecting? What did they expect?

They unlinked arms. Heidi touched her friend on the shoulder and started off towards the outer hall. Morgan followed her through a pair of glass doors, beneath a painting of a technicolour mollusc. She went into the washroom. He stood next to the door, pushed against the handle until the door cracked open. But he couldn't push it any further. What if her friend came looking for her? Morgan traced his hand against the door, just beneath the woman symbol. It would take the slightest push. He wondered what he'd say to her. Ask her if she was alone. If she knew where the other Morgan went to school.

Morgan drank from the fountain, washed the pitiful conversation from his mouth. The dry taste of vomit, something his toothbrush wouldn't be able to work off with just one brush. He felt, slightly, as though he was sinking.

Perhaps he should just kick the door open. Kick it hard and see what happened. Watch the blood trickle along the floor.

"You must be thirsty."

The voice came so unexpectedly, Morgan coughed on the water that tasted like metal and hit his teeth against the fountain's spout. He stood erect, hand to his lips, water dribbling down his unshaven chin. A spot of watery blood came off on his fingers.

"Sorry! I didn't mean to scare you like that."

"That's okay."

"You're bleeding?"

"No. It's fine."

"Are you sure?"

"Yes."

Heidi stood there looking at him for a moment, as if she expected him to say something more.

"Do you mind if I … could I step in there?"

Morgan backed away from the fountain. Heidi pushed her thumb against the spout and let it run for a moment. Morgan turned away, not wanting to see the cold water gushing into her mouth, her throat working it down. He looked down the hall, toward the gift shop. Glass walls, shelves stacked with reprints, photo frames, journals, stationary. The ceiling in this area was considerably lower than in the main exhibit area, and the floor, Morgan realized, had changed from tile to carpet. A kind of grey office carpet, like the one at work. Berber. If he stared in one place long enough, black and white spots began to stand out, sink in, move around. Morgan started to walk toward the gift shop, if only to get away from the shape-shifting carpet, but changed his mind.

"Are you Heidi?"

"Yes."

"Oh. I'm Morgan Wells."

"Excuse me?"

"I'm Morgan Wells."

Pause.

"Where's Morgan?"

"I am Morgan."

She laughed through her nose, then crossed her arms. When she smiled, she seemed to stop breathing.

"You're funny. I didn't realize he would bring a friend. I suppose that makes sense though." Heidi mumbled something about having a backup plan, tried to laugh it off. "How long have you known Morgan?"

"Not long. You?"

"We were friends in university. Lived in the same dorm. God, seems like ages ago."

Morgan nodded. Heidi wasn't looking at him. She was looking over Morgan's shoulder, as if she expected the real Morgan Wells to step out from behind him.

"I'm here with my friend Andrea."

Silence.

Morgan finally offered, "I have a pain in my leg."

"Oh yeah?" Heidi tilted her head, waiting for more.

"From walking."

"You walk a lot? I mean, are you a walker?"

"Yes."

"Smart choice."

Pause.

"So you don't own a car?"

"Don't need one."

She nodded, but didn't say anything, and again the silence invaded.

"Morgan's not here, by the way."

"Cool." Heidi started walking. "We can wait for him over there. I'll introduce you to Andrea!"

They walked into the gallery café. Morgan was unsure of his next move. He clenched his hands tight against his sides, afraid that if he let himself, he might reach for one of Heidi's hands. Heidi's friend was sitting at a white table, nibbling away at an enormous black cookie.

"Andrea, this is Morgan's friend ... sorry, I forget your name?"

"Morgan."

"Your name is Morgan too?"

Heidi frowned. "That's what he keeps telling me. This is Andrea."

"Nice to meet you Andrea."

Andrea had soft features, a paper white face. The tip of a purple tattoo crawled inconspicuously up the left side of her neck. A tail? A wisp of smoke? "What do you think of the art?"

"I don't think about art."

"Exactly. You don't have to. That's what art is."

Morgan enjoyed Andrea's polished chrome fingernails, the metal stud in her lip. His eyes travelled up and down the run of her legs. Andrea pulled her cup to her lips and took a slow sip of something frothy. A cappuccino? A latte? His wife would know the difference.

Heidi sat down. For a second Morgan stayed standing. The two women were facing each other, so he couldn't see Heidi's face. He wondered if they were talking about him with their lashes, the creases in their foreheads, the twitches of their lips.

He took a seat with his back to the wall.

There were two salt shakers on the table. Two of them. Morgan thought about moving them around. Thought about exchanging one of them for a pepper shaker, then thought better of it. Best not to draw attention to himself.

Heidi said something about her aunt, yes it was her aunt who owned the gallery, giving a talk about the featured artist in ten minutes. She spoke more now than she did before Morgan joined them, but she continued to look toward the door, waiting. He felt her words were waiting, as though she wanted to save her best sentences for Morgan, her Morgan.

Morgan pushed the two salt shakers together. Separated them. Pushed them together again.

He couldn't open his mouth at all. The words weren't there, or if they were, they weren't the right ones. He kept his hands hidden under the table. He had questions. She'd mentioned that she and Morgan lived in the same dorm. At what university? For how long? His hand grazed her left elbow.

Heidi turned, still smiling. For the first time, he realized her eyes were blue. Not brown. She waited for Morgan to speak. Her look burned holes in his cheeks, his ears, and then he wasn't thinking, only knowing that he couldn't stay. She wasn't the one he was interested in. She kept her hand curled tight around her purse strap. She knew.

"What's the matter?" Heidi asked.

"I have to go."

"What about Morgan? You're not going to wait for him?"

"I have to go."

He heard the women talking behind him as he walked beneath the electric red exit sign. He heard Andrea say, "Who the fuck was that?" and he heard Heidi say, "I don't know" and he heard Andrea laughing, and he thought he heard her say "You sure know how to pick them. What a loser." He thought he heard Heidi say she felt sorry for the woman who ended up with him as she wiped her lip with a napkin.

Andrea: The woman?

Heidi: The blind woman.

Andrea: The deaf woman.

Heidi: Near-dead.

Andrea: A fucking zombie.

Heidi: The fucking creep.

Andrea: No wonder his wife left.

Heidi: And did you hear why? Do you know what he did?
Andrea: It makes me sick.

Morgan began to steal more mail.

But it always ended up being more or less the same mail. Bills, bills, bills, junk, the same junk Morgan found in his own mailbox. Nothing worth responding to. All he'd learned about the other Morgan was that he'd studied Economics. He knew that he was married, because his wife, Nat, received mail under the name Natalie Wells. Beyond that, Morgan knew nothing of substance. He didn't even know the other Morgan's age, or where he worked.

One day Morgan found a parcel slip from Canada Post in the other Morgan's mailbox. He went down to the drugstore with high expectations, but it was only a book ordered online. Something worthless, written by a former prime minister. Morgan hadn't come across a hand-stamped envelope since Heidi York's.

He needed to choose a new mailbox. Find a new Morgan.

He could see no reason why the Morgan on Morton should be the only Morgan Wells worth looking into. There were probably other Morgan Wellses in the city that didn't have their numbers listed. Morgan could search for them later; at present, he decided to focus upon the other name he'd found in the phonebook. The Morgan who lived in the Annex had as much to tell him as the other Morgan. And the people who knew him, who still wrote letters. Who sprayed perfume on paper before folding it. Who used their tongues to seal their notes.

He made a rule. He would only steal letters from one house a week. He made another rule. He would respond to one letter at a time. It would be enough.

He wondered for how long it would be enough.

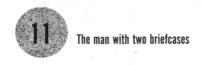

BLACKOUT, DAY 3.

At around noon, approximately ten minutes after I woke up, Val knocked on my door and asked me to go grocery shopping with her and Luís. A boring proposition, but how could I refuse? With Luís and his singing, and Val singing too.

August 16 (Late Afternoon):

> *"Cumpleaños feliz!"*
> *"Cumpleaños feliz!"*
> *"Te deseamos todo!"*
> *"Cumpleaños feliz!"*

I almost told Val that the grocery store wasn't my thing. I was anxious to begin interviewing people, and already felt as though I'd wasted so much time. After all, I only had a few days left in Toronto, and the world could explode at any moment. If our world became a blazing world before I even started my interviews I would've surely deserved a death of burning and smoke inhalation. But then Val wore a violet tank top with spaghetti straps and I could see her shoulder blades wincing against her amazingly deep and textured brown skin. Her skin between the shoulder blade and the spinal cord. When the blade is flexed, the skin suspended there is like a tarp, glowing in the sun and perspiring just the right amount. Caitlyn has let me touch this spot on her back several times, but it's not the same. Touching Val's skin would murder me. I'd be electrocuted.

So I agreed to walk with Val and Luís to the grocery store, and I spent most of that walk a few steps behind Val, glancing at the spot on her back, and then at her calves, and then at the spot again until

I put my hands in my pockets and pulled my shirt down with my thumbs and moved up in front of them to clear my head.

We were going to the grocery store to pick up some things for Luís's party, even though it was still several days away. Val said she didn't want to leave anything to the last minute. "No one wants a last-minute birthday!" she said, as if that was a saying.

I don't remember exactly what we put in the cart, but I do know that Val bought Tropicana orange juice. Later that day I tried to pour myself a glass, but Dave grabbed the carton out of my hands before I could, and told me I was only allowed to drink concentrated orange juice. When Val came into the kitchen and found me making orange juice, and then discovered why, she poured the Tropicana into a pitcher, and filled the carton with concentrated orange juice. I could've kissed her.

Besides the Tropicana, we also picked up some snack foods, which, thanks to Val, were without sugar and salt, and mostly made of vegetable or fruit or bread. A brick of bread that cost six dollars and was made out of brown rice. Val calls them treats and it blows my mind that Luís also thinks of them as treats. I've told him many times about candy bars, Wunderbars in particular, but he just looks at me like I'm speaking Chinese. I seriously wonder if he knows what I'm saying. Ross told my mom that compared to me, Luís is a genius child. But any kid who requests rice cakes for his birthday party must be slightly brainwashed. Or incredibly stupid.

August 16 (Late Afternoon):

[Background noise sounds a bit like an ocean breathing, and now and again is punctuated by someone yapping into a microphone: "Susan Gunther to Customer Service, Susan Gunther to Customer Service, please," and sometimes: "Attention shoppers," or "There's a blue Toyota parked in the handicap zone." And also a quiet hum of radio music, the type of songs you can't hear unless you turn the volume up full blast and zone out. Now and then, the sound of a can or a box hitting the bottom of a shopping cart.]

"*¿Cuáles quieres?*"

"*Estos.*"

"*¿Estos?*"

"*Sí.*"

"What do you think?"

"What are they?"

"Delicious. They have coconut in them."

"Whatever."

"*No importa.*"

"*¿Tomamos arroz con leche también?*"

"*Yo quiero tapioca.*"

"*¿Tapioca?*"

"*Sí, por favor.*"

"*¿Con pacanas?*"

"*Sí, ¡riquísima!*"

"Would you mind getting some tapioca mix?"

"Tapioca?"

"It's right … No, is that …?"

[The person on the loudspeaker says something about a sale. A blackout sale on snow peas and broccoli.]

"This stuff?"

"Can you reach? Great."

"Here."

"Thanks. It's one of his favourites."

"What is it?"

"You've never had tapioca?"

[I make gagging sounds.]

"Okay, I'll get the soy butter and if they have vegan marshmallows … would you mind …?"

"What?"

"Well, I was thinking some yogurt for dessert would be nice …"

Val started toward the dairy section with her arms pointing out in front of her. A guy walked past me carrying two briefcases. He had long, slinky hair, but was one hundred percent bald on top. He wore a long grey trench coat. My first thought was that his cases were lined with explosives, large knives, a mini bazooka, some pepper spray, agent orange, mustard gas, a biochemical cocktail that causes livers to disintegrate in seconds, a hypodermic needle filled with a concoction that shrinks the lungs to the size of a penny. He had no cart, just a dead look on his face, like he'd already seen the ending, and it wasn't pretty. He knew the world was ending, could end at any moment, had already ended and we were just catching up to the idea. He pulled the semi-automatic from the inside of his coat and held it to the back of my head. Did me execution style. Didn't even give me a second to say a prayer. My brains fell in pieces amongst the cabbage and radishes.

I pretended not to see the briefcase man as he walked past. Pretended to be fully amazed by the UPC codes I saw all around me. I was trying to think of some way to start a conversation. The man was a prophet. I hoped he might say something as he walked by, some kind of warning or prediction. Some kind of vision. A phone started ringing in his pocket. A phone, or some kind of explosive device?

August 16 (Late Afternoon):

"Hello? Hey sweetheart. Yes. No, I'm here now."
[6.7 second pause.]
"Okay. Baguette or rye? I know, but sometimes you go for rye. Ha! Okay. Sure. Yes. Yes, definitely. Be home in twenty."

After the weakling with the briefcases passed, I stood there by the shopping cart for a while, looking at the tapioca. Boring. I needed someone to interview.

I walked to the deli counter, the displays of meat glowing in fluorescent light like some science fair exhibit. Wrapped and stamped. I'd overheard Val talking to Dave the day before about her disgust with the meat industry. They were in the kitchen, and it was just before supper.

August 15 (Evening):

"Babe, can you make tacos tonight?"
"My nut seed tacos?"
"No. Real tacos."

[5.2 second pause.]
"Dave, when is the last time I made anything with ground beef?"
"I think my iron count has hit an all-time low."
[4.6 second pause.]
"I'm not making 'real' tacos."
"Why not?"
"First of all, the power keeps cutting out. Secondly, you know why."
[10.5 second pause. Sound of Dave opening and closing cupboards.]
"Val, people have been eating meat since the dawn of time. I just don't—"
"You like getting your meat from an assembly line? Where animals, living, breathing creatures, are treated like—?"
"Food?"
"Like objects."
"They are objects."
"They're living creatures. They're alive, Dave."
"They're also delicious."
"Enough, Dave. Seriously. We'll order in Chinese."
"Let me guess: vegetarian Shanghai noodles?"
"Why do you always have to bring this up?"
"Because I get hungry several times a day."
"Ugh. Do not take that tone."
"What tone?"
[12.3 second pause.]
"What tone, Val?"

Another conversation of theirs that ended with a discussion about tones: overtones, undertones, levels, volumes. How can so many conversations end like that without either of them aware of it? Don't raise your voice and don't talk to me like that. They must know the conclusions they will come to. To which they will come.

Although I do not often share any thoughts or opinions with the onion-faced Dave, I think it is worth noting that for this particular conversation I had to side with my brother. I also am a wonderful fan of meats and in the end I do not care how I get it, or how it gets to me. I like chicken, and beef, and pork, in that order. Chicken is famous for its versatility. Beef for its constancy. Pork for bacon. Even Val admits that everyone loves bacon.

I was standing near the meat display and imagining the meats didn't come from farm animals, but from human bodies. I imagined my own body being cleaved to pieces by the butcher, and the meat being pulled from the bones and slabbed onto Styrofoam plates and wrapped in Saran. I was thinking that it's too bad that Val doesn't eat meat. I was picturing Val cutting up parts of my brain on a plate when I noticed Luís standing a few feet away. He was wearing a blue shirt with red sleeves and a stupid little Blue Jays hat that was too small for his head, and he reached forward into one of the fridge sections and rubbed his fingers against a frozen chicken. Yes, and he rubbed his fingers against the ice crystals on the outside, like he was scraping up snow. Then he looked at me and put his fingers in his mouth. Stuffed his mouth with chicken frost. He swallowed. *Hey-Zeus.* So he was Dave's kid after all. He scooped up another mouthful, which was too much for me, I had to leave and go straight down the closest aisle. To get away from Luís, whose actions were this close to making me fall in front of a bus.

I walked down the canned food aisle. The grocery store was pretty much empty. Not a single person to interview. The power was up again, and either people had stocked up earlier in the morning, or they'd gone somewhere else the day before. Either way, the place was surprisingly empty, considering there was only so much time left for people to fill their bomb shelters with all the essential emergency items.

I wandered up and down the aisles for another ten minutes or so, and was eventually drawn to the shelves of magazines and newspapers. One in particular caught my eye, of a black New York skyline against a faded orange backdrop. New York or Chicago? Some

American city. The headline said, "Dependence Day." I wondered which of the publishers would be most interested in my investigation. I spent several minutes searching among them, looking for some kind of lead. I picked up the top copy of the *National Post* and flipped through the first few pages, not reading anything, just looking at the headings, wishing I could see my dad's name beneath a title. The pictures. Some old men in suits at a press conference. Baseball players swinging bats. A woman in a hospital bed who'd started having contractions as soon as the power went out, who gave birth on Highway 401 with the help of a stranded doctor. I wondered if her child was born with special powers.

I was staring at a picture of about nine strangers lined up at a pay phone on Dundas, wishing I could find them all and ask them exactly what they were thinking when that picture was taken, when Val found me. For a split second, I wondered who Val was, and why such a beautiful Mexican was speaking to me.

August 16 (Late Afternoon):

"Where's Luís?"
"With the cart."
"Which cart?"
[5.5 second pause.]
"The cart I'm pushing right now?"
"I told him to wait by the cart."
"You left him? Alone?"
"I was only gone for a sec."
[2.3 second pause.]
"He's four."
"Five in a couple days."

Val looked at me like she couldn't believe what I was saying, then pushed the cart toward me. We spent the next ten minutes tearing up and down the aisles, looking for Luís.

Val's like my mom in a way, because even though I could tell she felt like putting me in a headlock, or at least screaming at me, she remained calm, searched aisle by aisle, and only told me, after we found Luís eating green beans in the produce section, that I'd been "pretty irresponsible for leaving him." Dave would've surely massacred me right then and there. He would've taken the butcher's knife and stabbed out my eyes. He would've ground me up and made tacos. He would've surely massacred me after the fact if Val had told him what had happened. Only she did not.

The walk home from the grocery store was much quieter than the walk there. Luís was no longer singing, and Val was ignoring me. By the time we got home, I thought my arms would fall off from the weight of the bags. Just as Val slid her key into the lock, I saw the man with two briefcases from the grocery store walking down the sidewalk on the other side of the street. Although he'd already let me down once, I found it strange to see him twice in one day, and even stranger to see that he wasn't carrying any groceries. He'd told the person on the phone that he would pick up some bread, and unless he'd put the loaf of bread in his briefcase, he'd obviously been lying. To distract me? To trick me into thinking he *wasn't* some kind of terrorist?

As soon as my so-called sister-in-law got the door open, I went into the apartment and dropped the groceries I'd painstakingly carried for her onto the kitchen floor. I then started to leave, but Val stopped me before I got anywhere, and asked me to unpack the groceries. Normally, I would've told her to shove it, that I had more important things to do. But after losing Luís in the grocery store, I felt like I owed her something. In less than thirty seconds flat, I quickly unpacked the groceries and left them lined up neatly along the counter. I ran out the door without even telling Val where I was going, just in case she used the moment as an opportunity to make me put the groceries away.

The man with the briefcases was way down the street by the time I got outside, little more than a speck. I set off in that speck's direction, coming up with an introductory line.

Excuse me, sir, may I have a moment of your time?

Excuse me, sir, didn't you say you were going to buy some bread?

Excuse me, sir, is that a bomb I hear ticking in one of your briefcases?

I followed briefcase man down Dave's and Val's street for about a minute, until he turned down a side street. I wasn't worried about losing him, but quickened my pace once he turned the corner just to make sure he didn't get away. He'd turned down Dewhurst Boulevard North, a two-lane street peppered with squat two-storey brick houses, much like every other street in Pape Village. I turned down Dewhurst just as briefcase man made a left on King's Park Boulevard, another cookie-cutter residential street, except the houses were mostly single-storey. By the time I made it onto King's Park, briefcase man had disappeared.

I stood there on the sidewalk for a minute, sweating in the sun, scanning the street. I figured briefcase man must've lived on this street. There was a white van parked outside of one of the houses. I wondered if it was full of CSIS people, or better yet, the FBI. Maybe they already knew about briefcase man's top-secret mission. I walked closer to the van, but realized quickly that it was not there for surveillance. The back doors were open. It was full of painting supplies. Just as I'd suspected: a decoy. The real surveillance van was likely just up the street.

I was craning my neck to see where the real FBI van was parked when I heard the sound of breaking glass. It came from a house on the other side of the street. My first and only thought was that briefcase man was breaking into the house through the back door. He was planting an infection. Distributing the virus to housewives all over the city, one perfectly decorated home at a time. I crossed the street with major stealth. The steps to the house were just these two huge slabs of concrete stacked on top of each other, slightly rounded along the edges, like a wedding cake without the frosting. The window above the front door was stained glass, a picture of an angel. There was a crack in his forehead.

I grabbed the steel handrails and walked up the steps, concocting a plan. I imagined kicking the door open, and seeing briefcase man wearing a gas mask, standing over a woman in a bathrobe, about to inject her with a particularly vicious strain of the flu virus. SARS would be nothing next to the hell this baby would unleash.

I didn't kick the door open. I'm not Rambo. My strength is in my tongue. Besides, why blow my cover? I'd just knock on the door, and pretend like I was any other neighbourhood kid. Maybe I'd offer to mow the lawn or something. Make him think I wasn't onto him, and then as soon as he turned his back…

I knocked on the door. No one answered. I knocked again, then waited for a long minute. No answer. I peered through the window. The curtains were made of lace. The living room looked relatively normal, with white cloths on all the surfaces, school photos on the wall, what looked like a giant platter nailed over the fireplace. A family lived there. Poor family of dolts. They had no idea what this mass-murdering villain was up to. I went back to the door and knocked again. Checked the knob. It turned. I pushed the door open.

"Hello?" I called out as I walked inside. "Anyone home?" I said this just in case, but I knew no one was home. I stood still in the entryway next to a hat rack and a chair piled up with old newspapers, a few magazines. The floors were wooden, seemed to glow. Over in the corner of the living room, the stereo looked light, easy to carry off. I would have to leave the speakers behind. The television was far too large. But the stereo I could carry.

"Who are you? Hello?"

Terror alert red.

The woman was younger than my mom, but older than Val. She wore a housecoat and a pair of sky blue slippers. Her hair was wet. She held a fat black comb in her right hand. "Who are you?"

"Me?"

She looked at me with her eyebrows. "I'm calling the cops."

"I just …"

"Stay there!"

She turned her back on me. I walked after her, but she turned suddenly and grabbed a blue decorative bowl off a side table and brained me with it. The bowl was made of some kind of metal. It crushed the left side of my skull, left a big dent. I fell onto the sofa, blood leaching all over the pretty white cushions, and my vision started to fade and I plunged into a coma, from which I did not emerge. A month later, my mom stood at the foot of the hospital bed. She wept when the machines made that flat sound. Dead line.

Ross put his arm around my mom's shoulder. Val cried. They all felt that it was the right decision.

One time Dave wrapped his arms around my gut and shook me until I puked. Caitlyn was there when that happened, and she patted me on the back afterwards, and called Dave a jerk. I was a kid then, and Dave could still pick me up. Now he can barely pick me up, and so resorts to sitting on me.

After knocking, and receiving no answer, I did not go into the idiotic house on King's Park, where briefcase man may or may not live, or where he may or may not have been plotting the destruction of the human race. Even though I felt the world was ending, I saw no need to meet my own end prematurely. I decided—wisely, if a bit boringly—to retreat. I admit it.

And I was hungry, after the big chase, so I decided to cut through this pathetic excuse for a park to shorten my journey back to Camp David. It was called the Langford Parkette. Lots of empty swings and plastic toys left in the sand. Bags of dog shit near the entrance. I took a drink from the drinking fountain, then instantly spit it out. The water was warm, milky. Awful. I wiped my mouth on my sleeve and realized that the problem with Camp David was that Dave would be there by now. So I sat down on a bench. I opened my bookbag. I pulled out *The Blazing World*.

Nature is but one Infinite Self-moving Body, which by the vertue of its self-motion, is divided into Infinite parts, which parts being restless, undergo perpetual changes and transmutations by their infinite compositions and divisions.

I read these lines quickly, then read them again. But it was frustrating. Why couldn't I break the code? Was it just my low blood sugar? If the book was giving me clues about the coming Super Death, it wasn't going to make things easy for me.

I thought about what Val had said about books and went back to the beginning and read the first few paragraphs again. The part about the Lady-soon-to-be-Empress meeting the bear-men. I figured the story would be much more interesting if one of the bear-men was named Rundle. Rundle was the name of a character from one of my all-time favourite Choose Your Own Adventures, *The Blackest Night*. Like *The Blazing World*, it was about creatures, except creatures who live in enormous underground tunnels, and I had to help their leader, a cave dweller named Rundle, fight an evil band of killer worms. Rundle was super tough. Definitely one of my favourite characters.

In my version of *The Blazing World*, Rundle the bear-man would accompany the Lady, so that she wouldn't have to be on her own for her interviews, or while exploring the blazing and, let's be honest, pretty effed-up new world.

The bear-men take you as far as the sea of Atharanta, an emerald green body of water that separates the frozen tundra lands from the slightly warmer, more temperate lowlands of the continent. From there, however, they can go no further. As arctic creatures, they are incapable of leaving the icy lands, and, in fact, you've already noticed their hair changing colour, from a deep white to a dirty grey. Some of the bear-men are balding. Taking you this far has already constituted a considerable risk.

"Thank you, strong Rundle, for your help and your sacrifice. Without your assistance, I surely would not have lasted in this arctic winterland."

"The pleasure has been ours," says Rundle, gesturing with his enormous paws to the twenty or so bear-men who accompanied you on this dangerous crossing. "It has been over 337 years since a human has graced our shores. Many had begun to think of your kind as extinct."

"I assure you, we are real, and we are all too abundant. I only hope I may rejoin my people soon."

"As we said, the legendary Elysia are likely the only beings on this world that can offer you that assistance. If only we could lead you back from whence you came, we gladly would have."

"I understand and thank you, sir. Peace be with all your people. But before you go, I must ask: how might I cross this vast body of emerald green water upon which you leave me?"

"Ah," says Rundle, smiling broadly, revealing his fangs. "This minor detail has already been seen to."

At this moment, the waters along the shoreline start foaming. The foam is not the expected white, but a deep shade of blue, with bright specks of purple. And from the foam emerges an enormous black turtle with light blue eyes the size of small ponds. On the turtle's back sits an enormous bird's nest with sun chairs already set up.

"This is Olgrad. He is your transportation to the other side."

I was about to flip to another random page in Cavendish's book when a shaggy black dog ran up to me and started humping my leg. No leash. I looked around. No owner. I'm not a fan of dogs, especially not the humping kind. I tried to push him away, but he was panting and wouldn't quit. I was pretty close to giving him a sharp kick to the ribs when I heard someone calling out.

"Marvin! Mr. Marvin Gaye! Where are you?"

The owner of Marvin Gaye, I was pleased to see, was a beautiful red-haired fox with gorgeous green eyes. She easily could've been the Lady-turned-Empress. She wasn't tall or anything, but her portions were just right. She was holding a coiled blue leash in her hand, and there were beads dropping off her neck and down her shirt. Her nose was a tiny bit crooked, but she had an amazing smile. She wore a giant ring with a bright stone on her hand, and for a while I couldn't look at anything else.

When she first saw me, she sort of stopped in her tracks. She looked surprised to see me, as though it was her parkette and no one else's. She looked even more surprised when she realized Marvin Gaye was humping my leg.

August 16 (Early Evening):

"Oh God! Marvin don't! Marvin!"

[Sound of a dog's collar being grabbed and leashed. Lots of heavy panting, metal on metal, a moment of soft cooing.]

"I'm so sorry!"

"He's got his lipstick out."

[Quick, pitchy laugh.]

"This park is usually empty this time of day. That's why I let him off the leash. Marvin stop!"

"It's okay. No big deal."

"You must be a dog owner."

"Why do you say that?"

"If you weren't, you'd have told me off by now."

"Well …"

"What kind is yours?"

[3.3 second pause.]

"You should say was, not is."

"Oh. Oh I'm sorry."

"He's gone missing."

"For how long?"

"Almost a week."

[Marvin Gaye starts barking. The woman shushes him and he stops pretty quickly.]

"I'm sorry to hear that."

"I've been looking for days, but no luck."

"Do you have a photo?"

"No."

[Heavy panting.]

"You don't have a photo? You should."

"I don't."

"You really should."

"I don't."

[More heavy panting.]

"Why don't you have any?"

"I don't know. I guess I didn't need one until she got lost."

"I suppose. But that's why you take pictures, right? In case things get lost?"

"I don't know. I don't own a camera."

"What kind of dog is she?"

"I don't know."

"You don't know the breed?" .

"I, uh ... I don't think of dogs in terms of their breed."

[High-pitched beeps. The sound of the redhead checking the time on her phone, or writing a text message, hard to say which.]

"Oh."

I went on to tell the redhead all about my fake lost dog. A brown dog of medium size. With three white dots on her nose and a yellowish trail down her neck. Responds to the name Sammy and wears a blue collar. I was surprised at myself for coming up with so many details off the cuff, though the name I chose came pretty easily, it being the name of a girl from school who resembles a golden retriever in near exactness. Especially worth knowing is the fact that her too-cool-to-speak-to-me-at-school older sister is on the swim team, and when my mom signed me up for swimming lessons at the Y, I would watch her through the windows while I waited for my ride. She was on the synchronized swimming team. Her legs, thick and muscular, white and wet, protruding from the water like filets of halibut. If Sammy is a dog, then her sister is most assuredly a fish.

The redheaded wonder sat down next to me while Marvin Gaye went sniffing around in the bushes. She said her name was Maria. She kept giving me these weird looks, like sort of squinting at me while I told her all about poor lost Sammy. Tilting her head from side to side like she was trying to read my thoughts. I don't know, maybe she knew I was pulling her leg. But she seemed to believe me. To be quite honest, though she was beautiful, I began to wonder about her intelligence.

August 16 (Early Evening):

"I'm sure you'll find him."

"I hope so."

"Have you put any signs up?"

"No. I will soon."

"The sooner the better."

[5.6 second pause.]

"Look, do I know you?"

[4.4 second pause.]

"I don't think so."

"Oh. It's just. You look like this guy I know. Used to know. He would be about ... maybe ... well, quite a bit older than you. You sort of have his smile."

[4.6 second pause.]

"I have a brother?"

"What's his name?"

"Dave."

"Dave?"

"He's exactly fourteen years older than me."

[The redhead hums and haws, but doesn't say anything for 5.7 seconds.]

"No. No, never mind. Not who I'm thinking of."

[8.7 second pause. Marvin yawns a major dog yawn.]

"So ... is Marvin your first dog?"

[2.3 second pause.]

"No. Our first was a black lab. Got him for my twenty-fifth birth-day. His name was Poe. My ex named him. Do you know why?"

"Anything to do with—?"

[The redhead's cell phone starts ringing, playing this annoying tinkling song. Marvin Gaye barks twice.]

"Oh sorry. Gotta get that."

Our conversation ended when the woman left the bench to go stand by Marvin Gaye and talk on her phone. I overheard her tell the person on the other line that she was waiting at the parkette, had been waiting for almost fifteen minutes, and "Where are you?" I started thinking about what sort of question I would ask her about the blackout once she got off the phone. I was thinking I would lean into the topic, maybe ask her where her dog was when the power went out. Make her laugh. Or say something about dogs not really needing power in the first place, considering they pretty much have night vision built into their eyeballs. But she didn't come back. She didn't even end her call. She clipped her leash to the dog's collar and left the parkette, all the while yapping away on her stupid cell phone. Didn't even give me a wave.

I felt cursed.

I couldn't believe my idiocy. The lost dog story had worked to break her defences down, to make her want to talk to me. That's something I often forget about myself, my natural gift for storytelling, and, of course, the general attraction that beautiful women feel towards me. For the first time all day I finally had someone to interview, someone who had experienced the blackout, someone who reminded me of the Lady-turned-Empress from the book, and she was talking to me. Listening to me. The redhead went from being a complete stranger to eating out of the palm of my hand in less than a minute. But I blew it. I became so involved in the story that I forgot completely about my purpose. For a while, I thought I really was looking for my dog. I recorded a mental note to myself, reminding my brain never to lose focus, even when the person I'm speaking with, the person to whom I'm speaking, just happens to have a magnificent set of teeth, regardless of the gap between the big ones. I did not like her hair, because I do not like people with red hair. Their eyebrows do not exist, a disconcerting trait. In her case, though, I would be willing to tolerate the redness. I do not think a woman of her disposition would touch someone like Dave with a metre stick, let alone an actual part of her body. For this reason alone, I began to think that the redhead was that much better than Val and Caitlyn combined. Better simply for remaining untouched by Dave's decrepit hands.

I stayed on the bench for some time, thinking there was still a remote chance the woman would come back. The only rule that Val and Dave had made for me was that I had to be back before the sun went down. I stayed until it started to get dark, until the last possible moment. I decided I would have to come back to the parkette, and soon. I wondered if it would be possible to pick up a dog from the SPCA for our next encounter. I wondered if it would be possible to arrange an accidental next encounter.

When I got back to Camp David, Luís and some other little kid with brown hair and freckles were in the living room, lying on their stomachs in the middle of the floor, watching old Looney Tunes re-runs. The volume was high, way too loud. Bugs Bunny dressing up as a woman in order to trick the wascally wabbit guy into falling in love with him so he wouldn't shoot Bugs Bunny's fluffy white tail off. Yosemite Sam or whatever his name is.

I took off my shoes by the front door and walked to the other end of the apartment, away from the sound of the fake shotgun and cartoon scrambling feet, into the kitchen. Val and Dave and some friends of theirs were out on the back deck, drinking beer. They were sitting in a circle on the fake Adirondacks. Dave was in the blue one, Val in the green one, and their friends, a chubby guy with a crew cut and a not chubby woman with not a crew cut, were sitting in the orange and red ones. Dave had his back to the door; the other three did not.

It was approximately 7:30 p.m., and there was lentil soup on the stove. The whole apartment smelled like stinky sleeping bags. The kitchen was a bit messy, with bowls and things left out on the counter. Dishes piled up in the sink. I stood above the pot of soup, thinking that life couldn't get any worse. My stomach churned for a burger, pizza, chicken wings, anything normal. I grabbed a spoon, and took one sip of soup. For making such a terrible smell, it was surprisingly tasteless.

Behind me, I heard the sound of fingers tapping against the slid-ing door. I turned around. It was Val. She waved me out. I thought about how excellent it would be if I gave her the finger and went to my room. But, of course, that is not what I did. I slid the door open and stepped outside. Dave instantly told me to shut the door to not let the bugs in the house. I don't know what bugs he was talking about, but I closed the door, and as I did, Val introduced me to their friends. Unfortunately, I didn't catch either of their names, and my recorder was, in the interest of saving battery life, off. Mark and Brenda, maybe? The kid with the freckles belonged to them. His name started with a W. Walter? Winston?

After being introduced, I didn't know whether I was supposed to sit down or not, so I just stood there on the deck for a while, listening to Dave talk about some stupid book he'd read recently. I didn't know if they'd already eaten supper. Had their friends come over for dinner? Why hadn't Val told me what time to be home by? Was there anything other than lentil soup in the house? I wanted to ask, but couldn't get a word in with Dave talking so much. He'd had a few beers at this point, and was surprisingly unannoyed with my presence. I decided maybe it was worthwhile turning my recorder on after all. Sometimes Caitlyn gets me to play recordings of Dave saying stupid things. His stupidity is truly an endless source of entertainment for us both.

August 16 (Evening):

"I don't know how to describe it. I should find a way, because people keep asking me."

"Take your time, man. We've got all night. Or at least until the drinks run out."

[Polite laughter.]

"Well … it's a, like, a character study. About real life that's as strange as science fiction. I haven't got to the end yet, but it's not all that important what it's about, so much as its message, you know?"

"Which is?"

"It's sort of a postmodern, post-mortem, post—"

"Coital?"

[Everyone laughs at Val's joke except Dave.]

"Post office?"

[More laughing. Dave clears his throat.]

"Yeah, ha ha."

[3.5 second pause while Dave takes a sip of beer.]

"I mean ... it's really about the fragility of the human psyche. I don't know how to describe it without sounding too pretentious ..."

"We can see that."

"Okay, Val, can you just let me explain?"

"Sorry."

"It sounds pretty intense, Dave."

"I'm not completely finished yet. It's heavily, heavily research-based, which I'm okay with. One of my strong suits actually. But I think I just need more time to think about it. Like, it hasn't completely taken shape just yet. But it's about ... since it's about disintegration, there are lots of holes, *intentional* holes, like space. It's about space, sort of. And duplication. Doubling."

"Duping?"

"Yes, that too. Ugh ... I don't know. It's not that important. I'm making it sound like it's some kind of masterpiece."

"It sounds interesting, man."

[4.6 second pause.]

"Hey, have you guys ever watched the movie 'Las—?'"

"Mainly it's about the balance between presence and absence, and the filling of the space between those two ideas. Most books I've read are all about some central thing, but this one, this book, is about, like ... all about the supplement. About what's extra, and outside. It totally colours outside the lines."

[7.3 second pause. Val raps her fingernails against the arm of her plastic chair, then puts her other hand on Dave's back and gives it a pat.]

"Does anyone want some cheese? I gotta warn you, it's vegan! And yummy!"

"No need to warn us. Soy cheese is pretty much the only cheese we buy these days. I'm lactose-intolerant."

"Phew. Because Dave—"

"Yeah, I like it too."

[This is where I start laughing out of nowhere. At first the bald guy starts laughing too, then stops, but I keep on going. Uncontrollable, crazy laughter, like being in church.]
"Little brother, take it easy over there."
[4.4 seconds pass. My laughter gradually dies down.]
"Well. I'm going to get the cheese."
"Go help her little bro."
[5.4 second pause. Someone coughs.]
"*Today.*"

Evolution may not have put an end to boring stories, but I guess that's why people have feet. I went inside, not because Dave told me to, but because I didn't see the point in staying out there with a bunch of numbskulls listening to Dave yammer on about some boring book he was dissecting when there was a hot girl in need of my assistance inside. Val put me in charge of plating the rice crisps. She took a block of tofu cheddar out of the fridge and started cutting it into smaller blocks. She'd obviously had a couple drinks since dinner. She was smiling the whole time.

After Val went back onto the deck with the plate of food, I went into the living room and lay down on the couch. Luís and the W-kid were still watching Looney Tunes. The room was messy with crayons and scraps of paper. Dinky cars. More cheap toys. I wasn't really paying much attention to what was on the screen. Bugs Bunny kissing hearts into the air, flashing his/her long eyelashes. I put my headphones on, rewound the tape and listened to my conversation in the parkette with the beautiful redhead. Listened to her say her name, twice. Listened to her laugh, and call her dog. Listened to the part where she introduced herself. Maria. Maria. A truly wonderful name.

It was while watching Bugs Bunny, and listening to Maria say her name, that I pieced together a few essential details. Mainly, that the name inside *The Blazing World* was Myrna, but that it could've *easily* said Maria (the handwriting was really unclear). Plus, Maria said she thought she knew me, recognized me or something. I wished I'd had the brains to ask her if she worked at a library. It was totally possible that she was the same person who liked giving books to the dead guy on Palmerston, and that's why I was meant to meet her. Destined. I'd found the hidden book, and the estate sale, and I'd chosen to follow briefcase man, and I'd ended up meeting her. Two worlds aligning. Colliding.

Or: when she said she recognized me, was it because she knew Dave?

Caitlyn. Valeria. Maria.

You'll thank me later.

I got off the couch and walked slowly to the kitchen. I looked through the sliding door at the back of Dave's head. His big, square weirdo head.

It couldn't be because I looked like someone else.

27. On the day her father died. Remember how she called you from the hospital, and said, without hello, "I need you."
149. On the day she broke the coffee pot. Remember how the kitchen floor was made of broken glass, and then her patient hands, gently pulling slivers from your foot.

Who was knocking?

The voice on the other side of the door: "Mr. Wells? It's time we addressed the situation. You know what I'm talking about?"

Morgan opened his eyes. Closed them.

"Mr. Wells?"

It was his landlady at the door, her voice a bit like a tin can scraping against pavement.

"Mr. Wells? Are you inside? Please open the door."

Open. Close. Open.

Best to sit tight. Best to stay quiet, unmoving. The chain lock was latched in. Morgan leaned heavily into the couch. He hadn't had a good night's sleep since the art gallery episode.

"Mr. Wells," the voice called, a bit dimmer this time, almost to herself. "I know you're in there. I must speak with you. Please. I've tried calling. Mr. Wells?"

The man on the couch pushed back against the springs until he felt the fibres loosening, pulling apart, making way. His head bumped against the wall, but even that had softened. The consistency of heated clay. He pushed harder, felt the wall dissipate, and then he was blind. Perhaps deaf? He had a hard time hearing his landlady's words, could recognize only the occasional calling of his name. When he opened his eyes he was inside the wall, surrounded by the puffy, pink cotton candy of insulation, twisted electrical cables. He couldn't move, but he didn't feel claustrophobic. He felt safe, and as his eyes adjusted to the dark, he realized the wall was translucent. He watched the landlady unlock the door and open it, but the chain kept her from opening the door all the way. If she was still saying something, the man inside the wall couldn't hear her, nor did he care to. He closed his eyes, fell back to sleep, the insulation and web of electrical wires a most comfortable bed.

Morgan stood outside his other's home in the Annex, an enormous white Georgian, waiting for the lights to go off. The paint around the windows was starting to chip. The asphalt shingles on the roof were peeling. A retiree lived there. He must've subscribed to every department store catalogue he could find. Sears, JC Penney, The Bay. He received letters from the bank, letters from his insurance company, but never anything personal, other than one letter from a distant relative, a cousin. Apparently, the other Morgan's wife had died a year before. He'd given her his kidney, but it wasn't enough.

Morgan had seen the man only once, taking the garbage out. A rare sighting. He spent most of his day inside, watching television.

Most of the house was dark, except for the light from an upper floor window, cast onto the street, and a vague, blue glow coming from what Morgan guessed was the TV room. The light spilled through the window frame, and now it seemed brighter. More light in the deepening dark. But why was the light still on?

After observing the house from the other side of the street for more than twenty minutes, Morgan crossed the road to take a closer look. In the dark, he walked beside his other's house, pushed his fingers against the siding, peeled off flakes of paint. He peered through the windows of the other Morgan's car. He crouched down near the basement window and put his fingers against the glass. He applied some pressure. Just testing.

It was locked. The house was sleeping. But what about the light upstairs?

Morgan went to the garage to get a better look. He stared at the upstairs window. Was someone in that room? Sleeping with the lights on, some invalid or child? Or not sleeping at all. Sitting awake on the edge of the bed, staring through the window. At what? At the roof of their neighbour's house? At Morgan?

The thought of someone observing him from inside the house was unnerving.

Morgan returned to the other side of the street. He watched the house for another minute before making his way home.

After watching the elderly man's house for a couple days, Morgan decided he needed more. The old place reminded him of the feeling he had at the gallery with Heidi, that feeling of standing on the sidelines. Not digging in. The house, comatose, lulling him to sleep.

Luckily, the Morgan who lived on Morton Road, whom Morgan took to calling the young Morgan, was a different story. There was always something going on at the duplex. The young Morgan was active, up before dawn, a man with a wife and two kids, a steady income, a man who travelled, owned his own car, and never left the house without a travel mug of coffee. A man Morgan could aspire to be.

Mornings were the best time for watching. They left their house at the same time every day, their two kids in tow. A boy and a girl. The girl was younger, and Asian, presumably adopted. The boy looked more like his father than his mom, and though he was still too young to sit in the front seat he had a grown-up face. The girl would be running wild around the car while her mother got the seat ready, but the boy would stand silently to the side, picking the lint off his shirt.

The young Morgan's wife, Nat, was pretty, if a little thin, cheekbones too exposed against slightly sunken eyes. Wispy hair, straight hips. Not as attractive as Heidi York, but perhaps more intelligent. Morgan had spoken to her once as she waited in the car for her husband to come out. He knocked on her car window and asked for directions to the nearest streetcar stop. She was courteous, if a bit curt. Gave the directions without a moment's hesitation, but rolled her window up as soon as she'd finished. The first thing Morgan thought when he saw her up close was that she was younger than she looked from a distance.

The young Morgan had had surgery on his collarbone recently. The white gauze of the bandage protruded just above the rim of his collar. Some sort of sporting activity, or maybe he fell. Morgan saw his other slip in the tub, saw him crash against the rim, heard the bone snapping, saw the blood, all that blood. Blood all over the bathroom floor, soaking into the bath mat. Soaking the grout between the tiles. The other Morgan's wife running in, grabbing a towel, no idea what to do.

Couldn't find the phone fast enough.

Blood dripping down the side of her leg, her dress soaking red.

But perhaps the other Morgan had simply missed a catch. There are a million ways to break a human collarbone.

Every weekday, during his lunch break, Morgan rooted through the other Morgan's mailbox. Sometimes he would take the whole batch, but he mostly limited himself to taking just one, whichever envelope seemed the most promising. The mail didn't arrive until after noon, and there were a few occasions where Morgan had to choose between the mail and being late for work. Out of necessity he used the van. Sometimes he came in the morning, before his shift started. Not for the mail. Just to watch.

Although there weren't any personal letters, the mail revealed that the young Morgan spent $32.56 a week at the beer store. He had $2644.52 in his savings account, and collected dividends from a place called Fidel's Café & Bistro. Morgan could only assume that the other Morgan owned the café, though how he went from studying Economics to becoming a barista, Morgan could only guess. He was glad Heidi York hadn't known more about the other Morgan's actual career, otherwise she never would've believed the letter, though perhaps that would've been for the best.

From the phone bill, Morgan learned that the other Morgan made several calls a week to someone in Vancouver. His parents? Sister? Brother? Morgan couldn't be sure. There were several 2 a.m. calls to sex lines as well, which could only mean that Morgan and his wife weren't very active. Morgan wondered which of them was making the calls. Perhaps they were calling together.

Morgan filed the letters he stole in his filing cabinet, feeling a vague sense of disappointment. What had he expected to find? Another letter from Heidi York?

The only handwritten document he managed to take after weeks of stealing mail was a birthday card for one of Morgan's children. Arthur Wells. "Artie." Sent by one of Nat's sisters.

Happy Birthday Artie!

8 already! You're growing up too fast. Please send me a picture as soon as you get this, and tell me how you plan to spend your summer. I sure hope there's a trip to see me in there somewhere.

Love Aunt Jane.

One afternoon, the mailbox still empty, Morgan went around to the back of the duplex, to the back sliding door. He stepped onto the deck and approached the door cautiously. He put his face against the glass. The door led into the kitchen. He checked the handle. It was unlocked.

Morgan stood in the kitchen for five minutes after closing the sliding door behind him. He stood there not moving, afraid to go further, afraid to leave, torn between haste and hesitation. He hadn't expected the smell: closeted, dry, a richness, a thickness, the smell of many bodies living. Clean laundry, but compost bin overflowing. The clock on the stove said it was 12:17 p.m. The middle of the afternoon.

No one saw him go inside. No one could see him.

Morgan put his hand against the kitchen table. The house was breathing. Ticking. Everything beamed. He would need to start moving soon. In or out.

No one was home. He'd watched them leave.

Morgan took a few steps, stopped in front of the fridge. He'd almost expected to see something of his hanging there. The walls were painted white, the colour of bone. The paint on the ceiling was beginning to chip and peel. Signs of water damage? A mobile of clay animals hung above the door to the basement. An out-of-date calendar was pinned to the wall beside the door. Morgan looked more closely. It was still being used, apparently, to leave messages.

Call Sherman at the service centre.

Where did you leave the measuring tape?

There were carrot and potato peelings on the counter next to the stove.

Morgan made his way into a small, dark hallway, taking note of the empty flowerpot that held the kitchen door open. He noted the dry dirt in the pot and the presence of several teabags. Two pairs of children's shoes, one pair of beat-up sneakers, and two pairs of flip-flops, one blue, one green, were lined against the wall. Morgan kicked his shoes off and pushed them against the wall next to the others.

He took a breath. Let it out. That smell. Of laundry, fermenting apples, plastic toys, cleaning products. Pine. Lemon.

The NICU waiting room. The smell of the hospital floors, the bucket of soapy water in the waiting room, the custodian around the corner talking to one of the nurses. The bubbles in the water, steam hovering at the surface. Lemon fresh.

Morgan didn't remember how he got to the hospital. He didn't know which route they took. He saw only her hand in his hand, the sweatiness of her palm, the hair sticking to her forehead, and the blood on her legs the blood on his hands and the blood on the front of his shirt. He'd never seen so much blood. Her hand kept slipping from his grasp.

In the living room, Morgan spent ten minutes standing under the ceiling fan, prodding at the cups and glasses on the coffee table, remnants from that morning's breakfast. A bowl of half-eaten cereal, the milk warm to touch. A plate smeared with hardened peanut butter, another covered in crumbs. He picked up a day-old newspaper and flipped through the pages. The cryptoquote unencrypted:

War is beautiful because it establishes man's dominion over the subjugated machinery by means of gas masks, terrifying megaphones, flame throwers, and small tanks. War is beautiful because it initiates the dreamt-of metalization of the human body. War is beautiful because it enriches a flowering meadow with the fiery orchids of machine guns. War is beautiful because it combines the gunfire, the cannonades, the cease-fire, the scents, and the stench of putrefaction into a symphony.

—Walter Benjamin

Morgan read the quotation twice, thinking it was a strange one, not like the ones his wife used to solve. Orchids of machine guns?

Morgan folded the newspaper and tossed it onto a chair. He then followed it. Put his feet up on the coffee table. Smelled the cushions. He felt his veins loosening in his legs.

Porcelain geese lined the top of the plug-in fireplace. A pink one, a blue one, a yellow one.

His hands were trembling.

A series of lines had been drawn on the living room wall beside a kid-sized table and chairs. Measurements. And beside each, ages.

Artie: 8 (April 15, 2000)

Jia-li: 3 (February 2, 2000)

The house was beautiful. Terrifying. This simple living arrangement, this proof of lives. A thousand shards of glass in Morgan's stomach.

In the kitchen, a Lazy Susan. Lima beans. Jalapeno jelly. Aunt Jemima. Dirty dishes stacked up in the sink, rinsed but not washed. Morgan wanted to search through each of the cupboards, but he had no idea when the other Morgan or his wife might return. He would have to prioritize if he was to make the most of it.

In the bathroom, the wastebasket: crumpled tissues; shreds of floss; empty pregnancy test box; negative pregnancy test; torn business card; four subscription offers from *National Geographic*; bottle cap; Q-tips; a withered bar of soap, just a sliver.

In the boy's bedroom, he found a year-old scribbler. On the wall above the kid's desk, a school project about Canada's arctic animals, with a scratch-and-sniff grape sticker giving the thumbs-up.

The Caribou cafe is born in spring. The caribou cafe can die right when it is born in a snow storm Caribou milk has more protein than cows an adult caribou may eat 4.5 kg of lichens a day. they eat juicy grasses low leafy shrubs brightly coloured wildflowers. caribou have long hollow hair to help them swim The caribous coat helps them float like a life jacket a cup of a caribous blood gets sucked out of them by insects. when caribou are old enough they get new coats as they tire off there old ones as they go throw the pickers.

Morgan leaned in close and tried to catch a whiff of the sticker.

Morgan looked up to see a collection of Hardy Boys books lining the bookshelves. The spines looked well worn, cracked in places. Morgan took one of the books from the shelf and opened it to the first page. As he'd suspected, the books had belonged to the other Morgan. "Morgan W." was pencilled in a childish hand on the front page. The other Morgan must've handed them down once Arthur was old enough to read.

The boy's bed was in the shape of a race car. Morgan sat on the end of the bed. On the back of the bedroom door was a poster of a Nascar driver standing in an ad-plastered suit, holding his helmet against his thigh, smiling. Morgan pictured the other Morgan's son going to sleep each night with that image as the last thing he saw, one of his heroes smiling at him in the glow of a nightlight. The thought made him smile.

Morgan left the boy's room, stumbled over a fire truck on his way out. In the hallway, he found a child's drawing pinned to the side of a small red bookcase. A picture of impossible forms, bodies without heads, arms floating in space, a green sun and a ground without substance. He pulled the picture from the bookcase, folded it once, and shoved it into his pocket.

There were flecks of pink in the hospital floor. Flecks of pink in the white and green tiles. He was wondering if the flecks were placed randomly by a machine, or if some person in some factory had placed each individual fleck, each seemingly random pixel of colour. Then he heard a man's voice above him saying Mr. Wells, Mr. Wells.

The doctor, steady and calm, explained the procedure, what they'd done, how they'd done it. Morgan had no idea how long he'd been sitting in the waiting room, in that chair, that hard plastic chair. Morgan was looking up. The doctor's face was pale, purple lines under his eyes. He kept taking his glasses off and squeezing his nose at the bridge. They might've been there like that for days for all Morgan knew, him looking up and the doctor pinching the bridge of his nose, explaining how there had been a rupture of some sort. A splitting. A burst. There was blood in the lungs. They had tried to pump it out, but there was too much blood.

The doctor spoke in tongues, used words like "intubation," "surfactant injections," "anoxic," "placental abruption," and Morgan thought, It's a boy.

They'd given his wife something for the pain. The doctor said there'd been some internal bleeding, hemorrhaging, but she would be okay. She would need to be monitored for the next week.

Morgan went in to see her. She had a tube sticking out of her inner elbow. She was sleeping with her mouth open. They'd placed a band of white gauze across her belly. Morgan sat with her for a moment, then followed a nurse into the room where they were keeping the baby—they said it was important to see—in a glass case, a display case, thought Morgan, but no, not a display case. An incubator. An isolette.

Two nurses were standing over the baby, removing tubes from him. One of them looked up, saw Morgan, then instantly looked at the nurse who'd brought him in. Said something about bringing him in too early. Morgan walked across the room, felt the tiles moving beneath him, moving up and down. The floor with the consistency of heated clay. He kept sinking into it, sinking in up to the knees, and pulling his feet out, having to grab his legs from under the knees.

The master bedroom.

Morgan pulled the covers back, inspected the sheets on the king-size bed. They were rumpled, and one of the corners had been pulled away from the mattress. Morgan slipped beneath the covers for a minute, lay on his back and eyed the ceiling. He then rolled onto his side and compared Morgan's night table with his own. This Morgan's table was full of receipts, dog-eared Tom Clancy novels, and framed photos; Morgan's own table held little more than an empty water glass and a thin membrane of dust.

Morgan decided he would need to make a few more rules.

Do not take anything, unless it can be replaced.
Do not leave anything behind.
Do not lose track of time.
Do not leave without inspecting the refrigerator.
Do not open or close any blinds.

Morgan sat up. He thought he heard a noise downstairs. A door closing. He waited. It was nothing.

Down in the kitchen again, this time the clock said 2:21. Morgan stood there, dizzy, smiling, a dishtowel bunched up in his hand. He opened a few drawers. He found it on the second try, underneath a cheese grater. He spun the rolling pin once, then held it out in front of him, watched it come to a stop.

The slightest protrusion of gauze above the other Morgan's collar.

Morgan lowered the rolling pin to his side, watched the clock change to 2:23.

He heard the bone snap before he felt it, a dry crunch. The blood too. Blood without pain. The rolling pin dropped from his hand and thudded against the floor. He put the bunched up dishtowel against his collar, used his free hand to open the sliding door. He was careful to keep the blood from hitting the floor on his way out.

After you make it safely to the other side of the emerald sea, to the town of Gallanta, you thank your enormous turtle transporter and disembark. As soon as you step onto the wharf, the giant turtle wastes no time in turning around and swimming away. You watch him for a moment as he sinks slowly out of sight, until all that's left are bubbles on the surface of the sea. The big shelly bastard didn't even say goodbye. Not that you are surprised; he didn't say a word during the entire fourteen-hour crossing, quite possibly the most boring trip of your life.

You start down the wharf toward the town, all the while getting the feeling that something is up. Really up. Because the bear-men told you that Gallanta was a major port of call, with restaurants, motels, arcades, that sort of thing. In particular, there was supposed to be a hotel called the Palmerstonian. That's where the bear-men told you to find the fox-men, who were supposed to take you safely to the Imperial City. But pieces of the wharf are missing, and the place is dead quiet.

By the time you reach the shore, it finally hits you: the town that was once known as Gallanta is no more. Most of the buildings have been destroyed, and some punk kids spray-painted what was left. The town, once a thriving port community, was abandoned to vandals, but even they have left. The place is a total ghost town. The fox-men are nowhere in sight.

You walk down the main street, and follow the directions Rundle gave you to the Palmerstonian. In the place where the hotel is supposed to be, there's only charred wood and piles of dead leaves.

With the town abandoned, and no one to ask for directions, you do the only thing you can do and start walking along the dirt road that leads out of Gallanta, in the hopes that it will bring you to the Imperial City, the home of the Elysia. You walk for seven hours, and are completely bored, and there are rocks getting in your shoes, but you really have no other form of transportation, and simply have to walk, no two ways about it. No buses or streetcars out here.

You walk and your calf muscles become sore, and you start to feel incredibly sleepy, and you're not really paying very much attention to your surroundings, until night starts to creep in, and you realize that you are walking in a dense, totally creepy forest. You aren't sure when this change occurred, but it's too late to turn back, so you just keep walking, hoping to find a clearing soon.

You don't. The sky gets darker, the moon comes out, but it provides only a little light. Unlike our moon, the Blazing World's moon is navy blue in colour, and gives off very little illumination.

You walk until you hear what sounds like heavy breathing to the left. You look, but see nothing. Dark branches. You think the sound could just be leaves blowing in the wind, but then the sound is to the right of you too, and you know it's more than wind. The breathing is uneven, heavy, laboured. You stand completely still, unsure of your next move.

A moment later, six enormous pale white creatures emerge from the brush. Uh-oh. You've heard about these ugly bastards. The infamous lice-men. They are fat, but they are swift, have goatees, and wear stupid-looking glasses. You try to run, but are quickly caught by one of the lice-men. Once you are captured, the lice-men start making this terrible sound. Sounds almost like laughing, but more like someone clearing a lot of phlegm from the back of his throat, magnified times ten. You scream once, but are quickly muffled by a slimy white hand that leaves a clear paste on your lips.

"You," says the one holding you, "will make a delightful midnight snack."

You know you are done for, and pray that this is merely a bad dream, that the whole blazing world is a figment of your imagination. You close your eyes and pray and pray, and suddenly feel the hands of your captors loosen. You get dropped to the ground, hear the sounds of lice-men screaming, though it sounds more like a car engine not turning over, magnified times ten. Then there is silence.

When you open your eyes, you see six dead lice-men lying all around you.

"Don't worry," says a booming voice in the darkness, "you're safe now."

You look up to see a ten-foot-tall figure step into the moon-shiny-light.

"My name," neighs the horse-man, "is Bartholomew."

The day after meeting Maria in the park, I finally had a lucky break. For the first time since the blackout, Dave left the apartment. Got a call from his boss. The phone rang at 10:05 a.m., and at 10:10 a.m., just like that, Dave was gone. He left in such a flash that he completely forgot to lock his office door, which was part of his normal, paranoid routine. I waited to hear him start his car, then drank the last of the milk from my bowl of Count Chocula. I walked swiftly out into the hallway, and checked the office door just to make sure. Yes. It was unlocked. I wasted no time getting inside and closing the door behind me. The door clicked softly when it closed.

Once inside, I did nothing but stare. I'd never been in Dave's office before. Sure, I'd walked past and looked in, but I'd never been inside. Dave had told me from the moment I arrived that the room was off-limits. Normally, I wouldn't have cared, and would've been happy not to step foot in a room so concentrated in Dave's general stink. However, that morning I needed to get something done, and I needed his computer to do it. I'd been sitting at the kitchen table trying to figure out a way to get inside Dave's office. The call from Dave's boss was a sign I was on the right track.

But before getting to my task, I decided to poke around a bit. If Dave was hiding anything, particularly an affair with Maria, this would be the place to find the proof.

First impression: the room was dark, and sort of smelled like coffee breath. Mayonnaise. It was like walking into a person's bedroom after they've been sleeping for eleven hours. The whole room reeked of stomach juices.

The next thing I noticed was a map on the wall. An old, beat-up map of Toronto. Unmistakeable, all those straight lines stretching out into infinity. Sprawling, no end in sight. Pen marks everywhere. My first thought was that it was some kind of murder chart. Dave marking off the places where he'd hidden the bodies. But upon closer inspection, the map was way too disorganized to mean much of anything. It was just a mess, which was totally in keeping with Dave's general demeanour anyway.

Next to the map was a bookcase. I scanned the spines, thinking how weird it would be if I found another copy of Cavendish's book. No such luck. Just issues and issues of Green Lantern comics, and hardcovers with names like *The Truth in Painting* and *The Rule of Metaphor*. Boring. For a second or two, I did what I did at the estate sale, and started taking books off the shelf, opening them, looking for Myrna's inscriptions. Then I wondered if Dave had the books set up in a particular way, and if he'd notice the books weren't in their exact spot. I decided this might waste all the time I had in there.

In the corner between the bookcase and the window sat the stackable washer and dryer. I opened the washer. It was empty. I opened the dryer and found a single black sock.

After a minute, I became bored of just gazing around, so I sat in Dave's chair, at Dave's desk, and started opening some of Dave's drawers, to see what I could see. I found a stress ball. A few copies of Dave's resumé, printed on robin's egg bond paper. In it he used such adjectives as "diligent," "project-oriented," and "leader." I also found an unopened Learn Spanish computer program. Near the bottom of the drawer were a few university papers that Dave had written when he was pretending to be a genius. I flipped to the back of one of them, and saw that he'd received an A. Someone had written, "Avoid the royal 'We'" in red at the bottom of the page. What the hell is a royal 'We'? I also found a picture of Val, when they first met, back when Dave was still dating Caitlyn. To my eyes, she looked the exact same, except for her hair. Her hair was big in the picture. 1990s big. I think at one point it was called the Rachel. She looked quite idiotic, but her piñatas were still as Mexican as they've ever been. Malaria Valeria. I put the photo in my pocket for safekeeping. I figured Dave probably had millions.

I turned on Dave's computer and waited for it to boot up. Dave and Caitlyn. Dave and Val. But Dave and Maria? I'd been up all night thinking about it. About Dave and Maria, but mostly about Maria. About how I'd blown my chance with her. About ways in which I could make up for my previous stupidity. It took me until three in the morning, but eventually I decided to create a survey, an official list of questions regarding the blackout. I couldn't believe it took me so long to come up with the idea. If my dad had been working on the story, a list of questions is the first thing he'd have done. *From Their Eyes* wasn't a bust. Technically, it had only just begun.

I realized, though, that I'd need to change the title again. It was becoming longer and longer, but that seemed necessary. I changed it to the following: *From Their Eyes: An In-depth Analysis of a City Paralyzed by Fear; Blackout 2003.*

After I had created a survey, I could go around Dave's neighbourhood, and in the area near the parkette. I would find Maria again, and I would also get people talking. The survey was my key to the city.

Unfortunately, Dave's computer is an old desktop, and takes about ten minutes to boot. It took even longer knowing that Dave could walk into the room and boot my head from my neck. When a dog barked in some distant yard, or if I heard a horn beeping, I also heard Dave coming down the hall, or the front door opening. I kept getting out of my seat and looking around, looking out the window, but all I could see from Dave's office window was the brick wall of the house next door.

Finally, the computer was ready. I double-clicked Word, and had to wait another eighty-five minutes. It had to look professional, something a real surveyor might create. This would be difficult because I'd never seen a survey before. Were they like the kind of tests guidance counsellors give Special Ed. kids at the beginning of the year? Where they show a bear wearing blue glasses and ask the kid to point out the same bear in a lineup of three? I've never taken the test, but I've heard stories.

I decided to start off with some basic questions, to get a sense of who I was talking to. The people to whom I would be talking.

Do you live in this neighbourhood?
How long have you lived in this neighbourhood?
Do you know the name of our galaxy?
Have you ever spent an evening looking at the stars through a telescope?
Do you like this planet?
Would you move to a neighbouring solar system, if space travel of that magnitude were possible?
Rate your knowledge of your neighbours on a scale of one to five, one being "Not at all" and five "Very well."
Where do you work? Does your work involve looking at websites?
How much do you get paid?
Do you think it's at all possible that our world is joined to an alternate world at the poles?
Have you ever been the victim of a hate crime?

Then I included some questions about the blackout. This way, the people I spoke to wouldn't know exactly what my purpose was, and would give me honest answers. It's called control. The last thing I wanted to hear were concocted stories or things people thought might sound cool to a surveyor.

Did you feel like the world was about to explode on August 14?
Where were you when the lights went out?
On a scale of one to five, how greatly did the blackout change your life, one being "Not at all" and five being "Extremely intensely"?
Describe in your own words exactly what you did when the blackout occurred.

I typed the entire thing in about five minutes, including a section for name at the top, and left space for additional comments at the bottom. Beside the page number, I quickly typed "F.T.E." I worried that at any moment Dave might come barging in, swinging a battleaxe into my face. For this reason, the survey was a bit unspecific and incomplete. Also, the second question was missing a question mark.

I printed twenty copies of my survey. It felt like the right number. Then I closed the file, and accidentally clicked "Yes" when it asked me if I wanted to save "Document 1." My first thought was that I would have to find the file and erase it. Otherwise Dave might discover I was on his computer. But my second thought was that Dave had hundreds of documents on his hard drive. No way he would ever just happen to stumble upon my survey. Just in case, I still went into Dave's Documents and Settings folder and erased "Document 1."

While the surveys printed, I looked around for incriminating files. I saw one file named "Big Booty Smash Down IV," and another called "Bossy Beauties 39." I wondered if Val knew that Dave was an Inter-perv. But most of his documents had pretty boring names, like "Contact List" and "Minutes re: April 4." I didn't open any of them.

Just as the surveys finished printing, a file titled "Post: A Character Study" caught my eye. I moved the cursor over the file. The pop-up window said the file had last been accessed the night before.

For a moment, I just stared at the file. Then it hit me, a squirmy weight in my guts: the night before, Dave had been talking about a book he'd read. A character study. Or so I thought at first. *Post* was the name of the newspaper my dad last worked for. For which my dad last worked. I realized with a sickness that the post-coital story Dave was talking about wasn't something he'd read, but possibly something he was writing.

The pieces came together in my head in less than two seconds flat.

Dave spent almost every second of his free time in his office. He locked the door most of the time. I'd always assumed he locked the door because he was looking at weird bestiality sex sites. In the morning. Right after supper. Sometimes, at least in the days before the power went out, he'd be in there until two in the morning.

What a sleazecake.

The thought of it made me physically ill. Dave didn't respect Dad. Practically hated him. Caitlyn told me that Dave had called Dad a bastard. Said he was verbally abusive, incapable of having a family. Of being a father, much less a husband, and no wonder Mom left him. But now he was going to try and profit from Dad's story.

If you choose to print the file called "Post: a character study,"
turn to page 62.
If you choose to delete the file called "Post: a character study,"
turn to page 81.

I held the cursor over the file. I was about to double-click when there was a sound at the door.

Terror alert red.

I could sense the headlock to come, but when I looked it was just Luís, who didn't say anything. Actually, he said, "¡Hola!" and lifted a plastic sword into the air, but I ignored him. I could hear Val out in the kitchen, but not Dave. Was he soon to follow? I closed Dave's Documents folder and turned the computer off. Before it would shut down, Word kept asking me if I wanted to replace the existing normal. A strange message, I thought.

After gathering up my printed surveys, I patted Luís on the shoulder, slipped out of the office. I made a trip to the kitchen, ate an apple that I coated in peanut butter, then decided to give Caitlyn a call. Dave had taken the phone out of my room on account of my leaving it off the hook two nights before, so I had to use the living room phone. I figured Caitlyn might be as annoyed by the fact that Dave was writing a 'memoir' about my dad as I was. Maybe she'd be able to sort through the details a little better than I could.

The first time I called Caitlyn was after Dave left her. I found her number written on a piece of paper in Dave's old room. I didn't think he'd mind, and in fact, I didn't care if he did mind. Caitlyn answered the phone, and I could tell from the way she said hello that she was disappointed to hear my voice. Not disappointed to hear me, but I guess disappointed that it wasn't Dave. At this point, I hadn't yet found my dad's recorder so I unfortunately do not have a record of this conversation. Mostly I just told jokes, mentioned how Dave's new woman was a Mexican and all that. She let me go after about five minutes. The next time I called, though, it was after Dad had gone missing, and Caitlyn sounded a bit less disappointed. I could tell she was happy to hear my voice. She even said at the end, "I'm glad you called me." She used to say that all the time at the end of our conversations. Sometimes we'd be on the line for almost twenty minutes.

I sat down on the couch and dialled Caitlyn's number. Luís came in and sat down beside me but didn't say anything. The phone rang twice before Gary answered. My worst nightmare.

August 17 (Afternoon):

"Hello?"
"May I speak to Caitlyn please?"
[4.6 second pause.]
"What for?"

"I don't believe I need a reason. Friends talk to their friends. That's what they do."

[3.2 second pause.]

"Friends ... right."

[10.9 second pause. In the background, Gary calls Caitlyn's name. When he hands her the phone, he says, "It's that pervy kid calling again." Asshole.]

"Hey kiddo. This isn't the best time."

"Are you busy?"

"We were just about to—"

"Are you busy?"

"Not really, but ..."

"But what?"

"You left quite a message the other night."

[2.4 second pause.]

"Kind of annoying. I couldn't get voicemail for an entire day because I didn't realize you'd eaten up all of the space."

"Oh."

[In the background, Gary asks Caitlyn a question. She says, "Just a sec," then clears her throat.]

"Well what is it?"

"What do you mean?"

"Just tell me what he did."

"Who? Dave?"

"Aren't I the kid's help line for pissed-off little brothers?"

[4.3 second pause.]

"Look, I don't mean to be an asshole, but school starts in a couple weeks, and I've got a shitload of forms in front of me ..."

"I just ... it's hard to explain."

"Try me."

[9.6 second pause.]

I sat there with the phone against my ear. Luís was looking up at me, as though waiting to ask a question. I was holding one of the surveys in my hand, looking at the questions. I was thinking of the computer file, but then I wasn't. I was thinking of my dad, thinking of the type of pants he used to wear. Never jeans. Always slacks, pants that went up above his ankles when he sat down. I was trying to get one clear image of him in my head, but it kept slipping away.

Then the front door opened, and Dave walked in. He stood in the door to the living room and looked at Luís, then looked at me. He mouthed, "Who are you talking to?" I didn't respond. I was thinking that, in that split second, Dave looked maybe like what my dad looked like. Younger, but not that different from what my dad looked like. A second later, he left the room. Luís slid off the couch and followed Dave out of sight down the hall.

August 17 (Afternoon):

"Hello? You there?"
"Yes."
"So...?"
[2.4 second pause.]
"Never mind. It's nothing. Goodbye, Caitlyn."
[6.7 second pause.]
"Goodbye, kiddo."

57. Checkers over chess.
58. Refuses to dress warmly in the winter, then complains about the cold.
59. Never sits in the aisle seat.
60. Can't listen to a story without sharing her own experiences.
61. Cuts out headlines for the fonts.
62. Prefers mixtapes to mix CDs.
63. Moans at the sight of roadkill.
64. Can count to ten in over six languages.
65. Unwraps gifts as though she plans on reusing the wrapping paper.
66. Had her palms read once and believed everything she was told.

Scott stared at Morgan as he ate his ham and cheese sandwich. It was past one, but Morgan hadn't had a chance to eat when he was out. He'd been at the younger Morgan's house again. That's where he'd made the sandwich.

Morgan chewed slowly. He knew Scott was looking at him. They were at a red light, and Scott had been staring at him since they'd stopped. But Morgan didn't want to look. Lately, he could barely move without Scott saying something.

Morgan was relieved when the light turned green.

They drove for five minutes before they hit another a red. This time, Scott didn't wait for Morgan to make eye contact.

"It's like driving with a mute," he said, pulling at his seatbelt. "Working with you. Except you can talk. You just don't. Choose not to."

Morgan shifted in his seat.

"Even now, you just sit there. Like you're dead or something."

"Sorry."

"For what?"

"For upsetting you."

Scott snorted. "Who said you upset me? I didn't say that. You bore me. You annoy me. Fuck, you don't upset me. Two drops in a fucking bucket."

Green.

Scott pressed on the gas, but they barely made it past the cross-walk. Traffic slow and sticky. Stuck behind a streetcar. Scott lit a cigarette, held it outside the window.

"I don't know why I'm telling you this," he said. "If you don't already know, then you're worse off than I thought."

Morgan finally looked in Scott's direction.

"You'll be getting called in soon. Not sure why. Maybe you'll blame me." Scott adjusted one of his mirrors. "Which is fine. Don't give a shit what you think. But take my advice: don't deny it. Whatever he says."

For weeks Morgan had been skipping shifts and showing up late. He'd been more than an hour late for work twice that week. Both times because he'd been up all night, monitoring the older Morgan's breathing.

"What are you talking about?"

Scott put his blinker on, then pulled around the streetcar, nearly hitting a bike messenger, who swerved onto the sidewalk to avoid the van.

"If you don't know," he said, wiggling his fingers at the cyclist, "you're even dumber than I thought."

Less than a week later, Morgan found himself sitting in an uncomfortable plastic chair outside Cranley's office at The Letter Shredders warehouse. The chair threatened to snap in half each time Morgan shifted his weight. He wondered how many times the seat had been used before he came along. A quick accumulation of numbers left him dizzy, so he relented. Behind the door, Cranley coughed loudly. A few feet away, in reception, Tabitha answered the phone, and typed noisily on her keyboard. Made appointments, sighed heavily. Morgan placed his hands on his knees, and bent his head, wondering why he'd been called in.

Fluorescent lights humming overhead.

Morgan put his hand against his collar. The wound had pretty much healed on its own. Well, it didn't hurt as much now as it once did, he could at least say that much. It ached worst in the mornings, and he sometimes woke up in the middle of the night to a deep, wincing throb. But he'd grown used to its company.

He'd been keeping late nights.

Morgan leaned back in the chair.

Closed his eyes.

The stolen letters had accumulated. He had taken over seventy from the young Morgan, and about forty from the old Morgan. He photocopied each one just in case they got lost, then stashed them in different rooms throughout his apartment.

Morgan knew the younger man's duplex inside out, and was just beginning to learn the layout of the older man's house as well. He'd Googled "Morgan Wells AND Toronto," just in case there were other Morgans out there not listed in the phonebook. He got no results. Not that he needed another person to study. He had his hands full with the first two Morgans, and the recent discovery he'd made.

Every Saturday, the elderly Morgan went for a walk. This was, as far as Morgan could tell, the only time the old man ever left his house. Morgan had followed him on three occasions, once for two hours, his shock of white hair making him impossible to lose sight of. He also moved slowly, and stopped frequently, either to catch his breath or give his legs a break. He only moved quickly when crossing the street. He would stop in front of the crosswalk, look both ways twice, then start walking, hands at his sides, crossing four lanes in less than ten seconds, which was speedy considering how slowly he moved the rest of the time.

The only place the old man seemed to go besides the drugstore and the grocery store was a dog park nine blocks from his place. He'd walk around, dogless, stopping to talk to nearly every dog that walked past him. He'd see them coming down the path, would bend his body forward ever-so-slightly at the hips, hands on his knees.

He'd speak to the dogs in this withered, high-pitched voice; their owners would reply, more than happy to talk about their dog's name, the reason for the name, the type of food they fed him, and why their particular breed was more congenial, kooky, and lovable than all the others. Inevitably, they'd ask if he had a dog, and each time the old man would say, "Yes, I did. A big, beautiful Weimaraner. Had him for fifteen years." There was always the occasional owner who was too busy to chat, who would smile tightly at the old Morgan's advance as they pulled on their dog's leash. The old man would nod, follow the dog with his eyes, then turn and continue on his route through the park until he came upon a park bench that was just slightly off the path and beneath an enormous oak. He sat on the same bench every time. He would take a book out of his pocket, a different book each day, and read. Taking breaks to pause, put the book in his lap with his finger marking his spot, look up at the canopy above him. He would sit like this for hours, pretending to read, though it was obvious to Morgan that the old man was waiting for dogs to walk past. Waiting for a dog to come along and put its paw in his lap. The old Morgan rarely read more than the first few pages of the books he brought with him.

Morgan followed the older man three times. The routine was always the same. So one day he left the old man sitting by himself and went to his house in the Annex. All the doors were locked; he was thankful for summertime half-open windows.

The old man's house was nothing like the younger Morgan's. It was clear that this man lived alone, like Morgan, and also that he didn't get many visitors. The coat rack was mostly empty, just two coats, both men's. Morgan considered wiping the whole place down. It was tidy, but dusty, the air stale even with the window open.

Morgan went into the living room, which was attached to both the dining room and the kitchen through adjacent doorways. The room was large but felt small, stuffy. White walls that were yellowing with age. Tiny porcelain farm animals, two pigs, three sheep, a cow, and five chickens, on the windowsill; the plaid draperies were tied open, their colours faded by the sun. Decorative plates from a strange mix of North American cities lined the wall above the doorway:

Minnesota. Niagara Falls. Saskatoon. Had the older Morgan been to all of these places? When had he gone? With whom?

Morgan walked along the perimeter of the living room. He noticed that the ceiling seemed to dip to the right, making the brass light fixture look slightly off-centre. The furniture in this room, one long, sleighed-shaped couch and two high-backed armchairs, was covered in a beige, crushed velvet upholstery, worn on the seats. On the mantle, Morgan found three different portraits of the old man's Weimaraner. He studied them carefully, wondering if the old man was the type to cremate a dead but much-loved family pet. If so, where would he keep the urn?

Strangely, there were two bedrooms in the basement. Is that where the older Morgan's kids used to sleep? The mattresses were bare. The rooms were now being used primarily for storage. Board games and boxes full of bedding. Hockey sticks stacked up against the wall of one of the rooms. A damp smell. It was all so familiar. He felt as though he'd been there before.

Morgan went back upstairs, and was about to walk up to the second floor of the house when a strange thing happened. He was looking at a series of pictures on the wall, pictures of the old Morgan when he was a younger man, a man with a wife and kids, a son and a daughter, much like the younger Morgan. The pictures were arranged in such a way that as Morgan walked up the staircase, the people in the pictures started to age. It was only after staring at a photo halfway up the stairs, which was probably ten or fifteen years old, that Morgan realized he recognized the old man's son. That he knew that face. He stared at it for several moments, trying to remember, when it hit him: he was staring at the face of the younger Morgan Wells.

He'd been watching these two Morgans for quite some time, but only now did he realize they were connected, related, father and son. Senior and Junior. How had he not figured this out earlier?

Morgan went home and examined his collection of phone bills. Morgan discovered that neither of the two Morgans had called the other in over three months. Morgan wondered if it had something to do with the death of the old man's wife, the young man's mother.

Perhaps there had been some disagreement over the way she wanted her funeral handled, the flowers chosen for the service. Maybe it had been something worse.

It didn't take long for Morgan to get his answer. Just two nights later, he was at the younger Morgan's duplex. The young Morgan and his wife were out on the deck, talking and laughing. Playing cards. Drinking. Morgan crouched down at the side of the house, listened to the conversation. Maybe the younger Morgan was a drinker, couldn't control his addiction. He listened to the couple talk, first about their son's new school, then about problems Morgan was having with one of his baristas, and eventually about changes they wanted to make to the house. Morgan listened for an hour, until finally his patience was rewarded.

"You know, Arthur was asking about his grandfather today."

"... what do you want me to say, Nat?"

"Nothing. Nothing."

"... I didn't do anything wrong."

"I'm not saying that you did."

"But you keep bringing this up."

"I keep bringing it up? Me? No, okay, our kids do."

"You seem to be taking his side."

"I'm not, Morgan. Honestly. But it's been months, and you told him—"

"I know what I told him."

"I'm only thinking of the kids. Arthur's starting to worry that he did something wrong ... that his grandfather is upset with him."

"Stop exaggerating."

"Do you remember being eight?"

"My grandfather never cheated on my grandmother."

"It's not like he hid it from her ..."

"What?"

There was a long pause.

"He hid it from me. And *he* says she knew. Who knows if she really did? Who knows? And you know that's not the only thing. How many times has he been to the café?"

"Morgan, I just think—"

"I know what you think. Thanks for your input."

"Morgan?"

"Drop it."

Again, there was silence. Morgan stayed there for ten more minutes, listening to the sound of two people drinking together, alone. He listened until he heard them gather their dishes, their cards, open the sliding door, and go inside. Then he went back to the other side of the street and watched the house grow quiet.

Lights out.

"Morgan?"

"Are you ready?"

"Nervous?"

Morgan's boss, speaking to him, his voice sounding as though it was behind a sheet of drywall.

Morgan wondered for a moment what nervous looked like, putting his hand against the gauze rising above his collar, lightly, the lightest touch. Is this what nervous looked like?

Cranley said something about punctuality. But it was hard to hear him. Then Cranley said something about letters. Missing letters. Something had been stolen.

A thousand possibilities flitted through Morgan's head. They would turn him in, cut him open, destroy him. They knew what he'd been up to, had known all along. Had watched him walking through their rooms, crawling under their beds where the floor was cool, the air was dark, a place where lost things were found. They would hang him.

There was a black speakerphone on Cranley's desk. A red light kept blinking, on and off. Morgan thought he heard someone cough on the other end, but he couldn't be sure. Might've been a sneeze.

"Someone saw you," said Cranley. "Last week. Someone saw you steal a handful of letters. You took them out of the bag and stuffed them into your pocket. Didn't you?"

A week before, he'd been taking a bag of shreddies out to the van. From a downtown gym, the place the younger Morgan went to. He'd been carrying the bag down a flight of steps when he saw a piece of paper with his name on it. With the other's name on it.

"Didn't you?"

Morgan had opened the bag and dug around until he found the piece of paper. The other Morgan had just renewed his membership. Morgan folded the sheet then slipped it into his pocket.

"Morgan?"

"I took a piece of paper," Morgan said, barely audible. "An invoice."

"So there it is." Cranley pushed his chair back and stood, a satisfied man. "Did you get that, Eric?"

A voice on the speakerphone said something about everything coming in "loud and clear."

"Now," said Cranley, opening a folder, "your termination slip."

It was only once Morgan made it to the lobby that he felt like he could breathe again. He looked down at his hand holding the notice of termination, wondering for a second which Morgan it belonged to.

Morgan stepped outside just as a Letter Shredders van pulled into the parking lot. It parked just a few feet away. Morgan knew who it was, who it had to be, didn't even have to see him to know. Scott emerged, and slammed the van door. Crossed his arms. "Don't blame yourself, Wells. You're just a born fuck-up."

Her: No, it's not.
Him: I did this.
Her: Don't say that. How could you be responsible for this?
Him: Because I should've …
Her: …
Him: I shouldn't have...
Her: Listen to me. I don't blame you. You need to know that.
Him: But maybe you do. What if you do, though? And you just don't know it yet.

Morgan said nothing. He walked toward the overpass, Scott calling out behind him. He couldn't hear a thing he said.

Though I thought the survey would make me legit, it really only made people avoid me more than ever before. I noticed people crossing the street without using a crosswalk, just to avoid me and my clipboard. I would say, "Excuse me," and before I could even say "sir" or "ma'am" people would shake their heads, or point at their watches, or just sneer at me. Sometimes they would start running, would careen right into oncoming traffic just to avoid me. They would see my survey, see me holding it out at them, and they'd take off screaming, like I had SARS, like I was sole creator of the virus, out to get them. I forced three men to jump in front of a streetcar, watched their cracked bodies tumble and tear beneath the steel.

It's really not easy getting strangers to talk. It's especially hard to do that in the world's dumbest city.

I decided to go door-to-door with my survey. I figured people on the street generally had somewhere to go, and that was why they didn't want to speak to me. If a person was at home in the middle of the day, there was a good chance I could catch them in the doorway, back them into a corner. People so rarely knock on strangers' doors these days. They would think they were important for being chosen and interviewed in person by a real reporter.

The first house I visited was in Dave's neighbourhood, on Langford Avenue, a townhouse street. I chose the house randomly to help keep my investigation as scientific as possible. My method was simple. Walk until I counted to two hundred, then knock on the door to the house I was closest to. The house on Langford was yellow, had a white door and two potted plants on the step. The blinds were drawn in all the windows. Whoever lived there kept their barbeque chained up. It also looked like at some point they'd turned it on too close to the wall; the vinyl siding next to the barbeque was melted and peeling. The barbeque was slowly eating the house—which reminded me how the Milky Way was eating Sagittarius, that scientists have called our galaxy a cannibal, I saw a special on the CBC—and next to the barbeque was a dead fir tree, leaning upside down against the side of the house. The needles had turned orange, almost brown. It must've been sitting there since January.

It made me think that I had to agree with Val that Christmas trees are a definite threat to environment, not to mention a total waste of time. For example, last November, Ross came banging on my door, his high-pitched voice sounding even whinier than usual, insisting that we all go out to buy a tree—me, him, and Mom. I had to ask him to repeat himself—I said, "Pardon me? Could you repeat that?"—I couldn't believe my ears. The sun had almost fallen; it was getting dark outside, and the radio was calling for freezing rain. I wish I had my tape recorder on just to hear my voice saying "Pardon me?" after Ross knocked on my door. It was so preposterous. For the posterity of the thing. The preposterity.

I didn't say "No," even though that was the first word on my mind. I don't know a single person who looks for a Christmas tree in the middle of the evening—let alone almost a whole month in advance.

I put on my hat and scarf and climbed into the back of Ross's Infiniti. Mom was already in the front seat, sitting there with her pompom hat on, and her leather-gloved hands folded in her lap. We sat there for five minutes, waiting for Ross to come out, neither of us talking, the heat blasting and drying out our eyeballs. I knew the tree thing was her idea, and she knew I wasn't too pleased. She'd been trying for a while to force us to do things together. Not me and her—she and I—but the three of us.

November 29 (Evening):

[Sound of the driver's door opening. Ross relaxing into his leather seat. The door closing.]
"If there's one thing I love most about Christmas, it's the tree hunt."
[Mom laughs.]

"I've got the best eye of anyone I know. The important thing is not to be lured in by size alone. A smaller, fuller tree is better than an enormous, naked one. We've got the space for a monster, but it's quality we're after. Am I right?"
[Mom laughs again as though Ross is the funniest man alive. 15.9 seconds pass, then Ross starts tapping his hand against the steering wheel. Then singing.]

"In the meadow we can build a snowman. And pretend that he is Parson Brown. He'll say 'Are you married?' We'll say 'No man!' But you can do the job while you're in town."
[Here Ross does this trumpety thing with his lips, and a bad drum roll on the dash board.]
"Later on, we'll perspire, as we dream by the fire ..."
"Wait—what? Did you just say ...?"
"What? As we dream by the fire ...?"
"No, before that."
"Later on, we'll perspire."
[Mom starts cracking up.]
"That's not the lyric!"
"No?"
[Mom's intense crazy laugh.]
"It's 'Later on, we'll retire.'"
"Oh ... *really*?"
[The two of them fall to pieces right then and there, and Ross even has to pull onto the side of the road to keep from killing us all. He laughs until he gets the hiccups.]

The drive to the tree farm took about ten minutes. Dark ditches on either side of the highway, flurries of snow whipping around in the headlights. The tree lot was behind this old farmer's house. When he saw the headlights, the farmer came out wearing a raggedy, old doeskin jacket and waved at us. He walked over to the car and told us that he usually wouldn't bother bringing people around when it's almost dark, but Ross was an old friend of his. I tried to imagine Ross being friends with this grizzled farmer—did they drink lattes together? Coordinate their tanning sessions? He told Ross he had the perfect tree in mind and then whistled for his dog, a good-for-nothing beagle. They hopped into his truck and we followed them along a dirt road, basically into the middle of this huge field. There were rows and rows of Christmas trees, one after another, perfectly spaced.

We parked and got out. It was pretty much nighttime by this point, which made seeing pretty difficult, even though the tree farmer had all his floodlights turned on, not to mention he had two flashlights, one of which he gave to Ross to use. My mom kept saying, "What about this one?" to almost every tree we passed. The farmer repeated that he'd already picked one out, but she kept on saying that same line, again and again. She kept trampling further along the path, pointing out the next best thing.

The ground was cold, and wet, and any time Ross said something, it was always about the weather. And every time he said something about the weather, the tree man would laugh and say something wise, like, "You can't depend on the weather," or "Yessirree, it's colder than donkey's balls."

Ross and the tree farmer small-talked for an eternity before they realized that they hadn't heard from Mom in a while. Ross started calling her name, and he asked me if I knew where she was, which was a ridiculous question because I'd been standing right beside him the whole time.

I wasn't really worried, not at all, but within seconds Ross's voice went up a few octaves, and I knew he was about to start screeching his orange head off, so I went off into the field calling for my mom. I walked far enough away that I could barely hear Ross's voice, or the gruff voice of the tree man, calling out behind me. The tree farmer's beagle appeared occasionally from under a shrub, then would scamper back to the sound of his owner's voice. I called out for my mother a few times. Passed about a thousand trees. I didn't really know what else to do, so I just kept walking. I walked until I couldn't hear anything, until I knew I was in the deepest part of the woods. Then I stripped out of my clothes and lay down on the cold twigs and snow, and waited for the frostbite to take me.

I found my mom standing beneath a tree, in almost complete darkness. I saw her from a few feet away, her silhouette. She wore a white scarf over a white coat. A white pompom hat. She was just standing there beneath this tree, looking up at it, not moving at all. I walked up loudly, whistling "Walking in a Winter Wonderland," and stepping with thuds into the snow, so she'd know I was there, but still she didn't turn around. She didn't even acknowledge my presence until I was standing right next to her. And then she said the strangest thing. Something completely unexpected.

Mom said, "Jesus fucking Christ."

I had no idea how I was supposed to respond to this proclamation. It was the first time I'd ever heard my mom use the Lord's name in vain. Definitely the first time she'd used it in combination with the f-bomb. I kept my mouth shut, and wished until my ears got hot I had had my tape recorder.

I could hear Ross and the farmer calling from the path a few metres away. My mom put her face into her hands and stood there without budging an inch, more like a tree than all the trees around her. I was about to say something, but then she suddenly called out, "Over here." Her voice was muffled, so I decided to help her out. "She's over here," I said. Then she took her hands from her face and looked at me, and said, "Well, what do you think? Is this a tree or what?" Her eyes were red, and she sounded short of breath. I looked at the dark tree, its boughs covered in layers of snow. "Yes," I said, "it's a tree."

On our way back from the tree farm, Mom made Ross park the Infiniti next to the flower shop on Main Street. She came out ten minutes later with a large gathering of lillies in her arms, which she promptly stuffed into a vase once we got home. She put so much water in the vase that when she stuffed the flowers in, a tiny bit of water sloshed onto the kitchen counter. I watched her wipe the area around the vase dry with a dishtowel. She said "Goddamn it" twice before she noticed me standing in the door. Then she pretended to be in a good mood, and suddenly made her face smile, made her eyes look happy, and asked me how school was for the first time that day.

"Fine," I told her. "It was fine."

I knocked on the door to the yellow Langford house. No answer. I crossed my fingers and toes and knocked on the door a second time. I knocked and knocked and knocked. Then I heard someone yelling from behind the door. I stopped knocking and crossed my arms behind my back. The door opened. The man who answered wore a purple terrycloth housecoat, even though it was three in the afternoon. He did not look very sleepy, but a swatch of stubble covered his face like a cold grey hand. Also, the housecoat was not closed and, to my great chagrin, I could see the front part of the man's underwear.

August 18 (Afternoon):

"Can I help you?"
"Hi."
"What is it?"
"I'm conducting a survey."
"For what?"
"An in-depth analysis."
"On?"
[5.5 seconds.]
"Uh ... well, it's about neighbourhoods. Or, no. More specifically, it's about the coming apocalypse."
[2.8 seconds.]
"I was ... are ...?"
[Sound of door closing softly. And locking.]

I'm such a bottlefuck.

Stupidly, I had not thought ahead about how I would present myself. I didn't even have a plan for saying who I was working for. For whom I was working. Obviously, I couldn't say I was doing it for my own sake. As I walked to the next house, I came up with more details. I was doing the survey for a local newspaper, which would remain anonymous. No, I couldn't say that. I'd have to explain that I was doing the survey for my school newspaper. Though wouldn't that sound a little weird, considering it was still August?

The next house I went to was below Danforth, on Wolfrey. The owner, a middle-aged woman wearing a hockey jersey, was a bit more receptive, though she didn't let me in, and she didn't finish the survey. We were able to get through the first couple of questions though.

August 18 (Afternoon):

"Do you live in this neighbourhood?"

"Obviously."

"How long have you lived in this neighbourhood?"

"Four years."

"Do you know the name of our—"

"No, five years. We've been here five years. That wasn't the original plan, but it's fine. It's what we can afford, y'know? Would obviously rather live in Rosedale, but we can't all be rich Jews."

"Excuse me?"

"Nothing."

"Okay. Have you ever considered moving to a different part of the planet?"

"Yes. At least once a week. Ha!"

"Do you like this planet?"

"Like, the whole planet?"

"Yes."

"What choice do I have?"

"Is that a 'yes'?"

"Yes."

"Would you move to a neighbouring solar system, if space travel of that magnitude were possible?"

"Um … sure."

"Could you rate your knowledge of your neighbours on a scale of one to five, one being 'Don't know them at all,' and five being 'I know them very well.'"

"Uh, three, I guess."

"I hear a bit of hesitancy in your voice. That's probably more like a two, then."

"Are you writing two or three?"

"Two."

"But that wasn't my answer."

"Where do you work?"

"Why do you want to know where I work?"

"It's one of the questions."

"Sort of private, isn't it?"

"Only if it's illegal."

"I don't. Work, that is. I take care of the house."

"How much do you get paid?"

[5.7 second pause.]

"Uh, you know what? I think I hear the phone ringing."

[Definitely no sound of a phone ringing.]

"But we're not done."

"Yes. We are."

This sort of thing kept happening to me. Even when I made it to the end of the survey, the answers I got regarding the blackout basically made me feel like I was wasting paper. And tape. One person said he was out of town when the lights went out. Another woman claimed to have slept through the whole thing. These weren't exactly the answers I was hoping to get.

August 18 (Afternoon):

"Oh man. Let me tell you. I was on an elevator."

"Really? For how long?"

"Yes. Well, no, I mean I wasn't on the elevator. No. I was about to get on one. That would've been terrible. Can you imagine? Instead I had to take the stairs and go down like twenty-three flights. But, honestly, I mean, the doors were closing. Then the power went out. This close!"

August 18 (Afternoon):

"I was at home."

"When did you notice?"

"Um. Well, not for a few hours actually. It was the middle of the day, so I didn't see any lights go out. I don't own a microwave, and our oven is pretty old. No clock."

"What time did you …?"

"Oh, probably about three hours after it happened. Does that sound right, Max?"

"Yeah, about that long."

"Oh."

"Our milk went bad."

"Uh-huh."

"Yeah."

August 18 (Afternoon):

"It was just like in the movies, y'know?"

"Tell me about it."

"I was at my desk, doing work. Ha! Who am I kidding? I was probably downloading music or something. No, no, I remember. I was reading about this guy that had this, like, weird fungus growing on his skin. Yeah, the fungus was growing out of him, was hard. Looked like algae. Was seriously coming out of his pores. Ugh! Nasty."

"Okay. And then?"

"Right. Then the power just went out. Boom. Like that. I have a fan on my desk, and it stopped spinning. I have a laptop, so that was fine."

"What did you do?"

"I didn't do anything. I kept reading about the guy. I swear, it looked like these little mushrooms coming out of his arms and neck. No, barnacles! They looked like barnacles. Ugh!"

"How did you get home?"

"I actually live like two blocks from work, so I just walked home. Spent the night on our deck looking at the stars."

"Hmm."

"Had some beer in the fridge. Didn't want them getting warm, if you know what I mean."

Not exactly Pulitzer-winning stuff.

I interviewed this guy on River Street who kept wiping at his nose with the back of his hand. He seemed to be under a lot of stress, wore a tie with a dried piece of lettuce on the bottom edge.

August 18 (Afternoon):

"This is a weird survey. What's it for?"
"School newspaper."
"But what's the point of it?"
"I can't tell you. It would influence your answers and jeopardize the legitimacy of the experiment."
"I'm not doing it."
"Sir, it'll only take a second. If you like, you can leave the name line blank and your information will remain anonymous."
"Anonymous? There's no such thing."

This other woman I spoke to lived in Cabbagetown, in a house with a rather big front yard. Big for Toronto, anyway. I watched her buy a paper at a convenience store and followed her home. I waited for about ten minutes before knocking on her door.

She was a doctor. She owned two mini dogs, scrunchy-faced yappers. They yipped and snapped the whole time I was in her house, and I wondered if the lost dog story would've worked on her. She gave me a drink of water, and apologized for not having any cookies. I told her I didn't like sweets, which is a lie, but it made her laugh. She said, "Your mother must adore you." I decided to change the subject by placing the survey firmly on her kitchen table.

August 18 (Afternoon):

"How long have you lived in this neighbourhood?"
"Seven years."
"Do you know the name of our galaxy?"

"Yes. The Milky Way."

"Have you ever spent an evening looking at the stars through a telescope?"

"Yes, but not for a long time."

"Ever considered moving to a different part of the planet?"

"No."

"Do you like this planet?"

"It has its problems but, yes, I like our planet very much."

"Would you ever consider moving to a neighbouring solar system, if space travel of that magnitude were possible?"

"Is this some kind of joke?"

"No ma'am. I assure you this survey is put together with the most serious of intentions."

"These are some fairly strange questions. Did you come up with them yourself?"

"The questions were created by a team of specialists."

"Is that so?"

"Yes."

"What sort of specialists?"

"I can't really say."

"Why not?"

"It would jeopardize the answers you give."

"Are you some kind of young scientologist?"

"A what? I don't even know what that is."

"I'm not interested if that's the case."

"I'm not a scientologist."

"Okay."

[6.8 second pause.]

"Okay, go ahead then."

[Sound of me clearing my throat.]

"Rate your knowledge of your neighbours on a scale of one to five, one being 'Not at all' and five being 'Very well.'"

"Four."

"Where do you work?"

"I'm a doctor. I work at St. Michael's."

"Do you think it's possible that our world is joined to an alternate world at the poles?"

"No."

"But have you ever been the North Pole?"

"No."

"Then how can you know for sure?"

"Satellite images."

"Hmm."

[2.8 second pause.]

"Have you ever been the victim of a hate crime?"

"No."

"Did you feel like the world was about to explode on August 14?"

[The woman laughs.]

"No."

[5.1 seconds. Sound of my pen on paper.]

"Where were you on the day the lights went out?"

"At the hospital. Working."

"On a scale of one to five, how greatly did the blackout change your life, one being 'Not at all' and five being 'Extremely intensely'?"

"One."

"Really?"

"Yes."

"So nothing happened?"

"I didn't see much of the city. We had backup generators running at the hospital, but ..."

"Did anyone die?"

[4.3 second pause.]

"What does this have to do with your survey?"

"Can't tell you that. It would jeopardize the legitimacy of the operation."

"Yes. Someone died. But not because of the blackout. I work in the ICU."

"Who was he?"

"Young guy. Late twenties. He'd been deteriorating for a while."

"That's awful."

"He'd known for a long time, and his family was with him. He was in pain, but not for very long. It could've been worse."

I stopped asking questions from the survey. It seemed pointless, after hearing her talk about this dead guy. She said he was only twenty-three, had had several bone marrow transplants, but it wasn't enough. The cancer was embedded, he could barely move or speak, and most of the time he was out of it, barely awake. His mom and dad were with him when he let go, and then, and this just killed me, I guess once he was done his little sister went around the room and blew out all the candles. I can just picture the room, dark except for the light coming through the window, the smell of candle smoke floating up to the ceiling, and this dead guy, younger than Dave, completely and utterly dead. So sad too, his sister blowing out the candles, like she wasn't even aware of how clichéd it all was.

For a second, neither one of us said anything, and then I opened my mouth to speak, but nothing came out.

I thanked the doctor for her time, then left the house in a bit of a rush. To explain my eyes, I told her I was allergic to dogs.

Bartholomew the horse-man allows you to ride on his back, even though this is something that horse-men never do. Ever. But he lets you ride on his back, because the roads are dangerous, especially at night, and there's no time to lose.

The horse-man takes you into the kingdom of the Elysia, and on each side, all along the narrow and winding river of Zeina, there are cities made of marble, alabaster, agate, amber, and of course some unrecognizable minerals. As beautiful as these cities may once have been, they are now smoking ruins, broken-down places, abandoned, just like the town at the edge of the emerald sea.

"What's happening here?" you ask.

"Those slimy creatures that almost killed you are what's happening. They've been happening now for over a year."

"Why is no one stopping them?"

"They are sloppy, they are stupid, and relatively easy to kill in small numbers. But the lice-men do not know the meaning of 'small numbers.' Rarely will you come upon a pack as small as the one I saved you from."

"Why are there so many?"

"They're breeders. They breed all the time, and give birth to numerous spawn. They're a disgusting, despicable lot, but not half as bad as the slug-men."

"Slug-men?"

"Twice as tall and just as mean. Both groups are being led by the Rat-King. Curse the bastard's name!" Bartholomew spits on the ground. "Slowly but surely, they're destroying this beautiful countryside. They have no respect for others, and expect everyone to bow at their feet on the sole basis that their city is the largest in the land, and has the tallest tower in the land. To that I say, 'Big deal!' Kings of nothing. My father ..."

You say nothing, waiting for Bartholomew to finish his sentence because you know he's taking a long pause for effect to really dramatize the thing. In the short time you've known him, you've come to learn that he's got a flair for melodrama.

"They took my father. At least, we think that's what happened to him. No one knows for sure. He disappeared some time ago, almost two years. My mother thinks that maybe he's been taken captive, that he's a prisoner, but I don't know. These fiends aren't known for letting their victims live."

You can tell that Bartholomew is overcome with emotion, so you say nothing else. The two of you travel in silence for the next six hours, until you come upon a fifty-foot-high wall that appears to be made of diamonds. Tall guards in heavy armour made from a glassy blue material see you coming. They point their arrows at you for a moment, then relax. They wave to Bartholomew, who waves right back. A moment later, they set about opening the huge iron gates in the wall that keep the lice-men and their ilk from coming anywhere near.

You can already guess, but you ask Bartholomew where you are.

"This," Bartholomew says, as you pass through the city wall, "is the last bastion of freedom for those not already enslaved by the lice-men and slug-men. This," he says once beyond the gates, gesturing to a sprawling, graceful city composed entirely of bright blue buildings with vines crawling up and down the sides, "is the Imperial City of the Elysia."

At that moment, a blast of trumpets fills the air, announcing the arrival of a new visitor to the Imperial City. Little do you know, the Emperor has been waiting for you.

It was after a long day of disappointing interviews; it was after a long, hot day, when I still couldn't sleep, when I was still staying in a glorified closet, when I was reading *The Blazing World* in bed, when a part of the book fell open to a thin piece of paper. It dropped into my lap, a dead thing.

I closed the book and placed it next to me.

I then recovered the thin piece of paper, unfolded it, and flattened it out.

It was a letter.

Addressed to my father.

Although it was written legibly, for a moment my brain had a hard time making out what I was seeing. I had to read the first line a thousand times before I believed what I saw. But it was definitely my dad's first and last name. Definitely a letter to my dad, even if the rest of it didn't make any sense.

The letter had been written in pencil. It was dated about three months before my dad disappeared. The person who wrote it signed the letter, but I couldn't decipher the signature. It wasn't familiar, and neither was the handwriting. The contents of the letter were actually kind of boring, so I won't go into too much detail, but basically it said something about the person wishing he or she could've gone to my mom's funeral, which made no sense whatsoever. The person also mentioned my dad having only one son, which also made no sense. I read the letter again and again, but only became more confused with each reading.

Last year in Ms. Rossbach's we read this short story by the dude who wrote that raven poem. I think he also wrote the books about Sherlock Holmes. Ms. Rossbach did her Masters and was always getting us to read stories that no one else in our grade read. This one was about a Frenchman who steals something from someone else, but no one can find out where he's hidden it until this detective goes to his house and finds it in the most obvious place, right there on his table. Or something like that. It's not a very good story. I don't even remember the name. And it seems stupid that the thief would just leave the stolen goods right out in the open. Just because the author made it work in the story doesn't mean it would work in the real world. But that's pretty much what happened to me. Something I should've noticed right away didn't get noticed until a couple days later. And any doubts about there being a reason that I found the book in the back of Dave's kitchen drawer became extinct.

The blackout led me to the book, which was somehow connected to my dad, a woman named Myrna/Maria, and of course Dave because Dave had the book.

Right?

Or, clearly the book must've belonged to my dad, and he used this lame letter as a bookmark. Someone named Myrna, who was probably Maria, had written a note on the book, before she gave it to dad, which meant that *she* didn't necessarily live on Palmerston, but that maybe Dad did. Where the owners were dead.

Hmmm.

But why did Dave have the book now?

And Maria had said something about recognising me. Dad had spent a lot of time in the city on assignments.

I started flipping like a madman through every single page, but nothing else fell out.

Why was Dad pretending to be someone else, with a dead wife and just one son?

Was Maria Dad's mistress?

My sister?

I went to the kitchen, took the phone off the cradle, crouched down by the sink, and called home. My fingers were shaking so badly I dialled the wrong number and had to hang up and dial again. I wanted to ask Mom if she knew about Maria. Is that why she and Dad had broken up? Was he even really missing, or had he simply gone to live with his other family? In Toronto? Was it possible that Dad was still alive?

The phone rang five times, then clicked. I waited for my mom's voice to come on, saying her usual, "Oops, you must've just missed us." But her voice didn't come on. The voice I heard shocked me, sort of like drinking from a glass of water that turns out to be 7-Up. I half-wondered if I dialled the wrong number before I recognized the voice. Ross's voice saying, "Sorry, we're not in to take your call, but if you leave a message, we'll get back to you shortly."

For the second time in two days, I felt like eating the receiver.

We're not in? *We'll* get back to you?

I hung up before the beep.

16

34. On the day she made our first Thanksgiving dinner. Undercooked carrots, potatoes. You ate it anyway; the children in Africa.

629. On the day she took photos of our fingers, and used them to make a typeface. Letters to spell both our names. She framed them, and put them up on the walls of the apartment, one beside the other. Our names in frames.

342. On the day you moved into your apartment. Her sitting on the kitchen floor, scrubbing a mysterious black spot with a fistful of iron wool. And when she looked up, and when she looked up, and when she looked up

Morgan sat in the farthest corner of the café, his eyes on the door. He was behind them when they left their homes, locked up, checked their watches. He knew when they slept, knew their favourite meals, their favourite TV shows. He knew the name of the younger Morgan's cat, who'd died from feline colon cancer. Tugger III. He knew the name of the older Morgan's physiotherapist. Denise Fitzpatrick. He hadn't been to his own apartment in weeks. The nights were warm and mostly dry, so Morgan found places to sleep outside the other Morgans' homes. He was thankful for unlocked sheds. The older Morgan's shed was sparse, tidy, a few gardening tools caked with dried dirt. The younger Morgan's shed was messier, stuffed with tiki torches, a garden gnome, beach toys, and a lawn-mower. Bags of grass seed, fertilizer, two rakes, and a shovel. But Morgan didn't mind the clutter. He cleared a space on the floor and slept beneath a tarp. It was worth it to be close at all times.

The bell that hung above the café door jingled. A tall, fair-skinned woman entered, head down, looking for something in her purse. Not who he was waiting for, but she reminded him of the woman who cleaned the older Morgan's house. He'd met her once. Well, perhaps met wasn't the right word.

Morgan had been at the older Morgan's house one day, watching a program about the effects of brain trauma on two fictional characters that had just been in a car accident. He'd fallen asleep, or just wasn't paying enough attention, he wasn't sure which. One moment he was watching a computer-animated display of a blood clot forming in a human brain, and the next he was sitting up, hearing footsteps coming down the hall. He could tell it wasn't the elderly Morgan. The footsteps were too light, too hurried.

Morgan stood up quickly, then sat down again. He'd expected something like this to happen. Eventually, he knew someone would catch him. He'd be caught either looking through the window, or walking through the house, or picking something out of the mailbox. His voice came out weak at first, barely a whisper. He remained seated. Cleared his throat.

"Hey Dan, that you?"

No immediate reply. He wondered if he'd spoken loudly enough. He could hear the doctor's husband coming toward the room. Morgan called out again.

"Dan? Where've you been?"

"Excuse me?"

A woman carrying a bucket and a box full of cleaning supplies rounded the corner. She was tall, pale, hair cut short.

"You're not Dan." Morgan stood up.

"Who are you?"

"Scott Parker." Morgan offered his hand. The cleaner took a quick step back, nearly knocking over a floor lamp. Clearly, she had no intention of shaking Morgan's hand. "I'm looking for Dan," said Morgan, trying to put his rejected hand into his pocket without seeming obvious.

"Who is this Dan?" The cleaner had an accent. Russian, maybe Polish, Morgan couldn't tell. She walked toward the television, hit the power button, and crossed her arms.

"Dan Cox."

"Doesn't live here."

"Really? What's the address? The address here?"

The woman said nothing.

"Dan said the door would be unlocked so I just came in, I didn't even think .... Are you sure this isn't Dan's?"

The woman kept looking Morgan up and down, as though committing his features to memory.

"I'm sorry. I must've, I don't know. I'll ... sorry."

The cleaner followed Morgan down the hall and stood about a foot away as he put his shoes on.

"Tie them outside please."

"What? Oh. Sure. Of course."

Once outside, Morgan checked his pockets to make sure he hadn't forgotten anything. When he looked up, the cleaning lady was still looking at him from inside the house.

The bell on the door jingled again. Morgan looked up to see the elder Morgan Wells hobbling in like his shoes were made of wood. The clock on the wall said it was 12:52. Good. He was early.

The old man didn't immediately step up to the counter but stood near the front door for a moment, as though allowing his eyes to adjust to the light. Then he walked forward a few steps and scanned the room, obviously hoping to see his son. His eyes looked wild, a bit frantic. But in a moment he seemed to collect himself, then walked further into the café until he was standing in the middle of the room. There weren't any free tables.

"Looking for a chair?"

This was the first time Morgan had ever spoken to one of his others.

The old man looked over.

"You can have one of these. I don't need all four."

"You don't mind? My son should be here in a minute or two. He's supposed to be here now."

"Sure. No problem."

The elder Morgan Wells sat down.

"You say you're waiting for your son?"

The older Morgan nodded, kind of turned in his chair to survey the room, then turned back again. "Yes. My son." He was nervous.

"What does he do?"

"He's the owner. Of this place."

"I see."

"Well, he's actually an accountant, but this is what he's doing now. He used to be a bookkeeper. And by that, I don't mean a librarian."

Morgan started laughing, then stopped. The noise sounded hollow, forced, and he suddenly realized that his palms were sweating. He reminded himself that he had nothing to worry about. According to the other Morgans, he was just another stranger in a room full of strangers.

Fortunately, the elder Morgan was feeling conversational, if a bit jittery. He kept looking around the room, looking toward the door.

"You know why accountants don't read novels?"

"Why?"

"Because the only numbers in them are the ones at the bottom of the page."

Again, Morgan heard himself laughing, in a way that almost sounded like he was choking.

"My son hates these jokes, but what can you do? What's that you're drinking?" he asked.

"Coffee. Plain coffee."

"I could use a coffee. But my son insisted I wait for him to arrive. Why, I couldn't tell you. Maybe he wants to treat me."

"You know, I could get you a coffee if you wanted."

"No need," he muttered, embarrassed by the idea. "Thanks for the offer. But I'll wait."

Morgan took a few sips of coffee. It was getting cold.

He tried to remember what he knew about the older Morgan Wells, but his mind was blank.

Ten minutes passed. The younger Morgan was late. With each passing minute, the older Morgan seemed to get more and more agitated.

"Do you read novels?"

"What's this?"

"Novels?"

"What about them?"

"You said your son doesn't read novels. Do you?"

The older Morgan leaned forward in his seat. Staring.

"I only meant ... well ... I was just making conversation."

"Yes. I read novels." Here, the older Morgan paused, chuckled to himself. He reached into his coat pocket and placed a book on the table. "I've read most of the ones I've got at home. My wife, she used to get them for me. Now I've read most of them, some many times, except for this odd one. I never quite understood why she got it for me. Seventeenth-century science fiction."

"Wow," said Morgan, feigning to be impressed.

The older Morgan shook his head. "Novelty. Really."

"Do you read often?"

"I don't have much else going on."

"Fills up the day."

"Exactly."

"Like exercise."

"You could say that."

In fact, Morgan had overheard the older man saying it once to a friend on the phone.

Morgan looked around the café, wondering why the younger Morgan was late. It was now twenty past one. Morgan had carefully arranged for the older Morgan to be here, to think that his son had invited him. He wanted to see them together, he wanted to see what would happen if they were forced to interact. Would the young Morgan think he was being ambushed? Would the old Morgan apologize? Neither would know that he was the architect. Their namesake.

The older Morgan kept looking at the clock, tapping his fingers against the table. He kept sighing, adjusting the way he was sitting. Morgan finished what was left of his coffee, then excused himself. He approached the counter, the whole time keeping his eyes on the older Morgan. A line of heat radiated along the top of Morgan's head.

"Can I get you anything?"

"I was wondering when the owner would be coming in today? Wasn't he supposed to be here at one?"

The girl shrugged. "I dunno. Hey Jan, is Morgan coming in today?"

The other girl shook her head.

"Nope."

"What do you mean?"

"Well, he was supposed to come in I guess, but he called an hour ago and said he wasn't. Something with the kids. Maybe he'll drop by later?"

"When is later?"

The girl shrugged again, emanating boredom. She had slinky shoulders, tired eyes. She scratched at her elbow. "He's not here now. That's about all I can tell you."

Morgan turned away from the counter, just in time to see the older Morgan leaving his table and heading toward the door. He'd forgotten his book on the table.

Everything was happening too fast; it was Heidi York all over again.

Morgan picked his way through the tables, snatched up the old man's forgotten book. People kept looking up at him as he passed by. He glued his eyes to the other Morgan's back, and accidentally stepped in a puddle of spilled coffee and milk foam. His feet made a sticky sound as he followed the old man outside. He tapped him on the shoulder just as he walked out the door.

"Yes?"

The sound of traffic exploded all around them. Cars fuming and hissing. Even the sun seemed to radiate noise.

"Where are you going?"

"Excuse me?"

"Aren't you waiting for your son?"

The older man stared at him. "I was. He's not coming."

"You don't know that."

"He's late. As usual. This is some kind of joke."

"But—"

"Why the hell do you care anyway?"

Morgan watched the old man climb into a green and orange cab. He slowly lowered himself into the backseat, then brought his right leg in last, the hem of his pants riding well above his ankle. He reached into his pocket before closing the door. Took out his wallet and pinched it open, checking his money. The cab driver watched him. When he at last reached for the door, he looked up at Morgan who was still standing a couple feet away on the sidewalk. The old man said nothing. Their eyes met, but without understanding, or recognition.

Whatever Morgan had hoped to achieve had been destroyed. Then again, what had he really expected? That they'd all become friends? Form some kind of club? What exactly was he hoping to achieve?

As he stepped onto the sidewalk, he saw the café owner strolling down the street toward him. Late, but not hurrying. He was carrying a coffee. Is that why he was late? Because he was out sampling coffee at a rival café?

Morgan started toward him, and before he'd fully considered the implications, he slammed his shoulder into the other Morgan's shoulder, knocking the coffee out of his hand.

"What the fuck, man?"

This was the first time Morgan had ever touched one of his others.

"He was waiting for you."

"Who?"

"Your father."

"My father?"

"He was waiting, but you were late."

"What the fuck are you talking about?"

"Do you know what he does all day?"

"Who are you?"

"Do you know … don't you …"

Morgan was out of breath. What was he doing? He turned and quickly crossed the street.

The other Morgan followed him. For almost two minutes. Asking his name, repeatedly. "Who are you? Hey, asshole. Where are you going?" But Morgan couldn't answer his questions.

Who was he? Where was he going?

Morgan arrived home that night to discover that his lock had been changed. He slid his key into the lock, his own lock, his own flat, not anticipating the sudden stop. No give. He twisted the key two or three times. Why wasn't it working? The familiarity of the gesture pointed toward success, but the door wouldn't open. He pulled the key out to ensure he'd chosen the right one. He had. He then inspected the make of the lock. Schlage. Had his lock always been a Schlage? Morgan tried to fit each of his other-Morgan keys into the lock. Then he reinserted the correct key, closed his eyes and tried again. The familiar twist. Then nothing. Locked out.

A couple minutes later, Morgan was pulling himself in through the unlocked kitchen window, trying desperately to avoid scraping all the skin off his back. He clambered over the sill, and nearly fell face first onto the kitchen floor. He lay on his back, on the linoleum, catching his breath, adjusting to the dim light.

Morgan was home. But this wasn't his home. It couldn't be. Even in the dark he could see that his kitchen was empty. His table was missing. The microwave, the coffee maker. And the map he'd taped to the fridge. His Post-its. By this point, Post-its were in every room in Morgan's apartment, on the floors, the walls, the cupboards, the doors, the ceilings. But in this kitchen? No trace.

But it was his kitchen. His apartment. Morgan pulled himself onto his knees and sat back against his heels. Had she taken everything? Finally?

The living room hardwood floor had been swept. His walls completely naked, save the odd scratch from a nail or bit of chipped paint. The room seemed smaller. A closed box. A wave of nausea swept through him.

By the time Morgan got to his office, it had struck him what had happened. He'd half-expected it to happen. He'd found the notices stuck to his door, but ignored them, more interested, invested, in the mail addressed to other Morgans. And although he hadn't paid rent for two months, maybe three, he never expected to be locked out of his own place. Or that the letters would also be gone. His boxes and boxes of research. Even the old desk. Stolen, taken away, by others.

In the living room: *nothing.*

In the kitchen: *nothing.*

In the closets: *nothing.*

In the medicine cabinet: *nothing.*

He did find one Post-it, stuck between the window trim and the wall: *potted zebra plant.*

All his research, everything he'd done over the past six-and-a-half months, all gone. His apartment seemed to bear no life, no signs, and could have collapsed in on itself at that moment. There wasn't a Post-it big enough.

The phone started ringing. Morgan followed the sound into the next room. He found the phone console beneath the radiator, blinking and buzzing. It wasn't until he stood directly over it that he realized the phone was not in its cradle. But it continued to ring, and the ring seemed louder than normal, louder than necessary.

Morgan brought his foot down heavily upon the console, and the plastic exploded under his weight. He stomped on it until the light disappeared, until all that was left were tiny shards of plastic, filaments of stripped wires, cracked electronics.

It kept ringing.

Morgan fell to his knees and swung his fist against the remains. The impact broke his pinkie finger. He opened his mouth, but nothing came out. He kept swinging.

Somewhere outside, Morgan thought he heard the sound of someone singing. A pale yellow light spilled across the room.

17

The Imperial City is grander than any city you've ever visited in your life. The sky is not smudged with yellow smog stains. The traffic is reasonable. The green-faced residents are friendly, and they welcome you with open arms and hearts. Some even go so far as to bow on the ground as you pass by, and attempt to press their foreheads against your feet. A little creepy actually, looking down and seeing their shiny bald green heads, because they're all bald, even the women and children. But you try not to let that bother you too much.

Not a single piece of gum has found its way onto the street. The place is really quite impeccable.

Bartholomew tells you that he will bring you as far as the Dragon Palace's front door, but will go no further. "I do not go inside buildings. It's no offence to the Emperor, or to other species who enjoy the comfort of interiors. But horse-men have no palate for walls and ceilings. Reminds us of stables, you know. It's degrading."

You thank Bartholomew for his help. As soon as you step down, a green-faced woman greets you, and asks you to follow her into the palace.

The Emperor's palace is, to say the least, bigger than any house you've ever seen. It seems to stretch on and on for miles, a never-ending series of hallways, arches, and fifty-foot ceilings.

You are brought into a large antechamber, where the green-faced lady directs you to sit. About a minute later, a purple-skinned man walks in and proclaims loudly, "I give you, the great Emperor, Drogan Khaleil."

You stand up, and the Emperor walks in. He's wearing an absolute tonne of bling. He is tall, at least seven feet. His skin is Mexican, his eyes a cold blue.

Following him is a young girl, the Emperor's daughter. Her name is Luísa. You are fully prepared to bow, when all of a sudden both the Emperor and his daughter drop to their knees and bow before you. You have no idea what to say, so you look at the purple-skinned man who announced the presence of the Emperor, only to find that this man is also bowing.

"Okay," you say, more than a little confused. "What's going on?"
"You have come."
"Yes. And?"
"Finally. After all these years. The prophecies have been fulfilled."
"The prophecies? Hang on, what are you talking about?"

The Emperor, still kneeling on the floor before you, starts to explain. He repeats what Bartholomew told you about the lice-men, and the slug-men, and the evil rat-king leader. You listen patiently, waiting for the part about prophecies. The part that explains why an Emperor feels the need to bow before you.

"Okay," you say, "I get it, they're causing you some trouble. But so am I. Don't you get that? I don't belong here. I want to go home."
"We understand."
"I want things to go back to the way they used to be."
"As do we all."
"I was told you would help me."

"And of course we will. We will do anything to please you. But you must understand, your coming has been predicted for thousands of years."
"What do you mean?"
"Please, allow me to show you something."

Drogan finally stands up and leads you down a long glass corridor. The two of you walk until you come upon a blue wall, at which point Drogan puts his hand into a hand-shaped imprint, and the wall suddenly vanishes.

"Magic?"
"What you call magic, we call technology, and vice versa."
"Oh."

You walk into a light-filled room, which has nothing in it but a stand, upon which sits a large black book. Drogan leads you toward the book. You see the title, written in shiny red raised letters on the front of the book's smooth black cover. It's called *The Blazing World*.

Drogan mutters a few words as you approach the book, and suddenly the book springs open, the pages falling lightly until Drogan says another word, and then the pages stop turning.

"Do you see?"

You lean forward. On the page is a picture of someone who looks unmistakeably like you. Your entire head is covered in fire. The picture is basically you with a burning head.

"What … what is this?"
"This book is over three thousand years old. It prophesizes that our people will undergo a great scourge, then will be delivered

to them a human, but a human who has the power to enact great destruction against our foes through the follicles."

"Um … what?"

"Your hair," said Drogan, "is a weapon."

"I'm not sure I'm following."

Drogan says another word, and the pages flip again. This time, you see an image of you, or someone who looks just like you, with your foot on the neck of a large rat. You are pointing a sword at its throat.

"This is you."

"I can see that."

"You must help us," says Drogan.

You look at Drogan, fully prepared to say you can't, that you don't know how to turn your hair into a weapon, and that, quite frankly, you're not really up for killing a giant rodent and his hordes of slobbering minions. But before you can say anything, Drogan says, "You must kill the rat-king. That is the only way you will get home, because right now, he guards the gateway."

"What do you mean, the gateway?"

"The gateway into your world. For millennia it has been under the protection of the Elysia, until the rat-king destroyed and plundered the fortress where it was hidden. He does not yet know how to cross through the gateway himself, but he has magicians working on it night and day."

"His tech support?"

"Yes. His techies. And if he does figure out how to operate it …"

"If he does …?"

"If he learns how to use the gateway before you kill him, well … I'm sorry, but … you won't have a world left to go back to."

I called my mom six times the next morning. I would make the call, get the machine, then wait for ten minutes and call again. I kept thinking that she was just out running a quick errand, or maybe was vacuuming and couldn't hear the phone ringing.

I read the letter six thousand times.

Against my better judgment, around lunchtime, I called Caitlyn. The phone rang twice. Then Gary:

August 19 (Afternoon):

"Hello?"
[3.7 second pause.]
"*Hello?*"
"Gary, I need to speak with Caitlyn."
"You again?"
"Is she home?"
"No, she's not."
"You're lying."
"I'm not lying."
"Just put her on."
"What?"
"I don't have time for this."
"Time for what?"
"I need to speak with her, asshole."
"*Asshole?*"
[Gary chuckles. Clears his throat.]
"Okay, listen up you little dude."
"Dude?"
"We've had enough."
"We?"
"You need to stop calling."

"Maybe you need to stop answering the phone."

[8.8 seconds.]

"You think you're clever?"

"Is she there or not?"

"Wow. Are you listening to me?"

"I'm listening, yes, but—"

"Pay attention: stop calling. Do not call back. Okay dude?"

"Stop calling me 'dude.'"

"Just hang up."

"Go to hell. I'll call back if I feel like it."

[Gary laughs loudly.]

"Are you that fucking stunned? I mean, look, two years ago, when you were just some kid who lost his daddy, okay, understandable, you needed someone to talk to, why not turn to the pretty girl your brother used to date? But have you looked in a mirror lately?"

"Yes. Every morning at least when I brush my teeth."

"You haven't noticed the dirt on your upper lip?"

[4.2 second pause.]

"What dirt?"

"Think about it."

"You're a huge dick, Gary. You know that? I've never liked you."

"Whatever. Just stop calling. And buy a fucking razor, greaseball."

Fucking Gary, fuck him. What difference would it make if I shaved? It's not like Caitlyn could see me through the phone.

Although I knew Gary had motives for saying those things, I couldn't help but wonder if Caitlyn really thought of me that way. As just some charity case, not her friend, but some loser she felt sorry for. Some loser for whom she felt sorry. Some "greaseball."

Two years is a long time to pretend though. A lot can happen in two years.

Two years since Dave moved to Toronto and married Val.

Two years since my dad went missing.

My dad had been living a double life. Had been married, probably had kids, acted like everything was normal when he came back to

Nova Scotia, but couldn't stay, was always itching to get back to his other family. And Dave knew all about it. Was writing a book about it. Was I the only person in the dark?

Feeling totally deflated, I took a streetcar to the Eaton Centre, the mall that is one thousand malls, the A/C island at the heart of this hellhole city, the only place in Toronto that lets me forget I am in Toronto. I used what was left of the money Val had given me to buy Luís's present to buy an Orange Julius. I had just taken my first sip when I looked up and saw Dave on the other side of the mall.

Terror alert orange.

He was buying a coffee, and I could tell it was him from a mile away. Big fluffy head of hair, stupid goatee. I started to walk toward him, thinking I could confront him, or maybe just ask him for a ride home, but before I got to him, someone else did. A woman with red hair.

I stopped dead, thinking at first it was Maria, but no, definitely not. This woman was closer to Mom's age, had much thicker legs. She wore a black skirt and a yellow blazer, and reminded me of a large human-shaped bumblebee. She touched Dave on the elbow, and he turned around and smiled. Dave shook the woman's hand, then after a brief pause, she laughed.

At this point, I had no idea what to think. She did not have the looks of either Caitlyn or Val, so I doubted that Dave was sleeping with her. At the same time, she was more in line with what Dave should've been sleeping with, the bigheaded bastard. In a perfect world. The woman ordered a coffee and then they sat down.

When they sat down, the woman immediately pulled some papers out of her bag and laid them on the table. Dave opened his green spiral notebook. I didn't want to get too close in case Dave turned around and noticed me. He's the least observant person that I know, but I saw no need to confirm my suspicions. I had a better idea.

I went into a nearby shoe store, and sat down in one of the chairs. I took my shoes off slowly, and grabbed a pair of sneakers off the closest shelf. I put them on slowly.

Dave and the woman talked for almost two hours. I didn't stay in the shoe store the whole time. After trying on about ten different pairs, and getting these weird looks from the girl at the counter, I went into a bookstore, and then a clothing store that played sleazy techno, and then a magazine store.

I watched Dave. It seemed every minute was another opportunity to see him make a wrong move. I paid particular attention to his hands under the table, to see if they came within even an inch of the woman's rather rotund legs.

Was she my dad's secret widow?

They laughed quite a few times, but for the most part, they seemed more interested in the papers the woman had brought. Dave also kept flipping through the pages of his notebook, and making notes. They talked forever. They talked so long I almost forgot why I was watching them in the first place. It seemed like such a waste of time. But I think the last two minutes were worth the first hundred and eighteen. They'd finished talking, and the woman had stood up to leave. She put out her hand to shake, and just as Dave stood up to grab it, his knee hit the table and coffee spilled everywhere. It went all over the table, onto the woman's legs. Hilarious. Dave ran to grab some napkins, and dropped a bunch on the table, then gave the rest to the woman. She didn't seem too upset, but it was amazing watching Dave squirm like that. I was standing more than thirty feet away, but still I could hear him apologizing. Over and over. A truly beautiful thing.

The two of them left the mall together, Dave saying sorry the whole time. I was going to follow them, just to make sure they weren't just having a chat before booking a hotel room, but as I started toward them I saw Dave's green spiral notebook sitting on his chair. He must've moved it from the table after spilling the coffee, and had forgotten about it in the ensuing slapstick chaos.

Opportunities like this are rare. I didn't hesitate. I went straight to the table and looked around like it was me who forgot the book. Stupid me. I shook my head, grabbed the book off Dave's chair and tucked it under my arm.

I made it to the other side of the mall, and was safely inside a soap store when Dave came rushing back. The soaps all smelled the same, made me want to sneeze. Dave had this look like his face was about to fall off. He went straight for the table, then checked the tables nearby, as though he'd forgotten where they'd been sitting. He then went to the person behind the counter, who had dreadlocks, and looked like he wouldn't have known where the book was even if he was balancing it in on his head. Dave pointed at his table. That look on his face. Another customer came along, and the guy behind the counter stopped talking to Dave. I watched my brother go back to the table, just stand there, looking around. He put his hand through his hair.

Seeing him like this reminded me of the day we had the memorial service. Seeing Dave in his old bedroom, lying on his bed with his eyes open, hands on his chest, staring at the ceiling, not answering my knocks on the door. I had to open the door and turn the light on to get his attention.

"Time to go."

Dave stood there for almost fifteen minutes. Just stood around, like at any second his notebook would appear. He even checked the garbage.

I started to reconsider my decision. I could tell him I'd seen him, was going to say hi, but then he left, and that's when I found the notebook. Tell him I'd planned on bringing it home for him. But I couldn't. Dave would kill me if he even suspected that I was spying on him. Certain, absolute death.

If you choose to return the notebook to Dave, turn to page 189.
If you choose to keep the notebook and see what's inside, turn to page 122.

I left Dave digging through the garbage, and went downstairs to the food court. I found a table near the washrooms, and opened the notebook in my lap. For a second, I could only look at it. I knew that if I read anything in that notebook, I would face my most certain doom. But I figured I only had a couple days left in Toronto. If I didn't act soon, I might as well stick my head in the oven and get it over with anyway.

My heart was beating so fast. I reconsidered my location, knowing that it was entirely possible that Dave could at any moment come along and knock my head off with his forearm. But time was limited. I was sure that whatever Dave knew about our dad would be included in those pages.

I started reading, started with the first page, but the words I read told me nothing. Dave writes like a moron, and the parts I understood were scattered fragments of sentences.

Make more likeable—too dark.

Cut a.g.?

Greyhound at 2:30.

Pick up apples for dinner; Granny Smith?

I flipped through the pages, but it was all more of the same. A few creepy stick figure drawings here and there. Useless. There were a couple notes about some trademark infringers: a company called McRonald's, and another one named Z-Rocks. Is this what counted for research in Dave's snail-shaped brain?

Near the middle, there were a couple tables and lists. Lots of dates and times, basically a long chronology of events, but there were so many acronyms I couldn't make sense of any of it. If Dave was working on a story about Dad, I had no idea how this book would have any use. Impossible to decipher. Maybe that was the point. It was written in code that only morons who can't write would understand.

Or maybe it was really just work-related. Maybe none of it had anything to do with our father's disappearance.

I kept flipping. There were times when Dave used blue ink, times when he used red and black, times when he'd written his codified notes in pencil. What remained the same was the nonsense of it all, long, illegible paragraphs, arrows criss-crossing all over the place.

I could feel a hot line of sweat at the top of my head, slowly working its way down. Not only had I stolen Dave's notebook, but I'd got nothing for my efforts.

I flipped the notebook over. That's when I found a small stack of envelopes paper-clipped to the inside of the back cover. All of them were addressed to my dad, all with different addresses. Had my dad lived at all these different places? The contents of the envelopes told me nothing. Just bills, nothing personal. I sat there for at least five minutes, just staring at the different envelopes, different addresses.

What the eff was going on? I checked the postmarks. They were all within a few months of each other. Within months of Dad's disappearance. Did he live at all of these addresses? For what possible reason? If it was for an article, it must've been an important one. Why would he need so many different addresses though? Was he some kind of spy?

I suddenly felt something cold slide down my back. Then the room went dark. First blue, then completely dark. Another blackout. I looked toward the escalators, but I couldn't see anything. No, this was worse. The sun was gone. The sun had burnt out.

It takes eight minutes and twenty-three seconds for the sun's light to hit the earth. So as the flames died away, I knew that in fact our planet had already died. We just didn't know it yet. In seconds, it became very cold, which my hot skin initially appreciated. Then the winter storms came and I froze on the spot. Shattered into a million shards of glass.

Permanent blackout.

I went outside in the freezing heat, toward Yonge-Dundas Square. Past the Jesus weirdoes and Muslims handing out Islamic bibles. The place was swarming with maniacs, and there was some sort of show going on. People breakdancing and some Caribbean guy shouting nonsense into a microphone. All noise, lots of people to potentially interview, but I didn't let this slow me down or distract me. I was done with the interviews by now anyway.

The world was breaking into a billion pieces. The universe was snapping back on itself like an elastic band. It would all be over in seconds.

I was about to be struck by lightning.

I was about to be thrown through a plate-glass window by the tail of a tornado.

An asteroid, breaking through the earth's atmosphere, was about to come, from a million miles away, but headed straight for me.

19

For weeks Morgan slept on the beach. He never went back to his empty apartment. Wouldn't have gone back even if it was an option. The warm sand on his back. The soft waves pushing and pulling him out of sleep.

Someone had given him a blanket.

He kept thinking that he was waiting for someone, that any minute this person would arrive. His wife. Scott. A Morgan. It seemed inevitable that someone would find him.

He went down to the shore and wetted a corner of the blanket, which he used to wipe away the scum that had gathered on his face and hands. The mould that had started to grow along the contours of his neck.

He reached into his pocket, found a blank piece of paper. He turned it over in his hands.

He was thinking of the postcard, but couldn't quite remember where it was. What he'd done with it.

He woke up in the middle of the night to a dog licking his feet. He kicked it in the snout and rolled over.

Morgan went to the house in the Annex. To explain himself, explain what had happened. He owed the older Morgan that much. He arrived an hour after the postman arrived, close to one, at a time when he knew his namesake would not be home.

Morgan let himself in and closed the door softly. He wanted to wait for the old man inside. Greet him when he came through the door. He put his keys into his pocket, then removed his shoes and lined them up neatly against the wall. The phone was ringing. Morgan considered answering it, answering as Morgan, but didn't. He went into the kitchen instead to make himself a sandwich. The older Morgan didn't have much besides bread and margarine.

Step one: Remove two slices of bread from the plastic bag.
Step two: Put slices of bread in toaster, rounded side up.
Step three: Push lever down.
Step four: Count to sixty, then place toast on plate.
Step five: Spread evenly.

Morgan toasted the bread, spread the margarine on thinly, then sprinkled the bread with cinnamon. He ate the sandwich standing over the sink and rinsed the crumbs when he'd finished.

He washed his hands in the sink and dried them with a dishtowel. He made his way into the living room. He imagined the other Morgan drinking tea. He didn't like this room in particular, its plethora of useless trinkets.

The phone started ringing again.

Morgan walked up the staircase, up to the second floor. He pictured the other Morgan walking beside him as he went up. Would he hold the rail? With a firm grip? Or with loose fingers—sliding along the solid oak banister? Would he lean to the right? Keep his eyes on the stairs? Morgan limped in the way he'd watched the older Morgan Wells limp. Favouring his right foot, left hand close to the centre of his chest.

Morgan noticed that one of the three doors upstairs was closed. Perhaps he should've taken this as a sign. But he knew the old man was out, knew he was sitting on his park bench beneath the oak, waiting for the day to end.

From the landing, it took six steps to reach the master bedroom, nine steps to reach the bathroom, and thirteen steps to reach the closed door. He visited each in that order.

The bedroom had been cleaned. Morgan pulled the covers back. The sheets were missing. He made the bed, then laid on top of the blanket. He stretched his legs out, eyes on the ceiling. He had never fallen asleep at any Morgan's place. Trying every angle, imagining the different ways he could wake up. Morgan pushed his face into the pillow.

In the bathroom. Cool blue tiles, scum in the ridges between them. But an immaculate toilet bowl. Light grey flannel toilet seat cover. Morgan looked through the other Morgan's cabinet. He was noting an absence of certain prescription medicines when he heard a sound. A sound of falling. Something being knocked over. A book? From the shelf downstairs? But he'd left the books in their neat little rows, hadn't he? The noise couldn't have been caused by a falling book. Morgan closed the medicine cabinet. He listened, but couldn't hear anything other than the achingly quiet buzz of a vacant house.

Morgan stepped out of the bathroom. He stood for a moment in front of the closed door. To the laundry room? The study? The more he stared at the door, the more convinced he became that the sound had come from behind it. Something had moved.

Morgan examined the pores in the wood. The knob felt warm. Perhaps it was time to leave. It wasn't too late. If someone was home, he could still go. But no one was home. He was sure this was one of the older Morgan's park days. Besides, he couldn't leave without seeing what had caused the noise. If someone was home, then maybe that's how it was meant to happen. The discovery. Perhaps this Morgan could help Morgan after all. Perhaps that had been the point all along.

Morgan squeezed the knob. The door opened. He didn't even turn the knob. The door just opened. Light filtered through two large windows on the right.

The first thing Morgan saw was a body, suspended in the air. A body of sagging skin and bones, with grey whiskers, long hair, and enormous white wings. Black eyes. The angel hovered motionless in the centre of the room, then suddenly fell toward him, feet first, giving Morgan the nervous feeling that he was about to be kicked. He winced and fell back into the hallway, holding his hands protectively in front of his face. Nothing happened. No further noises, no disturbances. Morgan blinked, and in an instant the image of the winged man vanished. In its place, the elderly Morgan Wells hovered two feet above the floor, swinging his legs out toward the door. He was levitating. He seemed to be reaching, but then he stopped moving. In what tongue was he speaking?

Morgan realized the old man was not actually speaking. Neither was he floating. Rather, he was hanging by the neck from an extension cord tied tightly around an exposed water pipe. The old man's neck had certainly been broken. His limp body still struggled, in some cruel mockery of life, kicking rigidly against his nerves. Aftershocks.

Morgan took a moment. The old man had walked off his desk and into open air. He'd stepped into the noose, wearing nothing but underwear and a T-shirt. Morgan thought the man had said something before he fell. Had he spoken? Had he noticed Morgan?

As he stepped into death, what did he see? Who did he see?

Whatever words the man had spoken, he wasn't speaking now.

The elderly Morgan's body swung back and forth just inches from Morgan's elbow. He reached out to touch the corpse, to stop it from swinging. He missed. Fingers pulled back, balled into a fist.

The other Morgan had left a short letter on his desk, kept in place by a heavy brass paperweight shaped like an inkwell. His last words.

Gone to be with Myrna. Couldn't wait any longer. Everything to Morgan.

Morgan took it in. The way the other Morgan's feet pointed to the ground. The veins in his legs. The ex-Morgan's body swung back and forth, back and forth. A movement that was almost imperceptible, unless he stood close enough to smell the dead weight collected in the hanged man's underwear. He could see movement in the old man's toes. The rest of the room seemed to glow all around him. Everything there had once been touched by the dead man. The framed university degree. The pear-shaped vase on top of the radiator, covered in dust.

The phone was ringing—had it ever stopped?

Morgan dug around in the dead Morgan's desk for a pair of scissors. He then climbed on top of the desk, and cut the cord. He held the body, lowered it slowly to the floor. He untied the cord from the old man's neck. He put his hands under the dead man's armpits, and he was about to lift him into a sitting position when he heard a sound at the door. Sounded like someone breathing.

Moments before, Morgan had heard the front door closing, the sound of someone moving about downstairs, the sound of the dead Morgan's son speaking, saying, "Dad?" His voice reverberating in the empty house. Morgan had heard all of these things, but hadn't listened. "I've been calling all morning." Hadn't understood. It was all background to the present moment, the sight of the dead man's broken neck, the smell of his dead body.

Morgan turned around, and saw the dead Morgan's son standing in the door to the study.

"What the fuck are you doing here?"

20

It's the eve of battle. You and the Emperor and his forces, the mighty army of Elysia, have been marching for weeks, slowly but surely descending into the bowels of the rat-king's kingdom. The closer you get, the worse the air starts to smell. Smells like Tex-Mex and spoiled milk all mixed into one overwhelming stench. The people in these parts are rude, but who can blame them? They've been subject to a tyrant's rule for years. They've been living under a blanket of smog, it's always way too hot, and there's no room to move. Everyone is angry, but who knows, maybe hopeful to see the Emperor and his glorious army approaching the rat-king's lair?

You're travelling with your friend Bartholomew, who begrudgingly came along for the battle, because that's the way horse-men do things: begrudgingly. Although he claims to believe his father is dead, you can see he hopes that's not the case, but not because he wants to rescue him. No, he's told you that he wants a chance to kill him himself. It's recently come to light that his father may have led a double life, that he may have been married to another half-human half-horse hybrid, and probably had other sons too. If there's even a chance his father is still living …

You came along for the battle, not because you believed you were some kind of saviour, but because you didn't really have much of a choice. Of course, you did have a choice, and you chose to come. But the other option wasn't an option. If the rat-king was going to destroy this world and the one you came from, you didn't want to die knowing you did nothing to stop him.

So for weeks, you march until finally, off in the distance, you see the rat-king's city. It's a dark place, the exact opposite of the Imperial City, a place of dark greys and dirty whites, electrical wires hanging everywhere, highways and overpasses galore. One of those cities that just sprawls, no way to contain the mess. It's on a lake, but the lake is highly toxic, glows green, but not like the emerald sea. The waves are thick, acidic, and would burn the skin right off your body if you took a dip.

Roughly three kilometres from the city is where the Emperor's army sets up camp. The night you stop moving, you decide to visit the Emperor. You know you aren't meant to kill the rat-king, and he needs to know this. There's been a hell of a lot of walking, your feet are about to fall off, but no talk about just how you're supposed to set your head ablaze. The Emperor needs to know that his forces will be fighting the lice-men and slug-men without your help.

When you get to the Emperor's tent, you find him inside, speaking with his generals. They are talking about the plan of attack.

"We'll send our forces in from the east and west ends of the city. Take the Gardiner expressway and QEW, then move north from there. Once we've secured the lake, that's when we unleash you know what."

The generals are all nodding, and it's at this point that the Emperor looks over and sees you standing in the doorway.

"Indeed," he says, "and here's our secret weapon right here among us."

Instantly, all the generals turn and bow for an uncomfortably long time. Even though you've told them not to, the Elysia still treat you as a deity.

"Yes, well, actually, that's what I came to speak with you about, sir."

"Do not 'sir' me. I am yours to command."

"May I, uh … speak with you alone?"

Instantly, all the generals jump to their feet and leave the Emperor's tent. You sit in the chair across from the Emperor and try to explain what's happening. About the fact that you simply are incapable of turning your hair into a blazing fire.

"On the day of battle, that's when you'll know."

"But …"

"You are always free to flee. Free to leave."

"But that's not it. I want to fight. But I just don't want everyone counting on *me* to save you all. Can't it be more of a team effort?"

"You may not believe in yourself, but we believe in you."

"You shouldn't."

"We do."

"You're wrong to."

"But it feels so right."

"…"

"Look … we strike in the morning. Perhaps by then you will feel ready."

Back at your tent, Bartholomew is standing at the doorway, because, of course, horse-men never go indoors. You sit down on the ground, and you feel like crying, when you hear screaming. Screaming, and then what sounds like a million chainsaws buzzing at once, combined with the sound of two million lions roaring. Bartholomew stiffens. His ears perk up.

"What? What is it? What's happening?"

Bartholomew turns to you. "They're coming."

It's dark, but off in the distance, it's unmistakeable, that thick line of white moving steadily towards the camp. And behind you too. The multitudes are closing in on all sides.

The barbarians have left the gates of their rotten, soulless city.

They have come to feed.

The day before I left Toronto, or the day of Luís's birthday—or, to really make it clear, the day after I stole Dave's notebook: where I went and what I did didn't involve interviewing people about the blackout. It didn't involve much of anything actually.

I was stuck at the beach with the Val and Dave show, which is completely different than a trip to the cemetery, but similar in the sense that it also involves lots of unmoving bodies lying inert in the dirt. Because I was leaving soon, and also because it was Luís's birthday, Val demanded that we all spend a day together. A full day. She did not democratize the event, but said we had to do it because it was what Luís wanted. Otherwise I would've certainly voted against the beach. There is no need to spell out my misery, but of course the awful happened.

As soon as we arrived, before we even put our towels down, Val removed her clothes, stripped down to her bathing suit, the green one with the yellow flowers on it, and made me wonder why I had been avoiding the beach all summer, choosing instead to walk from one useless house to the next, conducting one useless survey after another. Dave removed his clothes too, which practically cancelled out Val's near nudity. I could not watch him rub the sunscreen onto her skin with his hairy sausage fingers. His grubby hands sliding beneath her bikini straps. I was drinking salt water when she rubbed the cream onto his back. Afterwards, her body gleamed like a shell. A soft, Mexican shell. But I couldn't get rid of the image of Dave's fingerprints covering her skin.

I was sitting there for maybe twenty minutes before I started to sweat through my T-shirt.

August 20 (Morning):

"It's hot."
"You're practically wearing a fucking parka. What do you expect?"

"I don't want to get burned."

"So wear sunscreen."

"It doesn't work."

"Doesn't work?"

"It doesn't."

"I'm sure. Actually, I'm not surprised. Of course you wear a shirt to the beach. Fits you perfectly."

"Whatever."

"How're your pits, by the way?"

"Sweetheart? Do you have the lotion?"

"No."

"Can you check?"

"Checked. Don't know where it is. Ask little brother."

"Do you know where he put it?"

"I don't know. Why would I know?"

"You need more?"

[Dave opens a can of beer, hidden in a blanket of napkins. Slurps foam from the top of the can.]

"I reapply every thirty minutes."

[7.9 second pause.]

"Oh, here it is."

"*Hey-Zeus.*"

"You should put some on little brother."

"I don't need any."

"This stuff is really good."

[Val clicks the lid open and squirts the cream into her hand.]

"Guaranteed you won't get burned."

"Val, don't worry about him. He's got it all worked out."

"What does that mean?"

"Have you ever taken your shirt off?"

"Of course."

"In public? Do you wear it in the pool?"

"I don't swim."

"What a surprise."

"I take my shirt off."

"Do you do anything athletic? Ever go for a run?"

"I walk."

"You have eczema, don't you?"

"Shut up."

"Some kind of rash? Scabies?"

"Dave?"

"Yeah?"

"Leave him alone."

"He knows I'm joking."

[Val closes the lid to the sunscreen.]

"You can use this stuff. I swear you won't get burned."

"I don't ... no. It's okay."

"Oh c'mon. You don't wanna sit there sweating all afternoon."

"I can't put it on."

"I'll do it. Take your shirt off."

I did not intend for Val to apply my sunscreen. But when she offered, I could not refuse. Which is not to say that I enjoyed the experience. The opposite, actually. My skin is quite pale, and as soon as I took my shirt off Val said, *¡Díos mio!* You're as white as a corpse. Practically invisible." I did my chest on my own, but when she did my back, I wondered if she was disgusted with me. The cream was cold and sticky. I couldn't see her face but I could tell she was disgusted by the way she rubbed the stuff on as quickly as possible, like it was some kind of medicine.

Ten minutes later, I was lying in the sun without a shirt on. Though I was more comfortable without my shirt than with, I still had a hard time relaxing. Since finding the envelopes in the back of Dave's notebook, I knew something strange was going on, that it wasn't just my imagination. Dad was alive, he was living in Toronto, had lived in a bunch of different places. I wanted so badly just to ask Dave about it, but I knew if I did, I'd have to tell him that I had his notebook. This would mean more than a simple headlock.

I must've fallen asleep thinking about headlocks, because an hour later Val nudged me with her toe and told me we were going home. I sat straight up, and surprised her with my agility and quickness. For a second I had no idea where I was, only that my neck hurt from sleeping on the sand. I rubbed my eyes, and was about to ask Val for the time when her mouth dropped open and she pointed at my chest.

I'd been burned. Sunburned. *Hey-Zeus.* Val had lied to me. The sunscreen hadn't worked at all. I told her so immediately. Except I didn't say anything. I just put my shirt on, shrugged like it wasn't anything much, and told her that I wanted to go home. Sort of unnecessary, because they were all ready to go. But I said it anyway, because it seemed important.

My entire chest was pink with the sun infection. It didn't hurt yet, but would soon. My skin would turn red, then purple, and then the itch would come. I did not speak the entire walk back from the beach. When Val offered her sympathies, I could barely look at her. It was obvious she was just trying not to laugh.

She clearly did not love me after all.

The birthday party started at two. If anything good could come from the sunburn, it was that I wouldn't have to help Val set up. She filled the tub with cool water and mixed it with half a box of baking soda and told me I could stay in there until the party started. I imagined pulling her into the water with me. I imagined her body entirely brown and toasty. I don't know if I wanted to drown her or make crazy sex love to her. I did neither. I didn't even take a bath. After she left the bathroom, I just sat on the closed toilet seat with my headphones on, and stared at the baking-soda bathwater, listening to my tapes. Through the bathroom door, Val recommended that I put aloe vera on my skin when I got out of the bath. She was in the kitchen getting things ready. I said I would, though I knew I wouldn't. Then a blender started blending, and that was the end of the conversation.

After listening to my tapes for a bit, I came to realize *From Their Eyes* was a total bust. A go-nowhere idea, full of stupid conversations spoken by worthless, uninteresting people. The world was going to end, and it would end without me knowing the truth. It would end without me speaking to Maria again. It would end, and the archaeologists wouldn't find my boring tapes. My tapes would melt with the rest of the city. But something told me they'd find Dave's memoir. They'd think it was just amazing. They'd learn all about

Dave from some incredible book I'd never get the chance to read. The thought was enough to make me want to stab my finger into an electrical outlet.

When I came out of the bathroom, Val was already dressed in a full pirate costume. A frilly white blouse, a curly-brimmed black hat, and tight spandex pants. She told me to call her Grace O'Malley, but of course I did no such thing. She then took me aside, whispering, "Come here." I followed her into the kitchen. She reached into a plastic shopping bag, and took out an eye patch and a fake sword.

August 20 (Afternoon):

"These are for you."
"Can I pass?"
"No. Put this on."
[Sound of me taking the sword and putting the eye patch on. Val laughing.]
"Great. Looks great."
"Thanks."
[3.1 second pause.]
"So … what did you get?"
[6.7 second pause.]
"Pardon me?"
"For Luís?"
[9.9 second pause.]
"I, well, um, I looked."
"Yeah?"
"Couldn't really find anything."
[7.1 second pause.]
"You're joking right? Tell me you're joking."
[4.2 second pause.]
"*Cabrón.* You and your brother. Two lazy peas in a lazy fucking pod."
[Sound of someone knocking at the front door.]

Val left the kitchen and thudded down the hall. She put her hand on the door handle, but didn't immediately open the door. Instead, she called out to me, asked me to press Play on the stereo in the living room. "Can you at least do that?" she asked. I went down the hall, into the living room, and hit Play. The sound of a sea shanty filled the apartment. Val had made a special pirate music mix just for the party. Lots of fiddles and cheering. Swashbuckling type of music.

As soon as the music came on, Val swung the door open. The people on the other side were the same couple who'd been over the other night. How disappointing. Val and Dave had even fewer friends than me. They came in dressed as Blackbeard, Blackbeard's first mate, and their kid was, supposedly, Captain Kidd. Their costumes were totally pathetic. The guy's black silk shirt looked like it belonged on his wife, and he was wearing really tight black jeans. His fake beard kept coming loose around the ears. His wife's costume looked like it had been bought at a Dollar Store, and was actually kind of slutty. Normally, this would be a good thing, but since she was not hot, the costume really wasn't doing anyone any favours. The kid's costume was homemade. A white T-shirt with a capital K drawn on it with a Sharpie. His black construction paper hat kept flying off his head whenever he ran, which was often.

After leading the Blackbeards into the living room, Val went back into the kitchen. The Blackbeards sat on the couch and started talking to Luís about turning five. The man said something about how soon Luís would be old enough to drive, then laughed as if that was the most hilarious thing he'd ever said. I sat on the floor next to the fireplace and crossed my legs Indian-style. Val had put up green and blue streamers all along the ceiling. She didn't believe in plastic balloons. In their place, she had cut balloon shapes out of construction paper, taped string to the end, and stuck them to the walls and ceiling with fishing line to make it look like they were floating. But the fake helium balloons weren't the worst of it. Val had also hung white sheets in the corners of the room. They were supposed to look like sails, but really they just looked like laundry hung up to dry with thumbtacks. One of them had an orange stain on it.

Luís was jumping up and down in the middle of the room. He was supposed to be Jack Sparrow, but really he just looked like a stupid kid pirate. For some reason his hat had a feather in it, and his vest was too big for him. After all the preparation Val had put into the party, I was surprised she hadn't come up with something a little more convincing.

We sat there for an eternity, watching Luís and the W-kid pretend to be pirates, play-fighting with their plastic swords. The Blackbeards laughed at everything they saw. At one point, the woman looked at me and said, "Aren't they the cutest?" I had no idea how to respond, so I said nothing. She looked away a moment or two later. Then Val came in, but not with Dave. He didn't come out of his office until twenty minutes later, and when he did he was dressed like Captain Hook, with a puffy white shirt, a vest, an eye patch, and a plastic hook on his left hand. He wasn't smiling. He sat on the chair near the doorway, next to Val, and said a curt hello to the Blackbeards, which obviously displeased Val. I could see it in her arms, something moving beneath her skin. She kept referring to his lateness, subtly, as though no one noticed, like, "Well, I suppose we're finally ready to eat. I hope no one has starved to death yet," and, "Dave likes to do his work at the craziest times of the day. Like right before bed … in the middle of a birthday party. I suppose you could call it dedication, hey sweetheart?"

I was thankful, this time, for the presence of the Blackbeards and the W-kid.

Not long after, Val went into the kitchen, and came back with a tray full of mini vegan pizzas, which Val called "tofuzas." She had them laid out on the tray, which she placed on the coffee table, along with glasses of juice. The Blackbeards immediately dug in, as did I, though the pizza tasted like cardboard. Val asked three or four times if the food tasted okay, and each time everyone lied and said "Yes." Everyone except Dave, who sat in his chair, arms crossed, not eating. At first I thought it was because he didn't want to start a fight in front of their friends. A fight with Val. But I noticed him on several occasions giving me the headlock look, his death glare. Normally I would have given him the finger for staring at me. But he had the upper hand. He must've discovered my transgression concerning his notebook. I kept thinking of other reasons he might've been angry with me, some other menial detail. I had let Val touch my back. Could that've been the reason? Had he finally discovered our affair? Had he discovered that Val gave me money to buy Luís a present? Did she tell him I had kept the money for myself?

I told myself that Dave was mad at Val, even though it was me that he kept his eyes on the whole time we ate. My terror alert elevated from yellow to orange. Dave finally reached forward and grabbed a tofuza. He took a bite but didn't stop looking at me, so I wondered if he was imagining biting my face off.

After we finished eating, Dave got up to leave, but Val insisted that we stay in the birthday room and play games. Dave said something about having a lot of work to do, at which point Val said, not so quietly, "And you think this didn't take a lot of work?" Dave sat back down in his chair, and Luís and the Captain Kidd sat around and played games, and we watched. Val asked every seven minutes if everyone was having fun. If the Blackbeards needed anything to drink. Mr. Blackbeard's wife kept adjusting her husband's beard every few minutes, and laughed hysterically each time, as though it was the funniest thing in the world. I had to sit there the whole time, listening to married people talk, and little kids laughing, and knowing the whole time that my brother was about to make me walk the plank. I was going to die, and this would be the last thing I remembered.

Some time later, Val got out of her chair and disappeared into the hall. Mr. Blackbeard made small talk with Dave, mostly about sports, something else about traffic on the Gardiner, but Dave didn't say much in reply. He nodded. That was about it. At one point, someone called and Dave picked the phone up within half a ring. He grunted "Wrong number" before slamming the receiver down. He tapped his fingers repeatedly against the arms of his chair, kept sitting forward, then leaning back again. I could practically hear Dave's thoughts.

From out in the hall, Val started singing "Happy Birthday" in Spanish. Luís and the other kid stopped playing, and Luís got very quiet. A moment later, everyone in the room started singing, everyone except Dave, and then Val came into view carrying the birthday cake. She walked into the living room slowly, holding the cake out as though it was the Olympic torch, something for the whole country to salute. The candles were sparkling a little, flaring up, sort of like trick candles. The cake was square, and low, and was likely made with carrots. The creamy topping was probably hummus. I wouldn't know, because before Val had even placed the cake on the coffee table for Luís to blow out the candles, Dave stood up and crossed the room, white sheets flapping in his wake.

My recorder was in my room. I figured the party was going to be so boring there was really no need to waste tape on it. If my recorder had been on, it would've recorded Val: *"¡Cumpleaños feliz!"* It would've recorded Dave: "You! Come with me!" It would've recorded the sound of my collar being ripped. It would've recorded Val and the Blackbeards: *"¡Cumpleaños feliz!"* It would've recorded me: "I have a sunburn." It would've recorded Dave: "Does it look like I give a fuck?" It would've recorded Val, interrupted from her singing, saying: "Dave, calm down." It would've recorded Mrs. Blackbeard telling the W-kid to come over and sit with her. It would've recorded me telling Dave to go fuck himself, which is not something I normally say. To people or to Dave. It would've recorded Val telling us both to leave the room.

It wouldn't have recorded anyone finishing the birthday song.

It would've recorded Luís: *"¿Qué te pasa?"*

As Dave dragged me out of my seat and pushed me down the hall toward his office, I remembered the time I nearly was in a car accident, when I was in grade seven.

I was driving with Mom and Ross. They'd just started dating. Ross was driving. He was telling Mom a story, not watching the road. The car in front of us, a black sedan, stopped suddenly, but Ross didn't notice; it had stopped suddenly without signalling. I remember how I yelled out, in the backseat of the car, "Holy frig!" and Ross swerved onto the shoulder, rocks pinging against the underside of the engine as we hit the gravel, tires spinning, losing grip as we fishtailed around the stopped sedan on the inside lane, coming within inches of its side-view mirror, and my mom wasn't wearing her seatbelt, I saw her bounce forward against the dash, bounce up and down in her seat, her long hair flying all around, the car jumping up and down over potholes until we'd passed the stopped sedan then pulled back onto the road.

In two seconds, I saw how quickly it could all end. We were fine, not even a scrape, but I felt dead. That moment solidified everything for me. That when I die, I'm going to scream like a girl, or say "Holy frig!" and then I'm going to shit myself. And Ross and Mom and Dave and Val and even Caitlyn will laugh when I'm gone. "A pussy in life and a pussy in death," they'll say. "We were right all along."

They'll sell everything I've ever owned for a song.

We got to the office, Dave pushed me into the door, and it opened and I fell through. The first thing I saw was my bookbag on his desk. I wished I had my recorder with me, to record my last words; just in case I didn't make it out alive.

If I'd had my recorder, it would've recorded Dave asking me if I'd used his computer. From the way he said it there was only one answer to the question. I nodded. He asked me what the fuck I thought I was doing. He then pulled a piece of paper out of his pocket. It was a copy of the survey. He accused me of ripping people off. He asked me if I was stealing again. I said no. He punched the piece of paper into my chest. I kept my eyes closed. I fully expected a headlock. I was waiting for worse. Waiting for the punch to the face. The knife in my gut. The bullet to my solar plexus. I kept waiting.

I opened my eyes. Dave was sitting in his office chair.

Dave reached into my bookbag. I thought for sure he was going to take a Lugar out and make Hamburger Helper with my brains. Instead, he threw his notebook onto the desk. "You stole my notebook."

"No."

"You followed me and you stole my notebook."

"No."

"Don't fucking lie to me."

"I'm not lying."

"I lost this yesterday. Now it's in your bookbag."

"So?"

"So? Are you fucking kidding me? Are you going to tell me Luís did it?"

"Maybe."

"Do you think this is funny? This stuff is private."

"I couldn't even understand it. I didn't read more than a few pages."

A moment passed. I just kept thinking about how much I would prefer getting a headlock over having this conversation. He sounded like our mom. I wondered briefly if he'd already phoned her and told her what I'd done. The look on his face told me he had.

"Anyway, I don't see why you think you can write about him."

"About who?"

"Whom."

"What?"

"It's 'whom,' not 'who.'"

"You. Smarten up. When will you just grow the fuck up?"

Of course, it's necessary to keep in mind that even as Dave acted all stern and serious, he was still dressed as Captain Hook, a fact he seemed to have forgotten completely. This alone was making it hard for me not to start laughing. What made the situation completely hilarious is the fact that he was telling me I had to grow up while dressed as the archrival of the boy who never grows up. It was too much. I knew it meant certain death, but once the laughs started flowing, I couldn't stop them. And just as suddenly as it had started, the sitcom in Dave disappeared. Bob Saget left the room and Dave jumped out of his seat. He pushed me against the wall and grabbed me by the hair. I pushed him off of me and ran into the hallway. I only made it about five feet before I felt his hands on my back. All five hundred pounds of him collapsed me into a heap, and I lay there on the floor while he pushed his hands against my throat. I felt the way a popped balloon must feel. Even though I could barely breathe, I started laughing against his hand as it crushed my vocal cords, wheezing against the pressure.

It would've recorded Dave: "You think this is funny?"

It would've recorded me: "You're … funny."

It would've recorded Dave: "Fuck you."

It would've recorded Val: "Dave, what are you doing?"

It would've recorded me: "Fuck … you … Dave."

The guests must've heard the commotion. They came out into the hallway to watch, Blackbeard, his first mate, and Captain Kidd. Dave pulled my shirt over my face like we were in a hockey fight and started slapping my sunburned belly. Captain Kidd started laughing and clapping his hands.

"You'll never learn, will you?"

Luís came into the hallway and started crying. It didn't take long for the other kid to follow suit. Blackbeard and his first mate were now just a few feet away, telling Captain Hook to relax. Dave kept sitting on me, and talked to them like everything was normal. "Sorry about this," he said, as he pasted his open palm against my stomach again and again. "It's so embarrassing, he's been acting out for years now. This is the only way to teach him."

Dave slapped me twice more. Felt like a million hot needles poking through my pores at once. He was about to slap me again, but Val put her hand on Dave's back. Dave looked up at her. He was breathing heavily. Val shook her head. Dave looked back at me, then at the Blackbeards, then back at me. Maybe he realized for the first time how he was dressed, I don't know. But he suddenly pulled his eye patch off, got off of me, and stood.

It would've recorded Dave: "I, uh … sorry guys. We were just horsing around."

It would've recorded Luís: "You're not crying?"

It would've recorded me: "No. I'm fine."

At this point, Dave put his arm around Val, the Blackbeards smiled awkwardly, and Dave said something to the effect of him needing to "blow off steam." He went into their bedroom to change. As soon as the bedroom door closed, the Blackbeards thanked Val for having them over, wished Luís a happy birthday, and left. Val said, "No, please stay, we haven't opened the presents yet," but Mr. Blackbeard kept saying it was getting late and that their kid needed his "nappy-time." He ruffled the W-kid's hair when he said this. They didn't even bother to tie their son's shoes before opening the front door and making their exit.

So then it was me, Val, and Luís. I was still on the floor in the hallway, sitting up against the wall. Val asked me if I wanted a piece of cake. I shook my head. She asked me why Dave had reacted like that, and I told her she should ask him. But of course she didn't bother. Even after seeing what a moron he could be, she still stood by him, still took his side. She said, "What did you do?" I said nothing. After a moment, Val took Luís's hand and they went into the living room together. She let Luís dig his fork right into the whole cake. His eyes were still red from crying. Val laughed when he got the white topping on his nose and chin.

I got up off the floor and went into the room I was staying in. I felt awful. I'd always known that Dave hated my guts, but Val too? Had I really ruined Luís's birthday? It's not like I was the one who started the fight.

I closed the bedroom door and sat on the end of the unmade bed. I sat there for a while, thinking of what an idiot I'd been. I stared at the desk in the corner, wishing I'd just found the candles when Val sent me looking on the day of the blackout. Wishing I'd just been able to avoid this whole sad mess that I was in.

I heard a knock at my window. The noise startled me, but I thought it must've been a bird or something. I didn't move at first, but then I heard it again, this time three taps in a row. I had to stand on top of my bed in order to look out.

It was Dave. He must've been standing on something. A garbage can? We looked at each other through the window for a while. What the hell was he doing out there? I made no move to open the window, and he made no attempt to force me. Then he looked down and it seemed like he was talking to someone, only I couldn't hear anything. I leaned closer to the window and I could see that he was holding my bookbag. He pulled *The Description of a New World, Called the Blazing World* out of the bag and held it up to the glass.

"Where'd you get this?" he asked me, muffled. I said nothing. He flipped the book open and removed the handwritten letter.

"Open the window."

I opened it.

Dave held the paper up. "Do you know what this is?"

"A letter to Dad."

Pause.

"I haven't done anything illegal, Dave. I swear."

Dave smiled. Then he asked me to meet him on the back deck. I did some quick figuring. Dave obviously needed my help. At the very least, he seemed ready to answer some questions.

Morgan stood up. The other man's eyes flicked down. He saw his father lying on the floor. He stared at the dead body for several seconds, uncomprehending. His eyes flashed back to Morgan, who still held the extension cord in his hand.

"I can explain," said Morgan, but when he spoke, no words came out. He pointed at the letter on the desk, hoping this would suffice.

The other man started backing out of the room.

"What did you do?"

The other Morgan was in the hall; the other Morgan was turning to run.

Morgan grabbed the inkwell paperweight from the desk. It felt cold and hard in his hand. He moved quickly, slipping out of the study and into the hall. The younger Morgan had made it to the top of the stairs. Morgan threw the paperweight and it struck the back of the other Morgan's head. He yelped, a sudden, breathless cry. An animal-like noise. He fell forward, and lay there twitching a bit.

There was a steady thumping in Morgan's ears. Morgan slowly bent toward the other Morgan, picked up the paperweight.

The younger Morgan rolled over onto his back, with some difficulty. His world was coming back into focus. He looked up at the man standing over him.

"Who are you?"

You, thought Morgan.

You drop to your knees, put your hand on the injured man's chest. Then you let the weight of your weapon carry your other arm forward. A heavy thud, right on the nose. You are delighted to discover that the injured man's head is made of soft clay. You strike again. And again. A bright ribbon of blood oozes from his face, pools around him, around you, on the floor.

You remember.

That trip to the lake, yes. A still, black lake, a place with orange and red leaves. The Adirondack Inn, and then a fight on the train. Nothing serious, but she didn't want to talk once you were home. You remember the blood on your chin from where she'd slammed the door into your face, shutting herself in the bathroom.

You remember how she said your name, and how suddenly you kicked the door back open. She wasn't expecting it. The door knocked her down. Knocked her backward, and as she fell she turned, put her hands out to catch herself. But she didn't catch herself. She fell against the rim of the tub, and then didn't react in time. Slowly crumpled against the wall, her hands on her belly, her mouth open in a silent wail. You had stood in the doorway. Something didn't feel right. You saw yourself in the mirror above the sink, but it wasn't you. And then, blood, trickling from her, fanning out on the floor. Blood on her legs and ankles.

You tried to find the phone. Looked everywhere for the phone. Threw the cushions off the couch, opened every drawer in the kitchen, but couldn't find it anywhere.

In the bathroom she said your name twice, quietly, under her breath. It was already too late.

Your arm is tired. You look down at the younger Morgan's busted face. How long have you been swinging? Feels like you might've pulled a muscle. You drop the paperweight. It hits the hardwood with a thud. You push yourself up until you're standing over the other Morgan's body. The bathroom is just a few feet away. You go inside and strip out of your bloody clothes. You take a shower. You watch the blood swirl down the drain, pick pieces of the other Morgan's skull out of your hair. You walk through the house naked until you find a towel, a large blue towel, hanging from the back of the older Morgan's bedroom door. You then change into some clothes you find in the older Morgan's closet. A plaid cotton shirt and a pair of brown corduroy pants that are too loose around the waist. You find a black leather belt in the top dresser drawer and put it on.

On the main floor, you sit at the foot of the stairs to put your shoes on.

You look up to see a man standing outside the front door. There's a pane of glass beside the front door; the man's face is pressed against it. He looks like someone you know, someone you've seen before, but the name escapes you. You pick yourself up off the stairs and drift toward the door. You want to do like the man is doing, and put your face right up to the cold glass. Instead, you reach out your right hand, and pull the door open. You step outside.

Leaving the door unlocked behind you, you go for a walk.

23 Blackout

August 20 (Evening):

"Where did you find this book?"
[Sound of Dave dropping *The Blazing World* onto the deck
table that sits between us.]
"I found it in the apartment."
"No shit. I mean, where specifically?"
[5.7 second pause.]
"Oh, c'mon. I don't have all night."
"Behind the kitchen drawer. When I was looking for candles."
"And the letter? The letter inside it?"
"It was inside the book."
"Hmm."
"Have you read it?"
"No."
"Well, it's about this Lady who—"
"It's not important what it's about."
"Excuse me?"
"Listen: You know that Dad used to live in Toronto. He had
a place here. Mom thought this was because he had another
woman. That could be true. When I moved to Toronto, I tried
to find his apartment. Out of curiosity. Mom wouldn't tell me
where, told me to leave well enough alone, you know how she
is. But I tracked this place down at the library."
"Camp David?"
"Pardon me?"
"That's what Val calls your apartment."
[4.6 second pause.]
"There were three people with Dad's name in the phonebook.
One of them used to live here. When I found out that the

apartment was vacant, I thought maybe this was Dad's place. That it was vacant because he'd disappeared. But it wasn't Dad, in the end."

"Because Dad lived on Palmerston."

"No."

"But—"

"I wasn't able to find out where Dad lived. I don't think he had a place. Just stayed in hotels when he was here. Or he was unlisted."

"Then why did you move into this apartment?"

"We needed a place in a cheaper part of town. It was available. Plus, at the time I still thought it could've been Dad's, because it had belonged to a Morgan Wells. But then, who knows how many Morgan Wellses live in the city of Toronto? Could be just a handful, could be a dozen."

"I doubt there would be a dozen."

"I wasn't sure. Plus, the landlady told us the guy had been evicted. She gave us a huge discount on rent for moving in and paying right away."

"But how do you know it wasn't Dad's place?"

"Because of the things I found out about the previous tenant afterwards. Things we found around the apartment. There was this map taped to one of the walls, all marked up in different coloured pens, like something a serial killer would do. Xs on certain locations. Some parts of the map were torn because lines had been drawn on too hard. That made me wonder about the previous tenant's state of mind. Plus, you know Val, she insisted on a 'deep' clean. We had to really scrub the whole place down. Found a bunch of Post-it notes in random parts of the apartment, with weird shit written on them."

"I still don't see how that means Dad didn't live here."

"I also found a stack of envelopes addressed to Morgan Wells. Found them tucked behind the radiator in Luís's room, held together with an elastic band."

[5.5 second pause.]

"And?"

"The weird thing was, none were addressed to this address. They were all addressed to the other two Morgan Wellses I'd found at the library. The one who'd lived on Morton, and the one who used to live in the Annex."

"You think one guy lived at all of those places?"

"No. I read the letters. Bank statements, mostly. They definitely belonged to different people, neither of them the guy who used to live in this apartment."

[6.7 second pause.]

"And your point is…?"

"My point is, I was confused. What was one Morgan Wells doing with the mail of the other two? So, a few weeks after moving in, I called the landlady. She was pretty secretive. Said it was illegal to give out information on previous tenants and all that. So I had to do some research on my own. I went knocking on doors."

"Seriously? Man, you've got way too much time on your hands."

"Actually, it took me no time at all."

"I find people in this city are impossible to start a conversation with."

"What can I say? Must be my journalistic genes, because for me it was easy. I found out pretty quickly where the guy used to work, but other than that no one knew anything about him. They knew he'd been married. That he had a wife, and that she left him. But that was about all they could tell me. Anyway, it turns out the guy worked for The Letter Shredders, so I went down to their warehouse. Asked around. I, uh … I had to pretend I was a relative just to make some headway. Ha! That's where the last name comes in handy, you know?"

[Dave chuckling to himself for a couple seconds, remembering his ingenuity with satisfaction.]

"Anyway, I spoke to this guy named Scott Parker. Bit of a rough type, but as soon as I mentioned the name, he started talking. Had a real hate for the guy. He used to work with him. Told me how he was divorced, a terrible worker, spaced out most of the time. He lost his job for, get this, stealing letters that were meant to be shredded."

[7.4 second pause.]

"So what?"

"It's obvious! The guy was some kind of letter thief."

"But, I'm confused."

[Sound of me tapping on the cover of *The Blazing World*.]

"Where does the book come into all of this? The apocalypse, and like—"

"Like I said, the book itself isn't important. What matters is the letter inside. The one to the Morgan Wells who lived on Palmerston. It's just further proof that the guy stole mail."

"And that he stole other things."

"What do you mean?"

"The book. It belonged to the guy who lived on Palmerston."

"How do you know?"

"Because I went there."

"You broke in?"

"Geez, Dave, no. They were having an estate sale. I went in looking for mini tapes. I found an entire library full of books just like that one, old books from this woman named Myrna to the guy who lived there. Which means, if your theory is right, that the Morgan Wells who used to live in your apartment not only stole mail, he stole other things."

"Oh my God."

"What?"

"He broke into their houses."

[3.1 seconds pass.]

"He stole their mail, broke into their homes. He probably watched them. He probably, like, he …"

"I don't get it."

"I used to think he just stole their mail. But I *suspected* he went further, you know, because of the crazy map, and the stories I heard from his co-worker."

"But you can't say for sure he broke in. Maybe he knew the other Morgans. Maybe the older guy lent him the book."

"Ha! What, like they belonged to some same name club?"

"That's not what I mean."

"I knew there was something more to this. But I didn't have definitive proof that the guy had been in the homes of his others."

"You're jumping to conclusions."

"I thought he was just a voyeur, because even with stealing mail he would've been staying outside. Just watching. Until I found the book—"

"Don't you mean until *I* found the book?"

"Well, sure. Anyway, now I know. And there has to be even more to it than that. This is a major breakthrough!"

"Okay, but you've forgotten one important thing."

"What?"

"Dad."

"What about him?"

"How can you be sure the letter in the book wasn't written to Dad?"

"It's obvious that it's not."

"But isn't there a chance the guy who used to live here also investigated Dad? He was also a Morgan Wells, remember."

"Probably not. I doubt it."

"You don't even think it's possible…?"

[Sound of Dave flipping through *The Blazing World*. 12.4 seconds.]

"… I want that book back."

"You'll get it back."

"But Dave—"

"You'll get it back when I'm done with it."

"You just said it wasn't important."

"It's not."

"So?"

[10.3 second pause.]

"Dave?"

[6.9 second pause. Sound of Dave getting out of his chair, and opening the sliding door.]

"I'm going inside. See you in the morning, little brother. Don't forget to pack your stuff."

What a ramrodded fuckerhead.

This whole time I'd thought Dave was working on a book about our dad, and it was the last thing I'd wanted him to do. Now I knew that he was actually writing a book about some weirdo pervert who had absolutely nothing to do with my dad, and I have to say, I was disappointed. Let down. This feeling was made worse by the fact that my finding *The Blazing World* really just helped Dave finish his stupid story. I'd provided him with the final key to finish his work of fiction. And fiction is all it was without definitive proof.

As I packed that night, I realized that it had been almost a week since the blackout. Nearly seven days, and still the world was living. No nukes, no biochems, no weapons of mass destruction. My prophecy was a dud, just like my interviews.

What made me even more unhappy was that Dave seemed happy.

I wondered what the weather was going to be like back in Nova Scotia.

August 21 (Afternoon):

[Car radio music, light, persistent beat. Sometimes a DJ's voice providing traffic updates.]
"When's your flight?"
"Two o'clock."
"Two exactly?"
"Check-in time's at one."
"Did you check the, uh … the thing?"
"The itinerary? Yes."
"Good. And it leaves at two? Right on the dot?"
"As long as we're there by one I should be okay."
"Yeah. Okay. We should be there on time."
[39.7 seconds of silence. Radio chat.]
"Who's the woman you met at the mall?"

"She's my editor."

"Editor?"

"She's part of the editing service offered by the publisher."

"The publisher? You found a publisher?"

"Yeah. Found them online. They gave me a good deal because they really liked my idea."

"A good deal? You mean they charged you?

"One thousand copies, plus the editing service, for only $10,000."

[4.6 seconds.]

"Plus tax."

"That sounds expensive."

"No, it's a good deal. Trust me. I did my research."

[Two minutes pass.]

"About the story. I think I know how to end it."

[Window rolls down, and the wind comes rushing in. My window.]

"Okay, how does *my* story end?"

"Let's say the guy came home one day and found his apartment completely gutted. How do you think he would react?"

[5.1 seconds.]

"Why would he have come back? He was evicted."

"But what happened to his stuff?"

"His stuff? I don't know. He took it with him. He left it behind. The landlady got rid of it, took it to the dump or sold it. Who cares?"

"But if this guy was such a good thief, then wouldn't he have gone to the landlady and stolen his things back?"

[7.8 seconds of silence.]

"You must be retarded."

"You don't have much to go on to write a whole book."

"I've been researching this guy for the past sixteen months. I've got reams of notes. Trust me. He didn't come back."

[One minute passes.]

"I'm just saying that you could look at all the facts you have, and pretty much come up with any story."

"Like what?"

"Like maybe … maybe all the places were being rented out by Dad."

[4.2 second pause.]

"Seriously?"

"That's why they all have the same name."

"Because Dad had three different addresses?"

"Maybe. Maybe *he* was working on a story."

[Dave starts laughing, then stops abruptly.]

"So you still think this is all connected to Dad somehow? I spoke with the neighbours, you know? The previous tenant was in his thirties. Gaunt, lean, pale. Sound like Dad to you?"

"Maybe he wore a disguise."

"Are you fucking insane?"

[2.1 second pause.]

"The guy on Palmerston was in his seventies. Committed suicide. Sound like Dad to you?"

"No."

"And the guy who lived on Morton. He runs a café on Danforth. Sound like Dad?"

"Maybe some of them were Dad, some weren't."

"Listen to yourself."

"You don't have any proof, Dave. That's my point. You can't prove anything."

"This has nothing to do with Dad. Nothing. I'm not even sure if I'll use the name."

"You're changing the names?"

"I might. I mean, I'm changing a few things, you know? My editor says I should, just to make the story more readable. More exciting."

[58.5 seconds.]

"And another thing, idiotfuck, it doesn't have to be *true*. It doesn't have to be the *right* story. The story's done. Done. A perfect ending. At least it will be when I write it. It ends with the guy going nuts."

"But you made it up."

"Go fuck yourself."

[14.3 seconds.]

"What if Dad had all those addresses because, I don't know, he was working on something super top secret."

"Super top secret? Seriously, you need to grow up."

"You can't prove that he isn't still out there."

"Oh my God, Morgan. Just shut the fuck up already."

About thirty minutes later we reached the turnoff to Pearson. Dave didn't want to look for parking, so he just dropped me off in front of Terminal 1 and said he'd send the manuscript in the mail when it was finished. As if I'd asked for it. One thing he didn't know was that I'd taken *The Blazing World* back while he was eating breakfast that morning with Val and Luís. In my brain, I told him to keep his story, and to suck his own ass.

On the flight home, I came up with at least three alternate endings that are ten times more exciting than Dave's.

You are caught spying. The daughter of the man you were spying upon saw you leave and called the police. They monitor the house for two weeks until you come back. You are convicted and sent to jail for five years. In jail, you become your cellmate's girlfriend. He punches you in the face every time you look him in the eye. Later, you are killed for refusing to share your cherry pie with your cellmate's friend.

The End.

One night, as you lean over the bed of one of your subjects, he wakes up. You run away but he comes after you. He reaches out to catch you, mistakenly pushing you down the stairs. You break your neck on the third step, then slide down the stairs. The man calls an ambulance, but before they arrive he puts on a pair of Doc Martens and kicks the back of your neck, twice, finishing you off.

The End.

On one of your midnight walks, you cross the street without looking and a large cube van smashes your hips apart and drags you by one leg for several blocks. You heroically try to sever your knee, so that only your foot will remain caught in the bumper, but the cartilage and bone is too tough, and the asphalt scrapes away your skull too fast.

The End.

A light came on above my head, telling me to put my seatbelt on.

That's when the knife cracked my spine, punctured my heart, my lungs.

That's when the aneurysm exploded in my brain, sent blood crawling through my tear ducts.

That's when I choked on a bullet fired into my mouth.

That's when the cabin lights starting shutting down. Rows 1-12. Rows 13-26. Rows 27-39. The airplane bounced, the emergency lights came on. One of the flight attendants started crying. People turned their heads, turned toward me, until everyone in the plane was looking at me. Then the lights went out completely, it was dark, and there was a tremendous amount of noise.

The other passengers were all falling into the aisles, gasping for oxygen, searching for life vests, vomiting shitty airplane food, pissing themselves. The closer I looked I realized they were also crashing into highway dividers, drinking themselves senseless, falling from the tops of skyscrapers. They were clutching at their throats, blacking out, swallowing rat poison, foaming at the mouth. I was finally dying with company. I saw my mom choking on a chicken bone, and Ross being stabbed in the heart. I watched Dave, Val, and Luís die of smoke inhalation as their apartment went up in flames. And I waited for my own death, knowing it would be the greatest death of them all. I waited for the death of burning jet fuel and blinding light.

When the great plague comes we'll rot from the guts to the skin until there's nothing left but corpses crumbling in the corners of rooms, floating bloated in the ocean, rotting slowly in the sand.

We're dead.

We're a fraction of a second.

We were never here.

Acknowledgements

I gratefully acknowledge the public funding I received from the Canada Council for the Arts while working on an early draft of this novel. Thanks as well to *The Fiddlehead*, *The Windsor Review*, and *filling Station* for supporting me by publishing my work, and for their commitment to Canadian literature in general.

I would also like to express my gratitude to all at Freehand Books, specifically Robyn Read for her editorial dedication, and Sarah Ivany for all things media. Thanks as well to Grace Cheong for coming up with such brilliant book design options that she made it hard for me to choose.

I would be greatly remiss not to send an enormous thank you to Nicole Markotić, my thesis advisor at the University of Windsor. Without her help, I highly doubt this book would exist.

Thanks also to all my friends at the University of Windsor, and also to my amazing family for reading early drafts and telling me what they thought.

Finally, thanks to Joanna Thurlow, my wife and best friend, for her translations, her patience, and her constant encouragement. Without her help, I know for a fact this book would not exist.

N.B. The quoted material from a back cover of a Choose Your Own Adventure comes from Ellen Kushner's *The Enchanted Kingdom* (Toronto: Bantam Books, 1986).

All citations to the original text of *The Blazing World* are from the following edition:

Cavendish, Margaret. The Description of a New World, Called the Blazing-World. London: A. Maxwell, 1668. 5 Dec. 2010. <http://digital.library.upenn.edu/women/newcastle/blazing/blazing.html>.

Michael Murphy lives in Halifax, Nova Scotia. His work has been published in *The Fiddlehead, The Windsor Review,* and *filling Station.* He has an MA in Creative Writing from the University of Windsor, and is currently studying at the Schulich School of Law at Dalhousie University. This is his first novel.